NIGHT OVER
MEXICO

NIGHT OVER
MEXICO

A HUGH RENNERT MYSTERY

TODD DOWNING

COACHWHIP PUBLICATIONS

Landisville, Pennsylvania

Night Over Mexico by Todd Downing
Copyright © 2012 Coachwhip Publications
Introduction © 2012 Curtis Evans
No claim made on public domain material.

ISBN 1-61646-153-5
ISBN-13 978-1-61646-153-9

Cover Image: Landscape © Dmitry Rukhlenko

CoachwhipBooks.com

CONTENTS

Introduction, by Curtis Evans   7

Part One   13
1 Sunset   15
2 Corpse Light   20
3 Wet Red Hair   26
4 Not Warmed by Fire   32
5 The Monk's Wife   40
6 Hall of the Mountain King   51
7 Painted Serpent   61
8 Airways   70
9 Cold Symbols of Evil   80
10 Exit without Shoes   90

Part Two   95
11 Prayer for a Stranger   97
12 Old Man of the Sea   105
13 Slayer of Dragons   115
14 Swan Song   122
15 Tainted Waters   131
16 Noche Triste   142

17 Death in Tampico   149

18 Night-blooming   155

19 This Mortal Coil   164

20 Scattered Ashes   170

21 Water Cure   180

22 Exit Mr. Woodmansee   186

Part Three   191

23 Sanctuary   193

24 Smoke Tears   200

25 Bars in the Mist   206

26 Kiss   213

27 Fear in a Handful of Dust   219

28 Rocket in the Sky   225

29 Secret Agent   231

30 Sunset   242

INTRODUCTION
CURTIS EVANS

"Mr. Downing is a born detective story writer."
—Edward Powys Mathers ("Torquemada"),
review of Todd Downing, *Vultures in the Sky* (1935)

THE RICHNESS AND DIVERSITY of American genre writing during the Golden Age of mystery fiction (c. 1920 to 1939) is much under-appreciated today. Golden Age mystery readers could choose from a wide variety of literary dishes, be it the tough stuff of the hard-boiled boys (most famously Dashiell Hammett, Raymond Chandler and James M. Cain), which has long received the lion's share of the attention that scholars have granted American Golden Age crime writers; the psychological suspense (or HIBK—Had I But Known—as it was once disparaged) of Elisabeth Sanxay Holding, Mary Roberts Rinehart, Mignon Eberhart and Leslie Ford; the urban sophistication of Rex Stout, Patrick Quentin and Rufus King; the madcap humor of Phoebe Atwood Taylor and Craig Rice (the latter making the tail end of the Golden Age); the eccentric extravaganzas of Harry Stephen Keeler; the police procedurals of Helen Reilly; the courtroom dramas of Erle Stanley Gardner; or the magnificent baroque puzzles of S. S. Van Dine, Ellery Queen, Anthony Abbot, John Dickson Carr, C. Daly King and Clyde B. Clason.

This listing of authors just scratches the surface of American mystery writing in the years between the two world wars. So many accomplished mystery writers from the period have undeservingly fallen into obscurity. One such individual is Todd Downing, the Golden Age chronicler of fictional murders in Mexico.

Todd Downing was born in 1902 in the town of Atoka, Choctaw Nation, Indian Territory (soon to be Oklahoma). Though one-eighth Choctaw and, like his father Samuel (Sam), an enrolled member of the Choctaw Nation, Todd Downing had what in many ways was a traditional, early twentieth century small town American upbringing. Both Todd's father Sam and his mother Maud were staunch churchgoing Presbyterians and Republicans and Todd was brought up according to the proper precepts of these two orthodoxies.

Yet the Downing family of Atoka was unusual in its great love of reading. From an early age Todd Downing could be found in nooks and corners of the family's two-story foursquare house with his nose buried in books. He particularly loved romantic tales of adventure, played out in settings around the globe. Beginning with Sir Walter Scott's and H. Rider Haggard's colorful sagas of derring-do, Todd moved on, in his teenage years, to crime and mystery, in the form of the short story collections of Arthur B. Reeve, creator of the virtuous scientific detective Dr. Craig Kennedy, and the novels of Sax Rohmer, creator of the diabolical criminal mastermind Dr. Fu Manchu.

After Todd became a student at the University of Oklahoma in 1920, he soon discovered Edgar Wallace, the awesomely prolific English king of the thriller. Todd devoured Wallace shockers at a prodigious rate. (His library of books, bequeathed at his death in 1974 to Southeastern Oklahoma State University, included sixty-five Wallace novels and short story collections, as well as Wallace's autobiography and biography.) Yet as the 1920s progressed, Todd, like many bright people in his day, became increasingly interested in fair play detective fiction, where the point is not emotional jolts but cerebration: the reader tries to solve the mystery for her/himself through clues provided within the text by the author. Over the decade of the twenties Todd purchased detective novels and short story collections by Anthony Berkeley, Earl Derr Biggers, Lynn Brock, G. K. Chesterton, Mignon Eberhart, Rufus King, Marie

Belloc Lowndes, Baroness Orczy, Mary Roberts Rinehart, T. S. Stribling and S. S. Van Dine.

Between mysteries Todd managed to find time to qualify for his B.A. and M.A at the University of Oklahoma, as well as to take classes in Spanish, French and anthropology during summers spent at the National University of Mexico. In 1928 OU hired the young Atokan as an instructor in Spanish. (Todd was fluent in five languages: English, Choctaw, Spanish, French and Italian.) In addition to teaching his OU classes and conducting summer tour groups in Mexico, Todd continued voraciously reading both detective novels and crime thrillers; and in 1930 he began reviewing mysteries of all sorts in the literary pages of Oklahoma City's *Daily Oklahoman*. Especial favorites of Todd's in the mystery line were Agatha Christie, Dorothy L. Sayers, Ellery Queen, John Dickson Carr, Dashiell Hammett, Mary Roberts Rinehart, Mignon Eberhart and additional worthy writers who likely are less familiar to many today: Anthony Abbot, Rufus King, H. C. Bailey, Eden Phillpotts and Anthony Wynne (for more on Todd Downing's mystery fiction reviews see my book *Clues and Corpses: The Detective Fiction and Mystery Criticism of Todd Downing*).

Encouraged by an older colleague at the University of Oklahoma, Professor Kenneth C. Kaufman, Todd Downing wrote his first detective novel in 1931, not long after he had begun contributing mystery fiction reviews to the *Daily Oklahoman*. Eventually published in 1933, *Murder on Tour* introduced Todd's most important series detective, United States Customs Service agent Hugh Rennert, who would appear in seven detective novels between 1933 and 1937. (A Hugh Rennert novella, probably written by Todd in 1932, was published in 1945.) Besides *Murder on Tour* these are: *The Cat Screams* (1934), *Vultures in the Sky* (1935), *Murder on the Tropic* (1935), *The Case of the Unconquered Sisters* (1936), *The Last Trumpet* (1937) and *Night over Mexico* (1937). All six of these later novels now have been reprinted by Coachwhip Publications.

The Hugh Rennert detective novels are primarily set in Mexico (the one exception being *The Last Trumpet*, where the action ranges from Cameron County, Texas to the Mexican state of Tamaulipas). Todd Downing's authoritative and fascinating use of Mexico as a setting in his detective novels makes him one of the most important regionalist mystery writers of the Golden Age and is his most significant contribution to the genre. Additionally, the Rennert novels are graced with teasing fair play puzzle plots, stylish writing and interesting characterizations. Hugh Rennert himself is a notable detective, modest, middle-aged, self-reflective and somewhat melancholy, yet resolute and determined. ("A good kind man," one character calls him in *Night over Mexico*, and he is.) Hugh Rennert is fascinated with Mexico and *vacilada*, the mirthfully stoic attitude of the country's people toward life and death; and over the course of the series Todd Downing explores what might be termed the metaphysical relationship of Rennert and Mexico in interesting ways. We learn a lot about both a man and a country.

After 1937 Todd Downing wrote two more detective novels, both with a different series detective (Texas sheriff Peter Bounty, introduced in *The Last Trumpet*): *Death under the Moonflower* (1938) and *The Lazy Lawrence Murders* (1941). He also published the work which he considered his crowning achievement as a writer, a non-fictional study of Mexico, *The Mexican Earth* (1940; reprinted by the University of Oklahoma Press in 1996). Sadly, Todd's attempt in the 1940s to write a mainstream historical novel about Mexico came to naught. Todd had resigned as an instructor at the University of Oklahoma in 1935 in order to devote himself professionally to writing, but after 1941 he would never publish another novel—indeed, after 1945 he never published any fiction of any kind again. In the 1940s Todd found employment as an advertising copy writer in Philadelphia. One of his ads, the tongue-in-cheek mystery homage "The Case of the Crumpled Letter," was chosen in 1959 as one of the 100 greatest advertisements.

In the 1950s Todd returned to the teaching profession, taking posts at schools in Maryland and Virginia, but after the death of his father in 1954 he returned to Atoka to live with his octogenarian mother and teach Spanish and French at Atoka High School, from where he had graduated thirty-five years earlier. After the death of Todd's mother in 1965, Todd lived on alone in the old family home until his own demise in 1974. The professional highlight of his later years was his appointment as Emeritus Professor of Choctaw Language and Choctaw Heritage at Southeastern Oklahoma State University (then Southeastern State College). Reflecting Todd's continued interest in his Choctaw heritage were his series of lessons in the Choctaw language, *Chahta Anampa: An Introduction to Choctaw Grammar*, and his historical pageant play about the Choctaw Nation, *Journey's End*, both of which were published in 1971, forty years after he penned his first detective novel.

Todd Downing is buried beneath a simple headstone in Atoka, the place of his birth. Fittingly, his writing lives after him.

PART ONE

EVERYONE WHO HAS traveled in Mexico knows that on its mountain-tops live the Tlalocs, old and peevish godlings who blind the innocent wayfarer with mist and drench him with rain. As long as the only sounds to disturb the solitude of their heights were the soft pad of sandaled feet and the clop-clop of unshod burro hoofs, the Tlalocs played their pranks mostly in the spirit of fun and were propitiated by little gifts left beside running water. But the opening of the Pan-American Highway caused a marked change in their attitude, and Yankee "Ohs" and "Ahs" and the clatter of contraptions from Detroit have made them increasingly malevolent.

The Tlalocs on a certain mountain in Tamaulipas held council one August afternoon and decided it was time to loose all their terrors. They looked south and saw me approaching from Victoria. They looked north and saw a man from Brownsville, Texas, crossing the desert. They got busy forthwith and demolished the macadam road with a landslide, so that nightfall should find the two of us, and all unfortunate travelers between, at their mercy on a detour.

—Heigh-ho, Mexico!
by Gulliver Damson, Ph.D.

13

1
SUNSET

Hugh Rennert was reaching into his pocket for a cigarette when the signpost reared its spade-shaped head out of the mist.

He grabbed the brake, hunched over the wheel and groaned as he read the letters picked out by the lights of the coupé:

DESVIACIÓN

Lowering a window, he leaned into the drizzle and groaned again. The sky was a solid black lid save in the west, where its closing had caught a ruffed serpent and left the bloody pulp outlining a distant ridge. In that direction a curving arrow indicated a widening of the road into a meadow of coarse matted grass which might end fifty feet or as many miles away, for all he could discern. On the other side rose jagged edges of rock, plumed with dripping tree ferns.

The raw air set him to shivering, and he rolled up the glass, speculating on what dire and unrepented sins had let him in for such castigation. Twice, in the sun-stricken deserts south of the Rio Grande, cactus spines had gone through tires like needles through gauze. An hour or so ago, as his ears were beginning to crackle in the thinning air of the mountains, he had been blanketed by the mists of the *chipi-chipi*, released by the warm clouds of the Gulf as they meet the cool coastal ranges in their westward course. And now, with Victoria and the junction with the Pan-American Highway not more than sixty miles ahead, as the

15

Mexican vulture flies, an arrow was shunting him off into—heaven knew what.

Rennert lighted the cigarette, advanced slowly toward a wooden barricade and started to turn off over a rickety-looking bridge.

From behind the obstruction emerged a man who resembled, in helmet, rain cape and boots of glistening black rubber, some ungainly carapaced creature whose element is water.

As he sloshed toward the car Rennert saw that he was a member of the Highway Patrol. The dark mask of his face was split suddenly by twin rows of gleaming white teeth, he pointed dramatically to the right and, as Rennert lowered the window again, pronounced proudly the English word "Detour."

Rennert nodded. "How long is it?"

The Mexican smiled more broadly and said, "Yes."

Rennert repeated his question in Spanish.

A booted foot was planted solidly on the running board, and a pair of black eyes fixed themselves on the glowing end of the cigarette. "*Poca distancia,*" was the negligent reply. "*Hay desliz formidable. Un cigarro por favor, señor.*"

Obligingly Rennert tendered cigarettes. As if by legerdemain the entire package left his hand and reappeared in possession of the brown fingers, which began extracting one with great care.

"Ten miles?" he hazarded a guess as he held out a lighted match. While long experience in Mexico had taught him the futility of endeavoring to obtain anything like precise information regarding distance or time, he thought that possibly this patrolman had acquired something from tourists along with his limited vocabulary. And he didn't care for the sound of that "formidable landslide."

The Mexican nodded, murmured "*Poco más o menos*" and thrust the end of the cigarette into the flame. He stepped back then and, deftly cupping his hand so as to shield the tobacco from the downpour, made a gesture of dismissal. "*Gracias, senor. Vaya con Dios.*"

Rennert watched his cigarettes disappear into a voluminous pocket of the cape. "How is the road?" he asked, determined to get something in the way of return.

"Bueno, senor. Muy bueno." With an inclination of head and body that would have done justice to a grandee, the man moved toward his shelter.

And that was that. Rennert "went with God" across the bridge. The statement that the road was good meant as little as the assertion that the detour was not a long one. A Mexican, being *simpático* and wishing all the world to be happy, invariably gives the answer which he thinks will please the questioner. Happiness is a fleeting thing at best.

Rennert's optimism, which was all he carried away from the meeting, lasted about sixty seconds, when the first jolt, catching him unawares, sent a shock up his spine and a gulp into his throat. Wheels of ancient carts and plodding hoofs had worn the soil into ruts and ridges which the sun had baked to the consistency of stone. In the depressions, where streamers of dirty gray mist had not yet been dispelled by the rain, tires and chains slithered wildly through black viscous mud.

He found himself swinging southward in a wide arc, following the tread marks of two or three cars which must have preceded him not long before. There was a poor sort of consolation to be gained from the knowledge that he wasn't the only reckless fool to traverse these mountains after dark.

Why, he wondered now, hadn't he been content to make the roundabout journey by train, stopping for the night in Monterrey and arriving in Victoria early to-morrow afternoon? It would have meant an extra day's travel, to be sure, but the business which was taking him to the capital of Tamaulipas had been dragging on for months now, and he had no real hopes of winding it up on this trip. A tract of land adjoining his citrus fruit farm in Cameron County was owned by a Mexican family (with every distant relative sharing, it seemed), and the question of irrigation rights had involved a maddening amount of negotiation. That morning's mail had been so exasperating that he had stuffed some clothing into a bag and set out to cut a few Gordian knots. And had let himself in for this.

He slowed down at another signpost, stamped with the word PELIGRO, and surveyed apprehensively the rain-swept world beyond, where hills raised camel humps among dark pits of vegetation. "Abandon all hope," he paraphrased, "ye who enter here."

It seemed that his worst expectations were going to be justified. The soil was sandy and loose, treacherously, studded with stones. All tracks had been obliterated by the steadily increasing deluge, and travel became a matter of guesswork, of halts to clean the windshield, of yard-by-yard progress, of frantic swerves from the brinks of deep *barrancas*. Not at all conducive to the peace of Rennert's mind were the occasional wayside crosses of sticks and rocks, each an eloquent *memento mori*.

It was at the edge of what seemed a delta-shaped mesa hemmed in by thick underbrush and broken cliffs that a sleek-coated deer bounded into his path, turned eyes liquid with terror into the headlights and vanished—

But not (Rennert sat up, alert) into absolute darkness. Somewhere in the waste ahead and to his left, fire glowed fitfully in the rain.

He repressed the impulse to jubilation by telling himself that he would probably find only a miserable goatherd huddling under a ledge, as innocent of highways as of things pertaining to another planet. But he was resolved to end this groping through country where a man with a broken limb might lie for days a few feet off the road, seen only by vultures. At the worst he could spend the night in the car.

He wriggled his aching shoulders back and forth and cut in the direction of the beacon, hurried on by the tattoo of the rain.

The glow grew brighter, became at last red-tinged smoke and sparks spewed by a huge stone chimney. Below was a dark mass which must surely be unreal, an image conjured up by the imps of the mountains to tantalize him. But instead of fading, it continued to materialize as he drew nearer: a square, one-storied, fortresslike house of adobe roofed with tiles. It faced south. To the rear on the west side, which he was approaching, was a matching building which he decided was the garage. Civilization!

Rennert parked in a graveled drive and ran through mud to the door.

It was a substantial door, of split logs bossed with nails, sheltered inadequately by a small projection of the roof. As he lifted and let fall a ponderous knocker fashioned in the shape of a hand, water dripped on the back of his hatbrim and spray drenched the nape of his neck. He pulled up his collar and waited, glancing at the two windows, shuttered so tightly that they emitted no chink of light. Standing here, one saw no sign at all that the house was tenanted. Snake cactus ran riot over the ground, climbed the walls and swayed back in the water that flowed from the lips of the tiles.

The rain had a hollow sound upon the roof, accenting the pervading stillness. The cold was penetrating, and Rennert buttoned his thin coat against, it and against the vague, unreasoned dismay which always took hold of him when he was confronted by the loneliness of mountains. He had observed the same reaction in others whose lives, like his own, were spent in the more intimate lower altitudes, where silence is a compound of countless tiny noises, not a part of the emptiness of space. It wasn't to be attributed altogether to the unaccustomed strain put upon lungs and heart by rarefied air. . . .

Why the devil didn't someone answer?

His hand was lifted to ply the knocker again when the door was thrown open abruptly and a man stepped out.

2
CORPSE LIGHT

RENNERT HAD a momentary glimpse of shadows dodging firelight over white walls and a dark-beamed ceiling, then the door was closed and he was blinking in the glare of a powerful electric torch.

"Hullo." It was a thick and noncommittal greeting from a thick-set, heavy-shouldered young man, who stood like a figure blocked out of wood and clothed, by dint of straining seams, in seersuckers.

Rennert had to lower his eyes. They stopped short on the right coat pocket, where the fellow's hand was buried. That hand was held stiffly and grasped an object which bulged the cloth and ended, a few inches from the pit of Rennert's stomach, in a blunt point.

Now there is nothing necessarily alarming about the fact that the owner of a house in such an isolated spot should have a gun in his pocket when he answers a knock at his door. And as Rennert explained his predicament, he reminded himself that his own appearance wasn't likely to instill confidence in a stranger. His blue serge suit and limp felt hat were discarded ones which he had unearthed for this trip. His face must look decidedly dark, tanned by the Texas sun and untouched by the razor since early morning. . . .

But—damn it!—granting all that, there wasn't any reason why the man should inspect his features so minutely, maintaining meanwhile his imitation of a wooden Indian.

"Can you give me any information about road conditions south of here?"

"No," the other shook his head and said in the same tone, "I can't."

Rennert found his manner puzzling. There was nothing exactly apprehensive or hostile in it, but it certainly carried no hint of welcome.

"Any other houses near by?"

"I don't know."

"Then," Rennert summoned a smile which he hoped was disarming, "I'm going to ask you to put me up for the night if you can possibly manage it. Any kind of accommodation. I'll be glad to pay." As an afterthought, noting the fellow's hesitation, he added, "I have my passport here if you'd like to look at it."

"All right."

A passport, Rennert had found, is more likely to create a favorable impression upon one's countrymen abroad than upon foreigners. It becomes a link with home, and they fail to consider how little evidence it carries of the possessor's integrity.

This was an American in his late twenties or early thirties. Judging by his speech he was from one of the Southwestern states and had acquired some of the labialism of the Mexican, but not the corresponding mobility of the lips to make his words distinct. He had short brick-red hair and a square homely face which might have been likable enough had it not been weighted down by such a sullen expression.

Rennert's smile had no effect on him. Instead he took the document, frowned and glanced up from the photograph.

Rennert was surprised. It was a rather good photograph, he had always thought, and although it had been taken years before, when his face was younger and leaner and the gray was not yet so apparent in the dark-brown hair at his temples, there could be no question as to the identity.

The young man stared at him as he handed back the passport.

"I see," he said slowly, "that you're with the United States customs service."

"I was until recently. I'm located in the Rio Grande Valley in southern Texas now. A citrus fruit farm."

"Oh." The stare lasted a moment longer. "I hate to turn you down. But we're crowded tonight—"

"If I may put my car in your garage I'll be willing to bunk there until morning."

"No, that won't do," the other said at once. "I suppose we can make room for you. By the way, my name's Kerwick." He started to extend his right hand, reconsidered, and kept it in his pocket. "I'll open the garage for you."

They walked in silence to the corner of the house, where they separated and Rennert dashed to his car.

Inside, he watched Kerwick's stride through the yellowish swathes cut by the headlights. The unpressed trousers gave his muscular legs a cumbersome look and made his reckless splashing progress across puddles an elephantine one. He held his head up but kept turning it to right and left with quick jerks that spoke of alertness.

He came to a halt before the sextuple folding doors of white-painted wood, wheeled about and peered through narrowed lids past the corner of the building, He was frowning, and his wet face had an angry harried expression, as if there were some personal quality in the night and in the veils of rain which baffled him.

Rennert let his window down and followed the direction of his gaze. The beam of the electric torch stabbed futilely at the darkness, revealing nothing but straight-falling rain and thin wraiths of spray that drifted slowly away into the windless night. Rain tapped on the car top and drummed on the hood. From a gutter water spouted, to batter monotonously against stones. There was no other sound.

Kerwick shook his shoulders, jammed the flashlight into a pocket and brought out a bunch of keys upon a ring.

Rennert allowed the car to glide forward, in order to give him more illumination. He had to stop, for the fellow was having difficulty with the keys. He sorted through them with fumbling fingers, trying to insert one after another into the lock. Once he dropped them.

From force of habit Rennert reached for the cigarettes which, in lieu of family and other strong personal attachments, did more than he realized to keep his somewhat egocentric life upon its even tenor. His hand came out empty from his pocket. That Mexican (highwayman, not patrolman) had taken the only pack which he had carried on his person. He'd have to wait until he could get at the carton in his bag

And then, as Kerwick was pushing back the doors, he felt a sudden misgiving. *Had he put that carton in his bag?* He remembered carrying it into the bedroom and tossing it on the dresser while he made up his mind what clothes he'd need. . . .

"Damn!" he said under his breath.

Kerwick was beckoning him on impatiently.

There was space in the garage for six automobiles. It held three now, all spattered with fresh mud: a coupe like his own, with a Texas license plate and no chains on the tires; a long dark blue touring car from Kansas, of an expensive make; a steel-gray roadster which hailed (Rennert noted with casual interest) not only from the Lone Star state but from Brownsville, judging by the tag of a familiar motor company.

He followed wet tread marks into a vacant place alongside the latter and got out. He hauled his grip from the rear compartment and was about to set it upon the cement floor preparatory to switching off his lights when Kerwick's command stopped him.

"Wait!"

He turned his head slightly and looked into the muzzle of a slim black automatic, held in a huge and muscular hand.

"I hope you don't mind if I look you over for a gun." The hand went over his body none too gently, slapping his hips and exploring his armpits.

Rennert repressed a surge of ill temper. There was nothing to do, of course, but submit gracefully to this search.

"A man of peace," he commented with a lightness which, to tell the truth, he was far from feeling. His host was so very grim and determined.

"So I see. Now put your grip on the running board and I'll give it the once-over."

Rennert obeyed, unfastened the clasps and stood back. He thought, as he watched the clumsy examination of the contents, that he could have given the fellow several pointers on how to go about it more efficiently.

"O.K." Kerwick straightened, pocketed his gun and produced the torch again. "I'm sorry, but we have to be careful out in these mountains."

"Prowlers?" Rennert asked, as a hasty glance told him that he was going to be reduced to cadging cigarettes that night.

"Uh—yes."

"How many guests do you have?"

"Let's see." Kerwick moved his lips as he counted to himself. "Six. You make seven. Then there are three of us staying here." He slammed the doors shut as if he were venting animosity upon them.

"I take it this is a hunting lodge."

"Yes." It sounded like an oath. The young fool had confused the keys again and was starting on the trial-and-error method.

Shoulders hunched, Rennert began to pace the gravel. He knew the Mexican border states had taken action recently to halt the depletion of their wild life by commercial hunters from the United States, passing stringent laws which prohibited the killing of game except on a man's own property. He knew too how quick Texas sportsmen had been to circumvent such restrictions by purchasing or leasing land and building lodges such as this, where they and their guests (often paying guests) could slaughter deer and other animals undisturbed. Perhaps Kerwick was shooting without a license or poaching on another's preserves and feared he was being spied upon.

He came to a halt at the southwest corner of the building and started to turn back. He was wet and cold, miserably cold, down to his middle-aged hard-used bones. He didn't give a damn what peccadilloes other people had on their consciences if they would only let him hug a fire. . . .

His ears were growing accustomed to the disturbances of the streaming night, so that its basic stillness was at him again, intensified. One sound alone he couldn't identify: a slow, persistent scrabbling, as of something crawling over loose earth.

Impulsively he stepped around the corner and tried to penetrate the murk at the rear of the adobe wall. The ground sloped sharply here, so that the water cut furrows about his feet. In it, the length of his own body away perhaps, was a faint but unmistakable luminescence which brought instantly to his mind the death fires of the Ancient Mariner:

> "The water, like a witch's oils,
> Burnt green, and blue, and white."

Like an impossibly long and thin glowworm it was working itself toward him, twisting with the rivulet around obstructing stones. It wasn't making those grating noises, however. They came from the unrelieved darkness beyond. . . .

"Say!" Kerwick yelled. "Where are you?"

"Here. Bring the torch, will you?"

"What in the hell are you doing?" Not until the light found him standing in mud that reached almost to his shoe tops did Rennert consider what a ridiculous figure he cut, giving way to his curiosity in this fashion.

Without replying he bent over, balancing himself with one hand while he sent the other swooping into the water. The beam flashing between his widespread legs told him what he had fished out.

He straightened and turned, dangling in front of him a string of illuminated beads with pendent crucifix. They looked now as if they were coated with ordinary whitish paint, the green glow having faded in the rays of the torch.

Kerwick gave a stifled whistle and took them in his hand. He turned them over and over and scrutinized closely the bottom of the cross. "That's queer," he mumbled, seeming in his absorption to have forgotten that he wasn't alone.

"I think," Rennert said, "the water's bringing something even queerer from behind your garage."

3
WET RED HAIR

KERWICK'S LIGHT darted up the incline, jerked to the right and became stationary.

Near the rear of the garage lay a man's body. It formed an acute angle with the wall, the bare head with its shock of black hair slipping downward more rapidly than the feet, which grazed the adobe.

"Oh-my-God-hold-this!" Kerwick loosed the words in one breath as he pressed beads and torch into Rennert's hands. He went bounding up the slope, lost his footing and clambered on all fours, like a bear impeded by clothing.

He came back more slowly, digging his heels into the soil. He was carrying without apparent effort a small Mexican, clad in overalls, faded blue shirt and leather *guarachas*. Head, arms and feet hung limply.

"Open those doors for me. We'll take him inside."

Rennert preceded him and folded back the doors for which the key evidently had not yet been found.

Kerwick lumbered past him and laid his burden on the floor. He got down on his knees and began an examination which for inefficiency matched his search of the grip. There never had been a pulse where his thumb was gouging.

"Let me do this," Rennert said shortly. "I've had experience." He sat down on his heels and transferred the light to his left hand. He stayed in this posture for a moment. "Are you familiar with Mexico?" he asked.

Kerwick sank heavily onto the running board of Rennert's car and stared at him dazedly. "What's that?"

"I say, are you familiar with Mexico—its laws and the way they're enforced?"

"I've lived here almost five years."

"Then I suppose you know we're committing a criminal offense by touching this man. I have no compunctions about it in circumstances like these if you haven't. But I thought I'd warn you."

"I've already touched him." Kerwick's head was lowered, and he was running his fingers through his hair. "You might as well go ahead. I'll take the responsibility."

"We'll share it."

The man was dead, Rennert ascertained at once. Bodily warmth lingered, and *rigor mortis* had not set in, despite the fact that he had been exposed to cold and rain. There was no blood, but a livid bruise as wide as his palm ran from the left side of the neck below the ear, across jaw and cheekbone and over the forehead. Rennert held the light close and passed his fingers over the skin. This was unbroken, and there were no noticeably deep indentations, although it was apparent that the prominent bones had received considerable pressure. He examined the back of the head and found, as he expected, a contusion where mud and rain had removed any blood that might have appeared before death stopped the flow.

He lowered the head gently and fingered for a moment a rosary of an altogether different sort which still circled the dark, scrawny neck. On a thin leather thong were strung a few smooth round stones: the supposedly petrified "deer eyes" with which aboriginal Mexico wards off attacks of *los aires*, the malignant spirits infesting water. Here was a Mexican, evidently, who had sought to play safe by garnering the blessings of both old and new religions.

"I'm no doctor," Rennert said as he rose and surveyed the three automobiles in a row with his, "but I don't think there's much doubt the man was killed by a car. Knocked down and run over. One tire passed over his face." He paused and glanced swiftly at Kerwick. "Which one of those is yours?"

The red hair was tousled now, and the young fellow didn't look at all formidable. More than a little sick, rather, and trying not to show it. "None of 'em. They all belong to people who're staying here for the night."

"I judge by the mud that none of them have been here long?"

"No, they all came within the last hour. Less than that."

"Do you know who the Mexican is?"

Kerwick didn't reply until he had got out his handkerchief, wiped moisture from his face and blown his nose stertorously. "The caretaker."

"When did you see him last?"

"About half an hour—forty minutes—ago. He came outdoors. I guess that's when he was hit."

"Which cars arrived after he left the house?"

"All three of 'em."

"None of your guests mentioned an accident?" Kerwick shook his head.

There was an interval of silence during which Rennert studied the automobiles. An observer would have credited him with a piety which wasn't his, for as he stood over the corpse his face was grave, and without his awareness his fingers were telling the beads on the string which he had kept wrapped around his hand.

"Mr. Kerwick," he said at last, "we might as well face the facts. The evidence is that one of your guests accidentally struck this man, then hid his body. The rain dislodged it, and these beads came unclasped from the neck. It was an action typical of a large percentage of Americans who visit Mexico. They come down here and consider themselves under a divine dispensation to do what they please. The man responsible for this probably lifts up his hands in holy horror when he reads of a hit-and-run driver back home. But here it's only a native who got in the way of his car. This sort of thing makes me wonder why the Mexicans treat us as courteously as they do." Rennert checked himself. "But I don't need to stand here preaching to you. It's one of the few subjects I get heated up about. We've got to notify the state police, of course. I'll drive on to the highway."

"I'll be damned if you do!" Kerwick was on his feet, his face darkened by a sudden infusion of blood, his blunt jaw thrust out aggressively.

Their eyes clashed. Kerwick's were light blue, with the narrowed lids acquired by men who are exposed to the sun a great deal. They glinted brightly in the light of the torch which Rennert still held. It was several seconds before the tightness about them and about the square mouth relaxed a bit.

"I mean," Kerwick said, "I can't let you go to that much trouble. These roads are dangerous. Wait till morning."

It wasn't at all what he had meant, Rennert felt sure as he appraised the obstinate determination in features which weren't as stolid as he had thought at first. The skin had a healthy scrubbed look and the mahogany coloring which comes from tan upon a naturally ruddy complexion. A slight mottling was probably due to the presence of freckles.

Rennert spoke as if to a freckled, red-haired boy: "There'll be enough trouble with the police as it is, without having to explain a night's delay in calling them," and started toward his car.

He side-stepped a blow which would have floored a much larger man than he. As the fist swished past his ear he wondered how long his little knowledge of boxing would keep him on his feet against this lusty fellow whom he had thought to be bluffing.

But Kerwick didn't follow up the attack. Instead he caught Rennert's arm and said in quick contrition: "I'm sorry. I didn't go to do that. It was a silly stunt to pull. I—well, I'm sorry."

"Forget about it. Let's see just where we stand, though. I'm ready to concede that you can prevent my leaving if you want to. But are you sure you want to? That's the point."

"Yes." Rennert's arm ached with the tightening of the grip, but the trembling of the big hand told him of the strain that was racking Kerwick. "Listen! I know you think I'm trying to cover this business up. But I'm not. I swear I'm not. I'm in a hell of a mess, but I want to see the guy who did this get what's coming to him. In the morning I'll go with you to tell the Police. Or I'll stay here and hold everybody while you go. But I can't have them coming here now. Help me out, won't you?"

"Do I have a choice in the matter?"

Kerwick moved back and planted himself directly in front of the car door.

"No," he said thickly, "you don't. You're not going to leave this place tonight."

Rennert shrugged, much as a Mexican would have done in like circumstances.

"Then there's nothing more for me to say."

"No. Will you hold the light for me while I put this body some place? We can't let him just lie here. Then we'll go in the house."

"You aren't going to take him in with you?"

"No. That's another thing. If we say anything about having found him, the ones that were in the car which killed him will try to get away during the night. So the best thing for us to do is keep still. Not mention it to a soul. You promise you won't?"

Rennert shook his head slowly. This abrupt shifting of attitude was disconcerting. Kerwick looked now exactly like a boy who is offering to share a secret with a senior.

"I'm not going to promise anything. But my intentions right now are to keep my mouth closed."

"Good!" Kerwick's gaze wandered about the room and came to rest on a narrow staircase set against the east wall. "I imagine he lives upstairs. I'll take him up there anyway. Let me have the light."

Thoughtfully Rennert watched him lift the body with one arm and carry it over the cement and up the stairs. If that were a slip of the tongue it was an exceedingly odd one, betraying a greater unfamiliarity with the garage than had the confusion with the keys.

Something was very very rotten in the state of Tamaulipas, Rennert told himself uneasily as he took advantage of the other's absence to inspect the cars by matchlight. He found no dent or scratch which would indicate a collision. The Mexican, of course, had been of slight build, easily knocked to the ground. . . .

When Kerwick returned, Rennert was standing a few feet from the rear of the row of automobiles. "Before we go," he said, "I wish you'd tell me the names of the owners of these cars."

"I don't think I remember."

"They're all strangers?"

"Yes, all of 'em stopped just like you did. Let's see. That one"—Kerwick pointed to the roadster from Brownsville—"came last. A man and a woman in it. A man and a woman in the next one too." This was the touring car from Kansas. "I believe their name's Elkins. The last one, the one like yours but without chains, had two men in it. That's all I know."

"Where's the other car that was in here this evening?"

Kerwick pounded the end of the torch into the palm of his hand. "What other car?" he asked without looking at Rennert.

"The one which left those tread marks under mine."

"Oh, that!" Kerwick hawked loudly and spat into the rain. "It's gone on down to Victoria. It belongs to Mr. Smith, the man who owns this house. He sent the chauffeur on an errand. Ready to go in?"

Rennert waited on the gravel while the other locked the doors and dropped the keys into a pocket.

"I hope Mr. Smith has chains on his tires," he said as they tramped toward the house. "Otherwise the chauffeur's having hard going."

"The hell of it is, he doesn't. Forgot to bring 'em. He can get some in Victoria, though." At the corner Kerwick stopped Rennert. "Do you mind giving me that string of beads?" he asked in a low voice.

"Of course not." Rennert handed it over.

"Thanks."

When they lifted their feet, the mud into which they had sunk made tiny sucking noises, as if reluctant to let them go.

Kerwick threw open the front door unceremoniously, and Rennert crossed the threshold. A chill little eddy of rain-driven spray went in with him and touched his ankles in passing. His quick sneeze was a trumpet blast announcing their entry, so loud that it drowned in the stillness of the room the click and thud of key and bolt.

4
NOT WARMED BY FIRE

FIRELIGHT FLICKERED CONFUSINGLY, so that it took Rennert a moment to realize that he was in no cavernous hall but a living room some sixteen feet by thirty or larger—a symmetrically arranged room, with another door straight ahead and at each end wide chimneys of uncut stones set between arched openings to what were evidently alcoves facing east and west.

Gradually shadows sorted themselves out, became distortions of hunting trophies on whitewashed walls, of unlighted hurricane lamps swung from square chiseled beams, of furniture shrouded in dust coverings. Illumination came from the fireplace on his left, where the head of a Mexican collared peccary, or javaline, thrust snout and tusks out over blazing logs that silhouetted the bodies of two men, both of whom were staring intently in his direction.

On the mantelshelf behind them a candle in a brass holder burned with a steady flame while its mate, on a table drawn up between the fire and a deep couch, made a gleaming white tonsure out of the bald crown of a man who did not turn around.

"You probably want to get warm," Kerwick said at his elbow. "Rennert, I believe you said your name was?" His voice was as inattentive as his eyes, which were roving aimlessly over the bare floor of dull red, unglazed tiles.

"Yes." As Rennert put down his grip and crossed the room with him he wondered if it were a trick of the firelight or if there was an increasing alertness in the attitude of the standing men, a swift composure of facial expressions in preparation for the introduction.

"This is Mr. Rennert." In an attempt at naturalness, perhaps, Kerwick had spoken so loudly that the walls boomed back his echo. He cleared his throat and said indistinctly, "I'm not sure I remember your names."

The first was a fat man in a suit of light-olive whipcord which had too many pleats and buttons and too wide lapels. His mouth was open and he panted slightly, as if he were having difficulty with his breathing.

"Bohannon," he pronounced and smiled. In the process his small eyes, like oiled blue agates, were almost lost amid folds of unhealthily pale flesh. "Another guy with car trouble?"

"My car's all right, but I don't like mountain driving in weather like this. What's your difficulty?" Rennert wanted very much to reach for a handkerchief. The man's palm had been soft and moist and had rested flaccidly in his own.

"No chains. We didn't look for this rain." Bohannon moved back toward the fire and took a comfortable stance, with legs wide apart and one hand smoothing sleek yellow hair over a thinning spot at the top of his head. The candlelight glistened on tiny dribblings of chili or some equally greasy substance on the protuberant front of his vest. "You're spendin' the night here?" he asked, still smiling meaninglessly.

"Yes, thanks to Mr. Kerwick's hospitality."

"I see. Lucky we found this house, ain't it?" The observation did not warrant the thoughtfulness which he seemed to give it. "Oh—meet my partner, Tom Lurcott."

Lurcott was a smaller man, wiry, with tar-black, sharply parted hair which gave his face the effect of a white and expressionless mask. He did not offer to shake hands but kept up an almost imperceptible to-and-fro movement on the balls of his feet as he scanned Rennert's features with cold black eyes.

"Where you from?" He spoke out of one side of his mouth, with a slight curling of the upper lip, so that Rennert saw the flash of gold bridgework on his teeth.

"Brownsville."

"Where you headed?"

"Victoria."

"Business trip?"

"Yes." Rennert turned away in distaste from the staccato questioning and from the pungent odor of garlic which enveloped the pair. There would be no warming of himself at *that* fire.

Of different caliber was the occupant of the couch, who sat with knees spread to afford room for the end table which he had pulled around in front of him and on which he was laying out cards in a game of solitaire. The candle shone full on his face as he raised bleak uninterested eyes to meet Rennert's.

At the time the latter supposed it was the amber light coming from below, combined with his first impression of a shaven tonsure, which made him think of those features as ascetic. When he went closer he saw instead the glum solid countenance of an elderly man who eased out the word "Elkins" as he extended a meaty hand across the table with more concern for the arrangement of the cards than for Rennert's convenience. The eyes returned to the table, and the fingers which had barely touched Rennert's picked up, with deliberation, a card.

Elkins. . . .

A sudden movement on Kerwick's part drew Rennert's attention away.

That young man had remained in the background, with downcast eyes which must have been scrutinizing a portion of the floor rather closely. For now he stooped swiftly to the fiber wood basket at the end of the fireplace, tore a forked twig from one of the logs and with it in his hand squatted down near the wall. Very carefully—and, it would appear, cautiously—he ran one prong along the shallow depression between two of the tiles. Something tiny and bright was thrown up, to gleam upon the dark square before his blunt fingers managed to get hold of it.

His lips moved as he rose, and Rennert could read on them the short explosive oath which he kept back. He dropped the twig and thrust into the lapel of his coat a common straight pin.

He glanced up, as if suddenly conscious of surveillance, and flushed with embarrassment or annoyance.

"Looking for something?" Lurcott's voice flicked at him. The tight surrounding muscles and the stationary points of light on their still jet-black surfaces made his eyes seem lidless. The only parts of him that moved were his short, spatulate fingers, which were slowly tensing.

Bohannon was breathing stertorously. His smile had gone, and his face glistened as if perspiration had been frozen on it.

Rennert felt the impact of their watchfulness as sharply and emphatically as if a cold draft had come down the chimney and crept past them to prickle his skin.

He sensed that Kerwick was feeling it too, for the first time perhaps, and that for all his bulk and hard-bitten exterior the young fellow was alarmed. He stared at Lurcott as if trying to fight off the hypnosis of that black unblinking gaze while his hand went to his pocket and closed about the butt of the gun. "No," he said, "not looking for anything in particular." He turned to Rennert and cleared his throat again. "Do you want to sit down or get washed before supper? We're going to eat in a few minutes."

"I'd like to get some of this grime off."

"All right. Come on. I'll show you to a room."

As Rennert retrieved his grip and went with him to the rear, followed by the eyes of Bohannon and Lurcott, he took occasion to verify an observation about that floor. It had been swept recently. Unglazed tiles "sweat" profusely in damp weather, and these were streaked by the gummy marks of a broom. The broom itself stood against the north wall, by the door which Kerwick was holding open.

Rennert passed through and found himself in a short bare passage, flanked by two doors and debouching on an open courtyard. The rain sent little currents of air to meet them and very gently to sway the lighted lamp which hung on chains from the low ceiling. The meager flicker burnished Kerwick's close-cropped crinkly hair and glistened on his wet shoulders as he paused a few paces ahead and looked about him in an attitude of uncertainty. In sudden decision, just as Rennert came abreast, he turned to the left.

The patio was square and gave access to the rooms which occupied the rear of the house. It was paved with flagstones, and in the center were big-bellied jars which held flowers or plants of some sort. Along the sides ran a gallery whose roof did not project far enough to afford adequate shelter from the spatter of rain deflected from the stones. There was more of the snake cactus, a half-wild species whose stems grew erect for a few feet, then bent over to twine about the railing and to clamber up the wooden posts.

At the corner Kerwick pulled the torch from his pocket and sent its beam ahead of them along the adobe wall on the west. He came to a halt at the door in the center, knocked and, when no response was forthcoming, turned the knob and went in.

Rennert stood on the threshold and watched object after object picked out by the light as it traveled across the tiled floor and upward: two suitcases side by side, a round wicker table on which rested a brace of candles, a Panama hat and a felt cap—

"I guess somebody already has this room," Kerwick's voice came back to him. "Wait a minute." He laid the torch on the table, knelt, opened one of the suitcases (a cheap cardboard affair) and began to rummage through its contents.

Rennert stepped inside, put down his grip and looked about a chilly uninviting bedroom with blank whitewashed walls. There were two brass beds, one between the windows on the west, the other by a south door which stood open upon what appeared to be a bath.

"These belong," Kerwick explained, "to those two men you met just now—Bohannon and Lurcott. I don't like their looks."

"I can't say I do, either. You weren't quite as cautious with them as with me evidently."

"I frisked both of 'em for guns. Each one had a revolver in a shoulder holster. After I found those I didn't bother with their luggage. I got to thinking it'd be better to make sure that's all they had."

Rennert moved to a position where he could study the down-turned face to advantage. The more he saw of Kerwick the less impressed he was. Superficially at least there was nothing to distinguish him from many another youngster with whom Rennert had come into contact in Mexico. They compose an undevious, essentially naïve crew who seek adventure and El Dorados south of the Rio Grande and find, in nine cases out of ten, only hard work, dysentery and homesickness. He wasn't altogether tolerant toward their failings: their sublime indifference to the subtleties and complexities of their environment; the gridiron mentality which governs their conduct; their silly Anglo-Saxon racial prejudices. But, he had to admit, they were seldom perverse. More like bulls in china closets. . . .

"Kerwick," Rennert became rather paternal, "what's wrong?"

The blue eyes rose quickly to his and clouded. "What makes you think there's anything wrong?"

"You told me out in the garage you were in a hell of a mess."

"Did I? Well, forget it. I was talking about that dead Mexican."

"I don't think you were."

Kerwick rose, his face congested, and propped both hands on his hips. "Listen," he said angrily, "you haven't got any copper's badge, have you? You're acting like Mr. God or something. Maybe I am in a mess. What business is it of yours?"

"None at all. I merely thought I might be of assistance."

"Well—" Kerwick's fit of ill temper began to subside. He shook head and neck like a dog throwing off water and blinked at the floor. "The best thing you can do is get some supper, then go to bed—"

"Mr. Woodmansee? Is that Mr. Woodmansee?"

Both of them turned toward the voice that fluttered from the door of the patio. A middle-aged woman with shingled gray hair was standing just outside, pressing the collar of a dark cloth coat to her throat as she squinted myopically within.

Kerwick picked up the torch and directed it upon her, whereupon she raised her left hand to shield her eyes. "Mr. Woodmansee isn't here," he answered. "His room is opposite this."

"Oh, pardon me!" she talked breathlessly. "I'm nearsighted. And I haven't any glasses. I was just feeling my way back to the living room. I wasn't sure which side of the court Mr. Woodmansee was on. But I came to this open door, and I thought I'd call, and if he was here I'd get him to take me in. It's so dark—and this rain—this awful rain! I can't see a thing."

Rennert glanced at Kerwick and, as the latter made no move to do so, offered his assistance.

"Oh, that will be so kind of you." The woman peered in his direction. "You must excuse me if I don't recognize you—"

Kerwick came to life. "This is Mr. Rennert, Mrs. Woodmansee."

She caught her breath sharply. "No! You've made a mistake. It's Miss Pirtle. *Miss* Pirtle." She turned her face away to hide its growing confusion. "I supposed that Mr. Woodmansee had explained. He's just—just driving my car for me back from Mexico City."

"Sorry," Kerwick was gruffly apologetic. "All he said was you wanted different rooms. I didn't catch the names when you came in." He looked at Rennert. "We'll have to wait till after supper to get everybody sorted out. I'm all mixed up. You go in that room off the passage. Not the one on this side, that's the kitchen, but the east one. It's a—well, it's not a bedroom, but it'll do for the present. You can use this bath here."

"Very well." Rennert summoned a smile. "Do you have a cigarette, Kerwick? I hate to bum, but I find I brought only one package, and a Mexican on the Highway Patrol relieved me of that."

Kerwick stared at him, wooden-faced. "The Highway Patrol?" he demanded. "Where did you see him?"

"Back on the main road. At the beginning of the detour."

"Oh!" There could be no mistaking the relief in the monosyllable. "No, I don't have any cigarettes. Never smoke."

Thoughtfully Rennert took his grip in one hand, Miss Pirtle's arm in the other and guided her along the wall. It wasn't an infraction of a gaming law which was worrying Kerwick, he felt sure now, or a mention of the Highway Patrol wouldn't have aroused such perturbation.

Miss Pirtle's arm, a good solid arm which his hand failed to encompass, was trembling.

"Miserable night, isn't it?" he made polite conversation. "You'll be glad to get back to that Brownsville sunshine."

"How did you know I was from Brownsville?"

"I saw the tag on your roadster. I happen to be from the same city, by the way."

Her steps dragged, and he thought she was going to stop. "What did the young man, say your name was?"

"Rennert." As the lamp in the passage illuminated her, he was wondering what heartless hairdresser had persuaded her that that coquettish shingle was becoming. He frowned. The woman looked almost sick.

"Hugh Rennert?"

"Yes."

"Oh!" She disengaged her arm and brushed a hand across her eyes. "I might have known," she said dully as she groped for and found the door.

5
THE MONK'S WIFE

WATER FROM THE flooded court trickled over the tiles of the passage, nibbling at the soles of Rennert's shoes and laying siege to them with a widening pool. Brought to awareness of spongy socks by a violent sneeze, he quit his speculative staring at the door through which his fellow-Brownsvilleite had gone with her puzzling curtain line, passed into the room on his left and struck a match.

Straight ahead was a wicker table with a candle. He lighted this, put down his grip and looked about his temporary lodgings.

This was a long narrow room which separated the east end of the living room from the patio. He shared Kerwick's uncertainty as to a name with which to designate it. Gun- or cardroom probably. In the corners to left and right of the door were a cedar chest and folded card tables. In the center of the north wall was an empty fireplace, similar to those in the living room but smaller, with leather club chairs, footstools, a hassock and smoking equipment grouped about it. Against the opposite wall, with a background of framed prints of hunting scenes, was a studio couch. On one side of it stood a case with a glass door, through which could be seen rows of brass brads doubtless intended to hold guns upright; on the other, built-in shelves on which were ranged books, a stack of magazines and a few pieces of ornamental Mexican pottery.

Overhead was another unlighted hurricane lamp whose loose base evidenced the fact that it held no fuel. On the mantel was a second candle, however, and with this Rennert continued his inspection.

The room certainly had had no recent ventilation. The air was dead, pervaded by the aguish dankness given off by adobe in wet weather. He sniffed and tried to isolate a foreign odor—an uncleanly pungent smell, not unlike that left by a hibernating animal. . . .

There were two windows: a small one in the north wall which would give upon the patio and a wider one in the east. He went to the latter and demolished several spider webs as he unfastened the catch, pushed up the lower pane and tested the transverse bars outside. They were inch-thick bars of iron, firmly embedded in the adobe. He reached through them and opened the shutters.

Impenetrable blackness balked his eyes, and the wetness on his face was like another web that couldn't be brushed away. *Noche triste.* Such darkness and dismal rain had added to the terror of Aztec snake drums the night Cortez's Spaniards fled headlong from Tenochtitlan.

He shut himself in again and turned to the door adjoining the fireplace on his left, thinking it must belong to a closet. Instead he found himself in a bathroom, small but fitted with shower and lavatory. The latter had been used but a short time before, for the enamel was damp and had about it the sharp hygienic fragrance of good soap and Eau de Cologne. Through the closed door facing the one through which he had entered came a low but spirited whistling of that ballad of death in the bull ring, "El Relicario."

Rennert stooped to examine the kerosene heater which stood in a corner. At the click of the metal top on tile, the whistling was cut short, and he knew from the absence of all sound on the other side of the door that Mr. Woodmansee was listening. For, according to Kerwick, those were the quarters of the man who was driving Miss Pirtle's car—Miss Pirtle, who had been so strangely distressed at a meeting with a humble grower of grapefruit by the name of Hugh Rennert.

Having ascertained that the reservoir was empty, the inquisitive grapefruit grower straightened and waited a moment. When his neighbor made no move to enter, he returned to the other room for a towel and toilet kit.

After getting them from his grip, his roving eyes lighted on the bookshelves, which would have been a magnet for him in any circumstance. With the aid of the candle he scrutinized the backs of the four or five dozen volumes: the collected works of Henrik Ibsen; a few mystery novels; a goodly number of books on Mexico. . . .

But the literary tastes of the owner of that house didn't interest Rennert much. He took down a copy of D. H. Lawrence's *The Plumed Serpent* because it was within easy reach and turned to the flyleaf. There was a bookplate, and his face grew graver as he studied it. It was a handsome thing, representing a Viking ship darting out of a gloomy fiord and breasting the sea waves. Below was a name in block lettering: Snorre Bjerregaard.

"Smith hell!" Rennert said to himself as he replaced that volume and found the same plate in half a dozen of its companions. He shook dust from the top magazines in the pile and looked at the address labels on months'-old copies of *Field and Stream*: Snorre Bjerregaard, with a street number in Corpus Christi, Texas.

Not conclusive, of course, but enough to crystallize Rennert's suspicions and send him back to the bath with less concern than heretofore for his personal appearance. He washed in water which dribbled from the taps ice-cold and discolored by rust, regarded his reflection in the mirror and told himself he needed a shave but wasn't going to have one, despite the good example set by Mr. Woodmansee.

Still no resumption by Mr. Woodmansee of the bullfighter's dying words . . .

In his own room, however, the door from the passage opened and closed, and light footsteps moved over the floor.

He adjusted his tie, donned his coat and went in.

A woman was standing by the table on which he had left a candle burning. He saw her in profile, with the fingertips of her right hand drumming very lightly on the wicker as her eyes made the circuit of the room.

Rennert's pause was involuntary, and he wondered, after an instant, how many years it had been since he had gawked in such open tribute at a full-blown feminine form. It was the unhurried turning of her head, perhaps, which made him think of a model in a fashion show (he had seen them in the movies) who wore, with the poise that comes from an assurance of perfection, a smartly tailored traveling suit of dark blue tropical worsted. Her hat was a brimless basinet of black feathers, real or imitation he didn't know, which had been so highly lacquered that they gleamed like wet scales. To his conservative bachelor's eyes it was chic but a little too suggestive of—well, of wet scales.

Her face came into view, and he had a momentary glimpse of arched lips parting in a smile. It was a problematic smile, unfinished, for, suddenly conscious of his presence, she turned upon him.

"I'm sorry if I startled you," he said. "I was in the adjoining room when you came in. I'm Mr. Rennert, staying here for the night. Mr. Kerwick put me in here temporarily."

Her face, although pretty, didn't bear out the promise of her body. It was saved from being dollish, he decided, only by her eyes. These were black and lustrous and probably didn't need the rather elaborate setting which their made-up lashes and brows gave them. If not intelligent, they were exceedingly shrewd and careful eyes, which had appraised men before as they were appraising him now. They inspected his clothing, his hands and returned to his face.

"Thank God!" she said, relaxing. "You look like a respectable man. You don't have a machine gun hid in here, do you? Or a black-jack up your sleeve?"

"No. And I wasn't aware until tonight that people were supposed to travel with them in this part of Mexico."

"I take it the red-headed young prize fighter searched your luggage before he let you in."

"Kerwick? Yes."

"He did ours too. I'm Mrs. Elkins. My husband's in the front room, I think, waiting to eat. I had no idea anyone was in here or I wouldn't have walked in the way I did. I was just curious to look around the house." From the pocket of her jacket she took a flat silver case and extracted a cigarette. Her manicured pink nailed fingers weren't quite steady.

"I met Mr. Elkins when I came in. I wonder," Rennert spoke as she was about to snap the case shut, "if you'd take mercy on me and give me a cigarette? I'm an inveterate smoker, and I find myself marooned here without a one."

"Of course." She held them out. "I don't suppose you'll like these. Most men don't."

He lifted the candle to hers, then lighted his own. They were Nektars, a brand imported, judging by the taste, from somewhere east of Suez.

She watched his face and laughed. "I was right, wasn't I?"

"Beggars can't be choosers."

Scented smoke gathered in blue-gray coils about the still flames of the two candles. To counteract it for him and to invest her with a very special charm came her perfume, subtly like that of the clove pinks at Xochimilco.

"Where are you from, Mr. Rennert?" she asked, in a tone which told him it was no casual inquiry. The faint flicker in her eyes was the reflection of rapid thought.

He spoke of Brownsville and the citrus fruit farm while a part of him floated on Xochimilco's waters.

"Mr. Elkins and I stayed in Brownsville last night. We drove down from Corpus Christi." She paused. "Are you well acquainted in Corpus?"

"Not very well."

"I wondered if you know a Mr. Bjerregaard there."

Her gaze had wandered or she would have seen the swift flash of interest in his eyes. "Bjerregaard?" he repeated carefully. "What's the first name?"

"Snorre. He's in the shipping business. A good-looking blond fellow in his thirties."

"No," Rennert shook his head. "I don't know him."

"No matter," she said quickly. "Shall we sit down, Mr. Rennert? Or do you want me to run along?"

"Of course not. I'm being a poor host, but I'm really glad you came in."

The remark might prove less banal than it sounded, he thought as he watched her go to the coverless couch and adjust pillows behind her.

"My, these tiles are cold!" She repressed a shiver. "Do you mind getting me one of those little *sarapes* out of the chest to put my feet on?"

Rennert's eyes were more guarded this time and didn't betray his surprise. "It's a good thing you've been taking stock of our resources. I hadn't thought of looking in the chest."

A fleeting expression of something like annoyance crossed her face, and the corners of her mouth tightened. When she laughed, it wasn't altogether naturally. "I was being housewifely. Finding covers for the night."

Yet he was sure, as he walked to the angle of the wall between gun case and door, that she had been in that room only a matter of seconds before he entered. When he pushed back the heavy cedar lid and heard the shrill squeak of its hinges, he knew that the sound would have penetrated to the bath. Her visit, then, had been before he arrived. . . .

It was a large chest, packed to the top with bedding and woolen Mexican blankets. "We might as well make ourselves at home," he said as he took out a rectangular *sarape* which would serve as throw rug or table scarf. Idly his fingers tested the excellence of its weave as he carried it over and spread it on the floor at her feet. It was of Oaxacan manufacture and depicted realistically the coat of arms of the United Mexican States: a royal eagle perched upon a nopal, with talons about a writhing serpent.

"Thanks," she murmured as she leaned back and inhaled deeply.

He sat so he could see her face. She was younger than her husband undoubtedly. A great deal younger. He had been thinking of her as of his own age, but decided now that she would be in her thirties. In her thirties . . .

Suddenly she slapped away smoke and faced him. "Yes," her voice was brittle, "we might as well make ourselves at home in this house. We have as much right to do so as anybody who's here tonight."

"I've had the same suspicion, Mrs. Elkins." *In her thirties.*

"You have?" Her eyes took on new interest in him. "How did you know these people don't belong here?"

"Kerwick is the only one of our hosts I've met. It was obvious that he's unfamiliar with both garage and house. I'm quite sure he didn't know there was a bath adjoining this room. It doesn't necessarily follow, though, that the Mr. Smith whom he mentioned isn't the bona-fide owner. Have you met him?"

"There's an old man and his daughter who call themselves Smith. They gave us to understand the house is theirs and Kerwick is staying with them." She laughed scornfully. "It's a wonder they didn't say he was Mr. Jones."

"Of course there *are* people named Smith."

She tossed her cigarette to the tiles and ground it out with her heel. "But I'm sure they're lying. They all came this evening, not long before we did. Their luggage is piled in the sun parlor, off the living room."

Rennert was trying to analyze her manner, which seemed to have an uncalled-for vindictiveness in it. He was trying to decide also how far he had better confide in her.

"The tread marks in the garage do show that a car entered after the rain started, then left," he said cautiously. "How long have you and Mr. Elkins been here?"

"About thirty or forty minutes. He's not used to mountain driving so insisted on stopping when it got dark and the rain came on. We had a chauffeur, but there was some trouble about his passport at the border, and we couldn't bring him across. We thought we'd hire a Mexican in Victoria who knew the road to Tampico."

"Was anyone outside when you arrived?"

"Outside? Why, no. Kerwick opened the door. He acted sullen, but there wasn't anything he could do but let us stay. He went to the garage with Mr. Elkins, and I waited for them in the front room."

"Who were there?"

"The Smiths and a couple of second-rate thugs, one fat and one slim. They'd just come. Old man Smith kept up a patter about the weather, but Bohannon and Lurcott, or whatever their names were, just stood and watched the rest of us. And the girl kept on sweeping all the time, as if it were a life-and-death matter. Things were pretty strained when Mr. Elkins and Kerwick got back."

"The girl was sweeping. Rather, an odd thing to be doing, don't you think?"

"It did strike me that way. But I thought maybe she was trying to act at home. Kerwick started to show us to rooms when another car drove up. He had the old gentleman take charge of us while he went to meet it. I looked into the patio a few minutes later and saw him escorting a man and a woman out. He gave her a room on the north side. It has a connecting bath with ours. She came blundering in on me, said she'd broken her glasses and was mixed up on directions." Mrs. Elkins glanced at her wrist watch. "I expect we'd better be going back to the living room before long. It's past Jesse's dinnertime, and he'll be fuming if he doesn't get something to eat soon. I'm glad I had this chance to talk to you, Mr. Rennert. Sort of stand by this evening, won't you, until we see what's going to happen?"

"Why, certainly. But we mustn't let the night and the rain work our imaginations too much."

"Listen, Mr. Rennert!" She stopped him and laid a hand on his sleeve. Despite the fact that she was keyed up to a considerable tension, there was a convincing firmness in her voice. "I know all that. Those were the exact words my husband used when I was trying to get him to drive on and not ask for lodging in this house. I told him, when we first saw it, there was something wrong here. He just laughed at me. But it's the truth. I'm positive that these people have no right in this house. Will you believe me?"

"I'm quite willing to believe that. But perhaps you have some reason for your sureness that you haven't told either Mr. Elkins or me."

Her lids were narrowed slightly, but her eyes were very keen in their scrutiny of his face. "You're married, I suppose?" she asked after a moment.

"No, I'm not."

"Well!" Her surprise was evident, and Rennert unaccountably felt ill at ease. She laughed and said, "That was rude of me, wasn't it? But I had you classified as a very uxorious husband. What would you say if I told you that my woman's intuition made me sure the Smiths don't belong here?"

"I'd lift my eyebrows very very politely and let you have it your way."

She patted his arm and spoke in easy camaraderie: "A very sensible thing to do, Mr. Rennert. 'Intuition' is a handy word. Women use it sometimes for—well, for convenience's sake. Some men have sense enough to take it at its face value, others don't. Lift those eyebrows of yours now, and when we go into the other room keep your hand on your pocketbook. I've got my rings hidden. And if you get a chance to warn Mr. Elkins, do it. Maybe he'll listen to you."

Rennert sat forward. "All right," he said. "We're agreed that the Smiths and Kerwick have taken over this house without authority. Does your intuition tell you what their game is?"

"No, it doesn't," she answered slowly. "They may be criminals hiding out here. What really worries me is that Jesse told them who he is. He got started on the subject of the Tampico oil fields, and I couldn't make him stop. I'm afraid they may try to extort money from him."

Rennert turned and looked at her. "I'm dumber than usual to-night," he said. "It's just dawned on me who Mr. Elkins is. The Monk of Tampico."

It was the magic word "oil" which had told Rennert in a flash why there had been something vaguely familiar about the tonsured man engrossed in the game of solitaire. In the Mexico of a quarter of a century earlier, "oil" and "Elkins" had been well-nigh synonymous.

Rennert, it will be seen, had a reason peculiar unto himself for remembering Jesse Elkins and such of his history as was common property. Journalists had been fond of comparing him to one of his own geysers of black gold, which broke from the sea-level swamps to rocket to the sky in spectacular display. Accounts of his landing in Tampico as a beachcomber or fugitive from justice in the States were probably apocryphal, a part of the legends that clustered about him later. Certain it was, however, that the Gulf port first became aware of him as a tool-dresser in an outlying camp—a tool-dresser of parts, who in more than one of the pitched battles which were being fought daily between rival interests proved his ability as a strategist and leader of men.

Elkins was rewarded by a position of responsibility and had risen swiftly in the councils of the company until he occupied one of the major executive offices. Balked, it was said, by knowledge that the top rung of that ladder was temporarily out of his reach, he had started out as an independent concession hunter. His success was phenomenal, his tactics daring but, it was generally conceded, scrupulous enough according to the jungle standards of that period. At precisely the right moment he had sold out to one of the international concerns which were beginning to squeeze out smaller operators. Quitting the scene with as little fanfare as he had arrived upon it, he had retired to the little Midwestern town which had been his birthplace and in which he had banked his fortune—Acropolis, Kansas. Rennert even remembered the name.

Old-timers still mentioned Jesse Elkins with awe or venom or envy, as the case might be, and spoke of him as a curious man whose true personality had always been obscure. The Monk was the nickname which he had acquired, as much from an appearance of which the ghost remained as from his ungregarious habits and strict celibacy in a tropical port where morals were nonexistent and attachments of any degree of intimacy or permanence were a matter of a few pesos. This last distinctive characteristic of his had been attributed to fastidiousness, to some plighted troth, to an accident which had impaired his virility. No one ever knew the truth. And the subject ceased to interest Tampico when the story became current of what had happened to a man in his cups when he made a jest of it to The Monk's face. . . .

So the cardplayer in the next room was Jesse Elkins, and this (Rennert was suddenly aware that he had been staring at her) was his wife!

She was probably accustomed to such gaping at mention of her husband's name, for she smiled matter-of-factly as she rose. "You must get acquainted with Jesse. He'll be awfully pleased that somebody remembers his name. He's going back to visit Tampico for the first time since he left." She offered him her arm and, when he had taken it, pressed his hand against her side. "Want me to give you some advice, Mr. Rennert?"

Rennert nodded. He was being pulled two ways. He was elated that chance had thrown him and Elkins together and at the same time felt the very strongest diffidence at the thought of a meeting which might result for him in anticlimax. Twenty-five years is a long long space. . . .

"When you are a married man," Mrs. Elkins was saying in a friendly, deliberate voice, "and you and your wife are driving through country that's strange to her—a country that you are positive she has never been in before—and you want to stop for the night and she doesn't—and she says her intuition tells her not to—drive straight on, Mr. Rennert. The chances are that you'll be a lot happier—although you will never know it. Now let's go in. You may have to squire me about this evening. Jesse will probably sulk over our little quarrel."

"Because you didn't want to stop at this house?"

"Yes. Because my intuition told me not to."

6
HALL OF THE MOUNTAIN KING

WARMTH MET THEM at the door of the living room. Like its genius, Kerwick was bending over the fireplace at the east end, thrusting another log upon those which already blazed and crackled there, spitting sparks and sending flames up the chimney's gullet with the roar of an approaching tornado.

Rennert realized for the first time what a cheerful room it might be, more so probably in cloistering weather such as this than in the dry and sun-warmed atmosphere for which adobe walls are intended. Whisk those ghostly dust coverings from the furniture. Light the lamps overhead. Most important of all, infuse some animation into the people grouped stiffly about the west fireplace while one thin voice piped ineffectually against their silence: "You'll have to give the Mexicans more time before they have road maps and information available every quarter of a mile. But what's the hurry? I say. When you have them you'll have so many signboards and filling stations and hot-dog stands you won't be able to see the scenery."

Kerwick observed them and came across the room with alacrity, adjusting his cuffs and glancing with obvious surprise from Rennert to his companion. "I was wondering if you weren't about ready." His manner toward Mrs. Elkins had a heavy touch of deference. "Let's go over and meet the others."

"Yes,"—her voice was edged with sarcasm—"we *do* want to meet all your guests."

Bohannon and Lurcott still occupied their positions in front of the fire, blocking both heat and light now that the candle had been removed from the end table. Bohannon looked Buddhalike as he pared his nails with a pocketknife and said: "Nice place you have here, Mr. Smith. Mighty nice place. How many acres do you own?"

In the middle of the couch, between Miss Pirtle and Jesse Elkins, sat a plump little man whose gray hair was roached back from an impressive domed forehead. His fine patrician hands were clasped about the head of a carved and painted Apizaco snake cane. "How many acres?" he repeated in the piping voice. "How many acres? I wouldn't know." He turned at Kerwick's approach. "Oh, there you are, Keith! Mr. Bohannon wants to know how many acres we have here. I keep forgetting. You tell him."

Kerwick's "Fifty" was accompanied by a level and defiant glance in Bohannon's direction. His face was darkly flushed—from his recent proximity to the flames or from anger.

Bohannon merely smiled fatly while his little eyes took on an insolent gleam. Lurcott, still teetering, gave a short mirthless bark of laughter, and Rennert was positive the pair both knew that Smith was an interloper in the house and were baiting him with their knowledge.

His gaze went on to the young man who was standing, half in the shadows, beyond Lurcott. A tall, straight young man, in a tan suit and tan shoes whose polish the rain hadn't effaced, for the large square toes gleamed in the fire's reflection.

Smith was on his feet and bowing with Mexican courtliness to Mrs. Elkins. "Glad you have joined us again, madam. Ah, this is a gentleman I haven't met yet. Keith, my boy, where are your manners?"

Kerwick made a wry attempt at a congenial smile. "Mr. Smith, this is Mr. Rennert. I've told him he could stay here for the night."

"Certainly! Certainly! We're delighted to have you, Mr. Rennert." The old gentleman moved forward a step or two, aided by the cane. His right foot was swollen, and on it he wore a carpet slipper of gray felt. The fire gave a lustrous sheen to his loose black alpaca suit and revealed the sagging of the right pocket of the coat.

The heavy object which he carried there was outlined on the cloth, the shape of a package of cigarettes but larger.

He took Rennert's hand warmly, and the latter thought of a diminutive Saint Nicholas, whose benevolence proceeded partly from the heart and partly from other grosser sources betokened by the ruddy cheeks and by the fleshy nose veined wine red. His blue eyes might have been those of a boy. An imp danced in them, a sprightly imp that would invent jests and ribaldry and horseplay— but nothing more. Rennert added another to his growing list of certainties: there was no harm in this man. It was absurd to think of him as sinister. Could some sort of a practical joke be in progress? he wondered suddenly.

As Smith released his hand and turned to Mrs. Elkins, Rennert found himself observing Bohannon and Lurcott again. If that were the explanation for all this subterfuge, something cold and deadly and unlooked-for had slid in out of the rain, to bask glittering-eyed by the fire. . . .

"Mrs. Elkins, you haven't met Miss Pirtle yet, have you? Oh, you've already met!" Smith seemed in fine fettle, perfectly at his ease. His hand was about Mrs. Elkins' arm and nestled, Rennert thought, rather intimately against her breast. "And, Miss Pirtle, this is Mr. Rennert."

Miss Pirtle had moved from the corner of the couch to its edge, where she perched peering up at him and clasping the thin folds of the coat about her. Her eyes, he saw now, were a watery blue, with inflamed lids. The stupid appearance they gave her face was deceptive, for had she been blindfolded her forehead, mouth and chin would have been indicative of a great deal of forcefulness. Too much perhaps.

"Yes," she said weakly, "I've met Mr. Rennert."

"Let's see," Smith went on. "Mr. Rennert, Mr. Elkins."

"Mr. Kerwick introduced us when I came in." Rennert's covert glances had told him how futile it would be to re-establish a contact with the flesh-laden man who stood impassively a few feet away. Elkins was a fraction of an inch taller than Kerwick and in his prime had possessed a compact and muscular leanness which would have made that young man's physique seem in comparison bulky and cumbrous indeed. There was no apparent softness about him yet, no paunchiness beneath the well-cut, conservative gray business suit. Rather an accretion of heaviness in waistline and hips and thighs that had been ("And Mr. Woodmansee," Smith was piping, "Mrs. Elkins, Mr. Woodmansee—Mr. Rennert, Mr. Wood-mansee.") as pantherlike as those sheathed by the tan tweeds of Mr. Woodmansee.

Woodmansee had awaited his turn with a soldierly stiffness, brown hands still at his sides, then inclined his head to each of the newcomers in informal fashion. He didn't speak, but his slate-blue eyes met Rennert's in penetrating scrutiny. The straw color of his smoothly brushed hair emphasized the bronze of his skin. His face was strikingly handsome, but without fineness, as if the blows which had hammered its features into symmetry had not been delicate ones. It told little of his age, but the incongruity between him and Miss Pirtle was more than one of years. It was impossible to think of any ties that would link them. . . .

"Mr. Lurcott, Mr. Bohannon," Smith finished off and paused for breath.

For a moment the silence was scored only by the roar of the flames, by the far-off drumming of rain on tiles, by the sizzle of stray drops that found their way down the chimney.

Kerwick stood apart, staring big-eyed at dry, worm-eaten logs, moving his tongue about inside his mouth and (Rennert was almost certain) listening.

Without ceremony Jesse Elkins sat down. It was for Rennert a revelatory movement, not a sitting down so much as the settling of a dead weight, physical and mental. For the half-sigh, half-grunt that escaped from his nostrils was an echo of the whiff of air which his heavy hams expelled from the cushion. Thereafter he simply occupied space, eyes glazed, staring oxlike—at nothing. And thinking, according to his wife, of eating. Profoundly disillusioned, Rennert turned away.

Mrs. Elkins caught his eye, freed her arm from Smith's hand and said to him, "Let's go over by the other fire."

As they went she spoke in a voice which must have been intended to reach the ears of the others: "What a nice little house party this is! Aren't we glad we dropped in!" She left him and walked with quick lithe steps to the two articles of furniture which stood against the north wall, just beyond the door leading to the rear of the house. She jerked away the dust coverings, revealing a cabinet phonograph and a wicker chaise longue. "Shall we have some music, Mr. Rennert?" she suggested, with a backward glance at Kerwick.

But her gesture of defiance, and such Rennert interpreted it, was lost on the red-haired young man, who presented them with the seat of the seersucker trousers as he stooped to pick up the fiber basket of logs. By the time Rennert gained the fireplace and turned, he was carrying it through the arched door to the room on the other side of the chimney.

If the oddity of the action failed to impress Rennert at the moment, it was because the latter had abandoned himself to warmth. Voluptuous tremors were going through his body. He felt a spell of expansiveness coming on and watched Mrs. Elkins with tolerant amusement as she hauled an album from the lower compartment of the phonograph, flicked over a page and drew out a record. She placed this on the turntable, turned the crank with vigor, set the mechanism and came toward him.

He was afraid for an instant or so that she was going to ask him to dance with her. She seemed more like the woman he had seen at that first unguarded moment in his room, her face softer, a trace on her lips of that same secret smile.

Behind her a steel needle scratched along the outer grooves of the disk. Then music was welling out of the little wide-open shutters. A low, measured throbbing.

Rennert's gaze became a stare of surprise. Deliberately or by chance she had selected "The Hall of the Mountain King" from Grieg's Peer Gynt Suite. Those were trolls circling about the frightened Peer, grimacing, leaping, bringing their obscenities nearer with every beat of their tiny feet. Trolls, embodiments of primitive fears, loosed in a mountain fastness and given a mortal to bait.

Singularly, singularly apt and denoting a flair for drama which he wouldn't have expected in Mrs. Elkins. For the smile which she flashed at him as she passed and sank upon the couch was a smugly triumphant one. She took out the case of cigarettes, offered it to him and, when he refused, put one between her lips and waited for him to strike a match. She laid her head back then, smoked and stared raptly into the fire.

Rennert glanced to the other end of the room. Bohannon and Lurcott had left the hearth at last and gone to stand against the south wall, on whose whitewashed surface their shadows staggered huge and scarecrowish as they whispered. The others were wax-works figures which for a brief moment had been given animation to perform a meaningless rigmarole of introduction and now had returned to waxiness. Above the back of the couch were visible Elkins' white round tonsure, Smith's silver dome and the gray crown of Miss Pirtle's shingled hair. At the end of the mantel Woodmansee's head wore a whitish helmet while his dark-suited body blended inconspicuously with the gloom.

Rennert fanned his coattails gently up and down and saw trolls dancing over the tiles—trolls transplanted from northern to tropic mountains, to caper when a woman whose husband had millions banked in Kansas turned a crank and set a needle in a groove; to dance faster and faster, narrowing their circle about their victim, until the adobe walls seemed to be trembling with their jagged rhythm.

There was a Mexican touch to all this which delighted Rennert: the fire-lighted scene, the barbaric theme music which by its very artificiality the better caught the prevalent mood of apprehension, the obligingness of the actors in posing in such striking tableau. Being somewhat of an esthete of Mexican nursing as well as a man of the flesh who responded to such a stimulus as a cozy toasted rear, Rennert did a bit of posing. Not quite as naturally as a Mexican would have done, perhaps, for Mexicans alone have what Flandrau called the "unconscious habit of quietly or violently 'composing' themselves at every moment of their lives into some kind of a framable picture." But he did give himself a little needed tallness by rising on the balls of his feet and straightening his shoulders. Had he been wearing a hat, he would have pulled its brim to a rakish angle over one eye. Had he been, instead of an unimposing Texas farmer, a medieval gallant of cloak and sword he would . . . he would . . .

Through the arched doorway to the right of the opposite fireplace he saw two figures. A girl was standing on a straight-backed chair and holding an electric torch directed upon the floor. At the periphery of the beam was Kerwick's red hair. He was bending over and (Rennert shifted his position to avoid the obstacle of Miss Pirtle's head) examining a log of wood. He held it by the sawed-off ends, very gingerly, it appeared, and slowly turned it over. He laid it down, straightened a bit and seemed to be tramping on something. He stooped then and picked up another log. . . .

Rennert's heels hit the floor as from the phonograph came the clear pealing of a church bell, a rumble and the crash of stones toppling upon luckless trolls. A needle was scratching, scratching in annoying anticlimax.

The instrument evidently had no automatic stop. He walked over to the cabinet, set the brake and lifted the diaphragm with the long steel needle which, he observed, had given the loudest possible tones. He left the lid up and went back to the fire. He stood for a moment over the wood basket which was there and kicked at the topmost log. A procession of tiny red-brown ants was meandering over the bark, in flight from the heat.

Rennert sat down beside Mrs. Elkins and said in a low voice, "You've been in this house before tonight, haven't you?"

There was no change in her face. Her head was resting comfortably on the back of the couch, turned in his direction, and she looked a little drowsy. Her eyes were cool and unhurried in their study of his features.

"What makes you think that?" she asked at last.

"Your familiarity with it. Your unwillingness to stop here. Your mention of Mr. Bjerregaard. His name's on the books and magazines in the next room."

She raised her head, glanced down the length of the room, then sank into her former position. "You're smart," she said with a slight smile, "for a farmer."

"Oh no." His smile was slight too and only complaisant. "It was pretty obvious, wasn't it?"

"I suppose so. But just the same you're not like any farmer I ever saw. At least not like the ones we have in Kansas." She caught one of his hands, laid it palm upward on the cushion between them and ran her fingers lightly over the skin. "You have very good hands, Mr. Rennert. I might believe they were a surgeon's hands or an artist's. But I don't feel any calluses. Did you ever touch a plow?"

Rennert said "No" and wished he had remained on his feet. The couch was one of those soft deep affairs designed for intimacy rather than the impersonal interrogation he had had in mind. "You see," he went on unwillingly, "it's this way. I bought some land in the Magic Valley recently. It had some very young fruit trees on it. I had others planted. But it takes several seasons for them to grow and bear fruit. So in the meantime I've been just waiting and"—he laughed and felt fatuous—"holding my hands."

Mrs. Elkins' eyes went from his face back to his imprisoned hand. She made a pretense of scrutinizing its lines and said: "I'll do palmistry. You correct me if I'm wrong. You're a broad-minded bachelor who's been on the primrose path?"

"Right."

"You're discreet?"

"Very."

"You don't have any foolish notions about blackmail or anything of the sort? Because"—she looked at him levelly—"there's no proof of anything I tell you."

"I'm asking because I'm becoming more and more convinced there's something queer going on here. I think you can help me find out what it is. I'm not trying to pry into your personal affairs. In fact I'd prefer you skipped over them if possible."

"All right." She released his hand, folded her arms and fixed her eyes on his lapel. "I *have* been in this house before tonight. I was on the point of telling you in the other room, but decided I'd better wait until I knew you better. My husband knows nothing about it. I don't want him to—for the pure and simple reason that he's the kindest soul in the world and I couldn't stand to see him hurt. This house belongs to Mr. Snorre Bjerregaard of Corpus Christi. He's a Norwegian and always greets his guests with that record I just played. If you had been acquainted with him, I'd have come out with this sooner. I saw him yesterday. He spoke of this place and asked me if I didn't want to stop with Jesse on our way to Tampico. He said there was no one here but the caretaker. I knew it wouldn't be wise, though, because the caretaker might recognize me. And"—she shrugged—"it would be too much like laughing up my sleeve at Jesse. So you can imagine how I felt when the detour and the rain and darkness forced me to come here with him—and when I found these utter strangers in possession. I've been seething with rage, but there's nothing I can do without giving myself away. It looks as if it were up to you, Mr. Rennert, to oust them or find out what they're up to. Snorre will back you up in anything you do. I'll answer for that. And he'll repay you for your trouble. You can consider yourself as his agent, if you want to."

"I think I'll do that. Gratuitously, of course." Rennert turned his head and watched Kerwick return with the wood basket.

"By the way," Mrs. Elkins said, "Jesse has a gun in the pocket of the car. Kerwick didn't look there. I thought it was silly to bother getting a permit for it, but it seems Jesse was right. Though I don't know how any of us are going to get at it."

"No, and I'd rather not force any measures for the present. Tell me, you've seen or heard nothing of the caretaker since you've been here?"

"No. He's a Mexican who lives over the garage. He may have gone off or they may be holding him prisoner. There wasn't any light in his room when we drove up, I noticed."

"There's a question I'd like to ask about this house, Mrs. Elkins. I scarcely know how to put it without sounding sensational."

"What is it?"

Kerwick had put down his burden, stood up and was dusting off his sleeves. "Supper's ready now," he called loudly across the room.

"I'll postpone it," Rennert said as he helped Mrs. Elkins to her feet. "It's not very pleasant."

7
PAINTED SERPENT

SMITH WAVED the red-and-green serpent stick as if it were a ceremonial wand. "Buffet style, folks. And very informal. So pass right in."

He was standing on one side of the doorway to the right of the fireplace, Kerwick on the other. During the general stir that followed his words there appeared between them the girl of whom Rennert had caught a glimpse a few minutes before.

"Keith," he heard her say, "bring that other candle, will you? It's so dark in here."

She seemed embarrassed at the sudden focusing of attention upon her and would have withdrawn had not Smith called: "Wait a minute, Wilma. You haven't met all these people."

He moved to her side with surprising agility, his infirmity considered, and threw an arm about her. "We won't take time for their names now. But folks," his voice almost caroled in pride, "this is my daughter, Wilma. She's been acting as your cook tonight, so you'd better treat her nice."

Unintentionally Kerwick threw both into the background. He had crossed in front of them to the mantel, taken down the candle and was standing with it in one hand, like a gauche incense bearer. Instead of illumining the door he only cast the shadow of his broad left shoulder and forearm across it. He loomed so large in his light clothing that the girl, in a dark dress of what looked like knitted wool, appeared petite and fragile. In reality she was as tall as her father and, although much more slender than he, had none of the ethereal about her. A graceful athletic body . . .

61

She gave one quick glance into the group, acknowledged the introduction with a jerky movement of the head and walked back into the other room, Kerwick following.

As Rennert and Mrs. Elkins came up, the former stopped before Miss Pirtle, who had got to her feet and was peering about helplessly. "Stay where you are and let me bring you a plate," he suggested, noticing as he did so that the lapels of her coat were turned back now and that on the left she wore one of the badges with which the National University of Mexico decorates those of its students who are badge-conscious and have the purchase price.

"Oh, if you will, Mr. Rennert. I'll be so much obliged."

Smith had maintained his post just inside the living room. He made some polite remark to Mrs. Elkins as she marched past, but pointedly she ignored him. Her husband moved after her with no alteration of countenance.

Bohannon and Lurcott had come around the end of the couch and advanced as far as the center of the hearth. Bohannon's moon-like face glistened in the fire light as if it had been douched with oil. He was breathing heavily, and his smile was slowly widening. Although Lurcott's lips retained their tight mirthless set, there was an answering glint in the jet-black eyes that never wavered from their fixed scrutiny of Smith's alpaca coat. Of the right pocket of that coat.

Rennert felt prompted to speak to the old gentleman, to warn him of that surveillance from behind. But Woodmansee had fallen into step beside him and was saying: "Thanks for offering to help Pirtle. That's my job—if you don't want to bother."

"I'm perfectly willing."

"All right, then. Poor old soul, she's having a hard time. Almost as blind as a bat." His voice was crisp, slightly metallic, but had an impersonal kindliness in it.

"She and I are both from Brownsville," Rennert went on. "She's a schoolteacher there, I believe."

Woodmansee hesitated. "I really don't know," he said, with a firmness which told Rennert quite plainly that he did not care to enter into conversation regarding Miss Pirtle. There was an equal firmness in Woodmansee's manner which compelled Rennert to take precedence in the room. It was almost, the latter couldn't help thinking, as if the soldierly young man in the expensively tailored tweeds shared the whiting's aversion to a stranger treading at his rear.

Rennert's surmise had been correct. It was an alcove into which they had entered. There were two windows facing the west and in the narrow north end a door which probably gave access to the kitchen. Here too the floor was of dark red tiles, and Rennert's eyes could detect nothing at all on the spot where Kerwick had been examining those logs and making motions suggestive of tramping on something.

"Excuse me," he said to Woodmansee. "A shoelace." He knelt, struck a match and let it burn for a few seconds before he extinguished it and fumbled with a lace. Among the little splinters and fragments of bark were the crushed bodies of three or four ants. That was all.

Rennert rose and gave his attention to the table. This was of the long refectory style and occupied most of the space. The two candles lighted a cloth of Aguascalientes drawnwork—and an incomplete supper. There was a large assortment of hors d'oeuvres and condiments. There were tinned sardines, salmon, dried beef, pork and beans, preserved fruits and vegetables. A large pot of coffee. No bread or butter. Nothing which had not been, obviously, in storage at the place.

Wilma Smith and Kerwick stood on the other side, the young fellow in a clumsy semiprotective attitude. The girl indicated silverware and plates of blue Jalisco glass. "I'll have to apologize for the food." Her voice was flurried. "There's nothing but canned things, you see. I expect you'll be more comfortable sitting in by the fire."

Opposite them was Mrs. Elkins, deliberately studying first the table, then the uneasy hostess. "Quite all right, my dear." There was a mocking undertone to her cool and measured speech. "Don't apologize. You've managed very well with all this unexpected company. Inconvenient, not having any corner grocery to run into, isn't it?"

"Yes, it is."

From the living-room door came Bohannon's panting voice: "Let's wait a minute, Mr. Smith. We don't want to crowd out there all at once. I've got something to ask you."

Rennert and Woodmansee took plates and silver. Woodmansee had extremely deft hands, well shaped and muscular. The nails of Jesse Elkins, just ahead of Rennert, were manicured to a gloss, but his hands were gross paws. Lank hairs clustered on their backs and became, on the thick plowman's wrists, a dark mat.

Mrs. Elkins was dawdling, turning the glass and pottery bowls about as if admiring their coloring, removing some of the contents with vicious little jabs of her fork. Rennert wished that he had counseled her against any further demonstration. Her friendship with Bjerregaard gave her a proprietary interest in the house, he saw, but as long as she couldn't avow that friendship openly . . .

"You don't live out here in the mountains all the time, do you?" she asked Wilma Smith.

"Oh no. Not all the time." The girl's nervousness was increasing, and she kept her eyes fixed on the base of one of the candles. They were blue eyes, candid and clear and young, like her father's, but had an unnatural glassy brilliance. There was no color in her face. It was an attractive face, Rennert thought, small-boned like Mr. Smith's. There was a suggestion of his healthy plumpness in the cheeks, which were rather high. Her light hazel hair, worn in a coil at the back of her head, was in some disorder.

"Your home is near by, I suppose?"

"Our home—" Miss Smith faltered and looked up at Kerwick, who was staring at Mrs. Elkins as if she were some strange and beautiful winged insect of whose stinging powers he was uncertain.

"San Luis Potosí." Thickly he named the capital of the adjoining state on the southwest.

"And what are Mr. Smith's initials?" Mrs. Elkins persisted.

"C.

"Oh!" She laughed deprecatingly as she raised a knife and scrutinized its handle. "Silverware is always getting mixed up, isn't it? This has—let's see—'SB' on it." She looked straight at Kerwick.

He swallowed and spoke as if he were tongue-tied: "Yes. It's some—that somebody left here."

Mrs. Elkins glanced down the line, at her husband, heaping his plate from each dish as he came to it, and at Rennert. She smiled. "Simple, isn't it? 'SB' stands for Somebody."

Something hissed through the air behind Rennert and fell with a smart rap. "None of that!" The cry was shrill with anger. As he turned, there was another hiss and rap and the thud of a body upon the floor.

"That will teach you," said Smith with satisfaction, "not to play tricks on an old fox like me." With the tip of the Apizaco cane he prodded Lurcott, very indelicately, in a convenient part of his anatomy. "Get up."

Lurcott didn't get up. He lay sprawled face down in the doorway, his head in the dining alcove. He was very limp-looking and very still. He didn't move when the stick, under the guidance of thin white fingers, explored him further, found his right forearm and pulled his hand from under his body.

"What happened?" Kerwick's voice, out of control, rose in a shout. He had gained the end of the table in two bounds and was facing the door, the muzzle of his automatic describing a wavering semicircle, then slowly sinking. Wilma Smith was at his left elbow, her fingertips moving over the seersucker sleeve as if trying in vain to find a hold on its tight-stretched surface.

Very calmly her father hopped over the prostrate form, transferred the cane to his left side and stooped down. He jerked something from Lurcott's hand, straightened and held it out to Kerwick. "Maybe I *had* better let you keep this, boy."

It was a rectangular box slightly larger than a package of cigarettes, fabricated from some metal that looked like lead. The lid was partially open, as if it had been wrenched loose, and there protruded a bit of white stuff which Rennert thought, from the hasty glimpse he had before Kerwick's palm closed over the object and he thrust it into his pocket, was absorbent cotton.

"Sly but not sly enough," Smith continued, bobbing his head up and down. "Look." He held up the right pocket of his coat for inspection. It had been slit neatly down the center so that the gaping edges left a V-shaped hole. "He did that with a knife while the other fellow kept me talking. But I caught him at it. Laid him out too, didn't I?"

"Where is the other one?" Kerwick asked quickly.

"Right here!" Bohannon came through the door with a waddling movement, his bright little eyes stabbing at Smith. His labored breathing almost obscured his words. "You killed him, damn you! Tom was just havin' some fun out of you. But we'll see what fun you have when the Mexican cops get hold of you."

Smith flinched as from a physical blow, then gave a quavering laugh as his eyes moved slowly to the floor. "Don't get excited. He's not dead. I just tapped him a couple of times over the head with this." He raised the cane, aimlessly, until it was close to the faces of Rennert and Woodmansee.

They were near each other, with the Elkinses behind them. At the commotion Woodmansee had whirled around, even more swiftly than Rennert, and planted himself with his back to the wall. Since then he had stood absolutely motionless, watching.

Rennert glanced at the cane, then at Bohannon, who had straddled and was bending over Lurcott.

The cane held no particular interest for him at first, except from a historical viewpoint. They are common objects in Mexico, these straight cedar sticks, both for use and ornament. Yet few *mestizos* who swing them over city pavements and fewer tourists who carry them across the Rio Grande are aware how essentially unchanged they have come from a remote and sacerdotal ancestry. When the Aztecs first came to stare in wonderment at the waters of Mexico, they found on the neighboring mountains priests who bore wooden snakes and with them sought to cajole the Tlalocs into tilting the rain jars which would bring fertility, not cobwebs and mildew. Already that motif had had its inception which so very persistently has textured all of Mexican life. Understandable even today because rain—

Rennert's eyes jerked back to the cane just as Smith let its tip fall to the floor. An inch and a half thick at the top, it tapered down to less than an inch. About it, on a background of bright red flowers, twined a green serpent, the spade head forming a grip for the white blue-veined hand. . . .

"Well," Bohannon wheezed and lifted Lurcott as if the latter had been a sand-filled dummy, "maybe you won't have to sleep in a Mexican jail after all. Old Tom's not ready for the graveyard yet."

"He's not dead?" Kerwick's words were rasped by the quick release of his breath.

"No, buddy. Just cooled for a while. Lucky for you." In the act of turning away, the limp body in his arms, Bohannon fixed his beady eyes on Smith. "Maybe you haven't heard the last of this, though. It mightn't be such a bad idea to call the cops in. We'll see what Tom says when he wakes up. He may want to file charges against you, who knows?"

"File charges!" Kerwick blurted out, for all the world like a small boy who is trying to cover up his lack of sureness by bluster. "I'd like to see him try that! He was picking Mr. Smith's pocket. *We* can have *him* arrested."

"Yeah?" Bohannon joggled the senseless Lurcott slightly so that the man's loose arm flapped to and fro. "All you'll have to do is show the cops your papers and tell 'em you're spendin' a nice quiet little week end out here. In your own house. Yeah, I think Tom'll be ready to call those cops any time you are." He started to laugh but choked. His waxy face twitched suddenly, as if at a seizure, and his lower jaw sagged as he gasped for breath. His eyes went shut, then opened wide, and for several seconds he stared glassily and in unmistakable fright at the shadow which the edge of the table cast on the floor.

"What's the matter?" Kerwick demanded uneasily.

"Nuthin'. Nuthin'." Bohannon turned his back on them and reeled with Lurcott into the other room. Miss Pirtle gave a small stifled cry as he moved toward the couch, whereupon he kept straight on for the chaise longue.

And there, Rennert told himself, would go the villain of any well-ordered melodrama. But on this confused stage it seemed to be Kerwick who was bent on assuming that role. For, if Rennert was any judge, Kerwick was in an exceedingly dangerous mood. Blood had rushed to his face, and the veins on his temples were throbbing violently. Whereas before his features had been homely, they were now unpleasantly ugly. And without any seeming volition on his part the muzzle of the automatic rose until the sight was on the middle of Bohannon's bulging pleated back.

Rennert heard the sharp intake of Wilma Smith's breath and saw her fingers tighten upon the seersucker sleeve. Abruptly Kerwick shoved the gun into a pocket.

The breaking of the tension had sent Mr. Smith's spirits soaring. He beamed and gave Mrs. Elkins an exaggerated wink. "You're a brave woman, madam. I'm glad to see you weren't alarmed." (During the episode she had stood close by her husband, all expression frozen from her face.) "We won't have any more trouble out of *that* pair. Not if they know what's good for 'em. You wouldn't think I packed such a wallop, would you? I'm always telling Wilma I'm not the old fossil she thinks I am. That wasn't the first rascal this cane has rapped over the bean. And let me tell you, when this snake strikes 'em they don't forget it any time soon. One night in San Luis I—"

"Oh, Father, don't!" The girl left Kerwick, took Smith by the arm and drew him with her around the table to the chairs ranged along the west wall. "Don't talk like that. You might have killed him."

"Might've been a good thing, Wilma. Might've been a good thing. Somebody'll have to do it some day."

"Exactly right, Mr. Smith!" Jesse Elkins' voice rang out. "You're a man after my own heart. There's only one way to deal with rats like those two. I've known they were up to something ever since I first laid eyes on them." This was the first utterance Rennert had heard from Elkins since the murmur of his name at the time of their introduction. A distinct change had come over him, as if he had been galvanized out of a lethargy. "I'll help you handle them," he said excitedly and started around the other end of the table toward Smith.

"Jesse!" His wife spoke sharply. "Better attend to your own business. Or"—she looked from Smith to Kerwick—"the police will be taking you in charge too."

Elkins stopped short and turned, frowning. Beneath the south window, near him, was a top-heavy wrought-iron stand shaped something like a candelabrum and holding a number of potted cacti, tiny *echinomasti* for the most part. His coattails caught on the spines of one of these, and he brought the entire affair crashing to the floor. The mishap seemed to deflate him, for he stood helplessly in the midst of the debris and glanced at Mrs. Elkins for guidance.

She laughed carelessly. "Don't worry, dear. Mr. Smith can send you a bill for the damage later." Her eyes went from him to Rennert and Woodmansee. "Are we ready to go in? I'd feel safer with a bodyguard."

The necessity of securing two cups of coffee and finding places for them on the plates delayed Rennert, so that for a few moments he was left alone with the Smiths and Kerwick. Both the young people disregarded him in their attentions to the old gentleman. The girl sat beside the latter, patted his hand and spoke to Kerwick: "Fix him a plate, Keith."

"Tut, tut!" Her father made a pretense of getting up. "He won't give me what I want."

"You bet your life I won't, Mr. Smith," Kerwick said as he scooped up silverware. "Wilma and I've got doctor's orders for you. No meat. No—" He faced Rennert and asked stonily, "Want anything else, Rennert?"

"Nothing more, thank you."

"Then you'll find it warmer in the other room."

"Thank you."

Thus dismissed, Rennert would have made his exit a dignified one. Unfortunately, as he walked away, his feet crunching on the loose sand and rubble which the breakage of the pots had scattered over the tiles, he was halted by a sharp stab of pain in the ball of his right foot. He winced and had to hobble ignominiously back to the table, set down the plates and seesaw to and fro as he extracted from the thin leather of his shoe sole a long cactus spine whose deep red tip was still further darkened by some of his own blood.

8
AIRWAYS

Rennert limped into the living room. Mrs. Elkins and Woodmansee were rather far apart on the couch before the fireplace at the east end. Jesse Elkins was standing in the shadows by the front door, eating and watching Bohannon, with what expression Rennert couldn't discern. Bohannon was sitting by Lurcott's feet on the chaise longue. His head was bent, and he held a hand kerchief wadded against his face.

Miss Pirtle sat alone on the nearer couch. She took her plate awkwardly, spilling part of her coffee. "What happened, Mr. Rennert?" she asked him agitatedly. "What did those men do? That fat one stood between me and Mr. Smith, and I couldn't see anything at all."

He told her briefly, setting an example by keeping his voice low. Little light found its way to the chaise longue, but he was sure there had been no stir from Lurcott. Despite his antipathy to the man and to his companion, Rennert felt that Smith and Kerwick were being foolish, to say the least, in dismissing the injury in such an offhand fashion. He had not witnessed the actual delivery of the two blows, but he had heard their sounds, he knew the nature of those Apizaco canes and he had been taught by experience what dangerous possibilities lie in seemingly insignificant head wounds. . . .

Miss Pirtle echoed his thoughts: "But he may be hurt, Mr. Rennert! Seriously! I don't care how wicked he is, they ought to get a doctor."

"Remember you're not in Brownsville, Miss Pirtle. It's very likely there's not a doctor nearer than Victoria. With the roads as they are, it would be impossible to bring him here before morning. If then." He took a few bites and said affably: "Don't let it ruin your meal. Are you in the high school at Brownsville?"

Miss Pirtle stared at one of the buttons on his vest while her fingers tightened upon the rim of the plate and she sank back as far as possible on the couch. "How did you know?" she asked unsteadily.

"I noticed the badge of the National University of Mexico. I remembered that its summer session was over about this time. Most Americans who attend are teachers. So I jumped to the conclusion that you were a teacher. Of Spanish probably. Is that right?"

She nodded and left him in doubt as to whether or not she was attempting facetiousness. "I suppose," she said, "that's an example of your method."

"My method?"

"Yes, in detection. I—I never read mystery stories or accounts of crime, so I don't know whether you call it the inductive or the deductive method. Which is it?"

It was Rennert's turn to stare. "Why, I doubt whether it could be dignified by either name." He munched away on an olive for a moment while an improbable suspicion shaped itself in his mind. "You're the very person to help me, Miss Pirtle," he went on with the conversation. "Rolf Jester, the president of the school board, is a friend of mine. He and the superintendent have been getting up some sort of lecture program for your weekly assemblies this fall. Without my knowledge or consent they've put me on. I'm skittish at the prospect. I don't know anything about kids and haven't the faintest idea what to talk to them about."

"I know, Mr. Rennert." Her voice was stifled, and she made slight pretense of eating. "It was announced last spring. You're to talk about Mexico. Your experiences. The children are so anxious to hear you. It will be so much more interesting than the usual sort of thing we have."

"Thanks for the compliment. But I'm the world's worst talker. And it's been my observation that travel lectures are the hardest kind to put over—unless one shows pictures. And that's liable to be dull because everyone has seen better ones in the movies."

"Oh, but we hope you'll tell us something about your—your adventures down here. Your experiences in the customs service and in crime detection. It will have such a good moral influence on the children. You see, we've all read about you. And one of the little Mexican girls in my class calls at your house for your laundry every week. She's quite an admirer of yours, and one day when I had the class giving oral reports on current topics she told about you. It was mostly"—Miss Pirtle had the grace to blush slightly—"about your taste in clothes and your—she called it *singularidad*—in not wanting a lot of starch in your shirts. I—really I couldn't get her stopped. Of course she talked so fast most of the other children didn't understand all she was saying. But they have a rather personal interest in you now and are looking forward to seeing a real detective."

Rennert groaned inwardly at the thought of little Concepción, with Mexican candor, making his dirty linen the subject of classroom discussion. He wouldn't, he knew now, ever have the courage to step on that platform. He'd caught a tartar in Miss Pirtle. Her voice had risen toward the last, and he was uncomfortably conscious that it had brought the attention of the entire group to focus on him. There was silence from the couch occupied by Mrs. Elkins and Woodmansee, and the heads of both were turned in his direction. Bohannon had looked up. Jesse Elkins had got rid of his plate and advanced to the center of the room.

"Mr. Rennert!" he called, and the ring of metal in his voice made it sound like a command.

"Excuse me," Rennert said hastily to Miss Pirtle and went toward him.

Elkins' greeting almost literally swept him off his feet. The hand which he put out in response to the other's invitation was grasped and wrung by two powerful ones, so that the contents of the plate which he held in his left threatened to go sailing onto the floor.

"Hugh Rennert!" Elkins exclaimed. "Of the customs service. My God, man, you don't know how glad I am to meet you! I had no idea who you were. Why didn't you tell me? I heard you say you were a farmer."

Rennert was thankful they were standing so that the light showed him something of Elkins' face but left his own in obscurity. For he felt—again—the full impact of the man's personality and would have been visibly affected, while Elkins, of course, retained no memory of that previous, long-ago meeting. But even without that association, Rennert told himself, he would have responded immediately to the warmth which infused the smile and the square, comradely gaze. Being prone to protective self-analysis at moments such as this, he wondered if he weren't in reality being snobbishly pleased by the compliment that it implied.

"But I *am* a farmer, Mr. Elkins," he said with unintended stiffness. "I left the customs service some time ago."

"Oh!" Elkins looked at him for several seconds, then glanced quickly around the room, and his voice fell to a stage whisper. "I'm sorry. No excuse for me being so stupid." He laid an arm across Rennert's shoulders and spoke in a manner which puzzled the latter profoundly because it had a quality in it that he could only think of as wistful: "If you need any help, count on me, will you? My room's the northeast one, off the patio."

"Why, certainly," Rennert answered in some confusion. He felt he must be mistaken, for any emotion such as he was attributing to the other was utterly at variance with the Elkins character. His wandering gaze came to rest on Bohannon, who was listening to this interchange, and he saw that the handkerchief which the fat man had taken away from his face was drenched with blood. . . .

"I've got a gun," Elkins went on. "In my car. If you want me to I'll climb over the roof from the patio, break into the garage and get it. Shall I?"

"No," Rennert said firmly, his eyes still on the cloth which dripped as Bohannon wrung it. "That would be asking for trouble. Let's all take this as calmly as possible tonight, go to our rooms when supper's over and stay there. I don't think we're in any danger."

"As you say, Rennert." Elkins sounded disappointed. "You know what you're doing, of course. But don't forget where I am. I'll be waiting on you." With a farewell pressure on Rennert's biceps he returned importantly to his position on the couch beside Miss Pirtle.

Afterwards Rennert blamed himself bitterly for his seeming coolness, for his failure to grasp and clear up the obvious misapprehension under which Elkins was laboring. Perhaps, he always thought, it was because his attention had been distracted by Bohannon's distress.

Bohannon rose and watched him closely as he approached the chaise longue. "Hello, Mr. Rennert," he spoke with a slight note of respect. "You've put on weight since I seen you last. I didn't know you, neither."

"I'm afraid you have the advantage of me."

"I didn't expect you to remember. We didn't meet in no social gatherin'." Bohannon sniffled and passed the back of his hand across his nostrils. It came away darkly streaked. "It was up in Laredo, about six years ago. When you were with the customs. You thought I was tryin' to smuggle some dope across the line. God, you were hard-boiled. You made me strip off all my clothes and pretty near pulled 'em to pieces. No hard feelin', though. That was your job. And you were decent enough to apologize when you didn't find nuthin'."

"Don't tell me you put one over on me. People are always doing that now."

"No, I didn't have nuthin' that time. Think I could talk 'em into givin' me something to eat, Mr. Rennert?"

"I expect so. What's been the trouble with you?"

"I don't know. I got kinda scared there for a minute. Thought I was goin' to have a spell. I couldn't get my breath. My nose's been bleedin', and I feel some better now."

"Used to this altitude?"

"No, I never been up this high before."

"Then it's your heart. Better take it easy. Your partner's still unconscious?"

"Yeah. Dead to the world. What was that you were sayin' about a doctor?"

"I doubt very much that there's one nearer than Victoria."

"That's a long ways off, ain't it?"

"A long ways in this weather. Do you mind if I take a look at Lurcott?"

"Sure not. You know anything about medicine?"

"Very little. But I've seen a few men with head injuries."

Rennert found a precarious resting place for his plate on the turntable of the open phonograph and bent over Lurcott. The man's breathing was ragged, his pulse irregular but fairly strong. The light was insufficient for anything like a thorough examination—had he felt competent to make one—but with the aid of a match he located the marks of the cane. Both were on the left side, one high up on the temple, the other midway to the crown. The skin had not been broken, but they were nasty contusions.

"How bad is it?" Bohannon asked him anxiously as he straightened.

Rennert shook his head. "I wouldn't undertake to say. I don't think there's any fracture, but I can't tell as to a concussion. If he doesn't come to in a few minutes, put him to bed as easily as you can. And get him to a doctor in the morning." He observed the other obliquely. "What's in the box he tried to get out of Smith's pocket?"

Bohannon puckered his lips as if he were going to whistle unconcernedly. His little blue eyes switched to Rennert's vest and began a zigzag course upward.

Search me," he replied after a moment. "That's what Tom wanted to find out. He wasn't aimin' to steal nuthin'. He just let his curiosity get the better of him. See?"

"I see. He took nothing from the box, then?"

"No." Bohannon had got as far as the point of Rennert's chin.

"But he must have had an idea about the contents?"

"Maybe he did. You'll have to ask him when he wakes up." Bohannon's eyes swung swiftly over Rennert's cheekbone and for a few seconds met his steady gaze. "I told you, Mr. Rennert," he said as he stuffed the handkerchief into a hip pocket, "that I didn't have no hard feelin's for you. But you're not sittin' in Uncle Sam's office now, with a gun on your belt and a bunch of guys standin' around ready to take orders from you. Just remember that, won't you? And don't ask too many questions." He glanced toward the dining alcove. "How's that coffee?"

"Fair," Rennert told him. "In your place I wouldn't drink any, though."

"Why not?"

"On account of your heart. You don't need any stimulant."

"I'll only take a little." Bohannon paused and looked Rennert up and down. "Thanks for the tip," he said with a return to his tone of respect.

"Thanks for yours," Rennert answered dryly as he picked up his plate and moved away.

Mrs. Elkins and Woodmansee, having finished their meal, had both risen and seemed to be on the point of quitting that end of the room. Woodmansee, however, left her and stepped toward Rennert. "What about the Highway Patrol?" he asked in clipped syllables.

"What about them?" Rennert watched Mrs. Elkins open a compact by the firelight and thought she looked a bit displeased by her tête-à-tête with the tweed-clad young man.

"Yes. Aren't they supposed to come along the road at regular intervals?"

"The main highway, yes. But I doubt whether they'll give much attention to this detour tonight."

Woodmansee's laugh was hard and had in it a note of bravado. "Then we're pretty much cut off from the world, aren't we?"

"You came from the South, didn't you?"

"Yes."

"How far does the detour extend in that direction?"

"Almost twenty-five miles."

"Then"—Rennert was regarding him thoughtfully—"we're very much out of the world at present, Mr. Woodmansee."

With his free hand the other drew his coat snugly about his hips and fastened the lower button. "Wait here for me, will you, Mr. Rennert?" he asked. "I want to talk to you."

"Yes," Rennert said readily, "I'll wait."

While Woodmansee escorted Mrs. Elkins across the room, he took a few hasty bites and drained his coffee cup, eying with disfavor the javaline head that matched the one over the west chimney. No hunter himself, Rennert had never been able to understand this propensity to nail up bits of bone and hide as mementoes of personal prowess or a full belly. An unsavory survival of the Stone Age, was his private but unexpressed opinion. This trophy was altogether repulsive, with its tiny pig eyes and sharp white tusks glittering evilly in the firelight. . . .

He put cup and plate on the mantel, saw that Woodmansee was in conversation with Mr. and Mrs. Elkins and that Bohannon was out of sight. Hoping that he was unobserved, he slipped through the archway to the left of the chimney. Here was another alcove of the same size. It contained wicker furniture, he discovered when he struck a match, and the luggage which Mrs. Elkins had mentioned. He went swiftly about an examination of this.

There was a compact and expensive leather case such as women use for short trips, initialed "W. S." in gold. A voluminous Gladstone scarred by usage. A lightweight airplane fiber bag, almost new, with "K. K." painted upon it in big block letters. One of the two labels pasted upon the sides of this last was that of a large New York hotel widely advertised outside the metropolis; the other, that of the Pan-American Airways System.

The match began to warm Rennert's fingers. He let it fall and lighted another.

All three articles still bore, plastered over their openings, the long strips of white paper with which the Mexican customs officials seal all incoming luggage. They had been stamped at Matamoros that day. . . .

"Better be careful," a low voice warned from the door. "Here comes the watchdog."

The side of Woodmansee's mouth moved in a grim smile, and he sauntered away. When Rennert gained the living room, he was standing with his back to the fire, lighting a cigarette.

Kerwick was with Bohannon by the chaise longue but was looking at Rennert rather than at Lurcott. "He'll be all right in a few minutes," he said gruffly and walked toward Rennert.

Bohannon had a plate in his hands but had not begun to eat. He stared after Kerwick, his eyes narrowed. "He'd better get all right," he called softly. "There are a lot of witnesses to what happened, remember. And there'll be a lot of witnesses if anything happens to me."

"Aw, shut up!" Kerwick slowed his steps but didn't pause. He opened his mouth as if he were about to say something to Rennert, but his speech seemed obstructed by his growing anger.

"A cigarette?" Woodmansee offered a package to Rennert, and at sight of his own brand the latter felt like clasping in gratitude the steady brown hand.

"Thanks. You're a lifesaver."

Woodmansee held a match for him; then, with a faint click of the heels which somehow gave irony to the gesture, extended the pack to Kerwick. "Smoke?"

Kerwick shook his head.

Woodmansee smiled and assumed a surface appearance of affability while he gave intent scrutiny to the other's face. There was a leashed-in tension about him, not visible in the slightest unsteadiness of voice or body, but nevertheless charging the atmosphere electrically. "We've been admiring your trophies," he said. "Mr. Rennert thought you might have some more in the other room. Ferocious-looking beast, that javaline up there."

As Kerwick's head moved slowly backward on his short thick neck and he raised his eyes to the peccary as if seeing it for the first time, Rennert knew how great was the disparity, at least physical, between the two men. A combat (and, curiously enough, he thought at once of an antagonism in which he was no partisan) would be one of size and strength against stripped swiftness.

"Um-huh," Kerwick grunted.

"They say"—a crackle ran through Woodmansee's voice like the singing of a thin rawhide whip—"that javalines, are the only dangerous animals in this corner of Mexico. They take the offensive when others are on the defensive. I know because I've hunted 'em in Nicaragua. A partner of mine got lost. They treed him, then tore down the tree. When we found him there was nothing left but bones." He laughed and deftly flicked cigarette ashes behind him into the fire. "They always run in packs, though. One of 'em alone or with a family is easy enough to spear or club or net—even if you don't have a gun. The javaline's got sense enough to know that and leaves a man alone unless he has lots of help. Get the point?"

Some reply was coming, slowly, from Kerwick when Wilma Smith's sharp cry cut across the room: "Keith! Come here!"

9
COLD SYMBOLS OF EVIL

THE GIRL WAS STANDING, dimly outlined by candlelight, in the doorway to the alcove where the supper table had been set. There had been excitement in her voice, Rennert thought, rather than fear or alarm.

Kerwick turned and went to her on the double-quick, caught her by the arm and they disappeared, leaving a vacant aperture whereupon were trained a battery of eyes. The Elkinses continued to stare, as if in expectancy of the fellow's return. Mrs. Elkins was sitting near her husband now, in an armchair drawn up to the fire, and neither was paying any attention to Miss Pirtle. Bohannon stared too as he sat on a corner of the chaise longue, eating ravenously and drinking a great deal of coffee.

When Woodmansee sank down upon the couch and frowned into the flames, Rennert felt sure that, for all his air of assurance, worry was nagging at him.

"Sit down, Mr. Rennert," he invited.

When Rennert was beside him he took another draw on his cigarette and pitched his voice low: "Know who these people are?"

"No."

Woodmansee was silent for a moment, then abruptly shifted his position so that he could observe Rennert's face. "I want to ask you a question. Does your stopping here have any connection with them?"

"None at all."

The eyes of neither wavered as they studied each other.

"I think," Rennert went on quietly, "that you're being led astray by Miss Pirtle's talk about my being a detective. I'm not engaged on any such business now. And anything I've done in the past has been the rankest amateurism—forced on me by the circumstances, usually."

Woodmansee's smile was fleeting, but it was engaging and took years from his face. "You're too modest, Rennert. I've heard about you in Mexico City. But like everybody else here, I didn't know who you were. I'm damned glad you're here. I don't suppose"—he cast a quick glance behind them, and when he turned there was a slight sparkle in his eyes—"that you'd consider taking on a job tonight? A purely business proposition. To put it bluntly, I'll pay you and pay you well to team up with me, give me the benefit of whatever information you get and help me out in case there's a scrape. Kerwick pulled a fast one on me and got my gun. I'm lost without it. I'd feel better having a good man to stand beside me. What about it?"

Rennert digested this. "I infer," he said, "that you're anticipating trouble of some sort."

Woodmansee shrugged and gazed into the fire. After a moment he nodded. "But not"—he picked his words carefully—"with the police. You have my word for that."

Rennert watched his companion's virile hammered profile but gained no idea of what the other was thinking. The faraway look in his eyes was one which comes into any eyes that stay fixed too long on flames.

"Woodmansee," he broke the silence, "I'm not going to do it. When I say I'm a peaceful farmer, I mean it. I see no reason, however, why you shouldn't call on me for help if necessary and let me give it voluntarily."

Woodmansee nodded slowly, his face still without expression. "Good enough. Where's your room?"

"Temporarily at least I'm in the one on the right, off the passage."

"That's fine. I'm next to you—the east side of the patio. We have a connecting bath. Keep that room if you can. If there has to be any changing about, we'll move together. Satisfactory?"

"Certainly."

"Say, tell me, what's your impression of Miss Smith?"

"A very nice and normal young girl, I should say, passing through some abnormal experience."

"That's the way she struck me. I'm going to try and get a chance to talk to her. Maybe if I can get her away from Kerwick and her father she'll tell me what's wrong. I looked at their luggage before you did. See if you agree with me. Kerwick flew down from New York, maybe getting into Brownsville early yesterday evening or this morning. There are two planes a day. Smith and his daughter met him there, and the three of them, with a chauffeur or other person, started to San Luis Potosí. They got this far and something happened. They stayed here, and the fourth member of the party took the car on to Victoria. To get help maybe. Is that what you decided?"

"I haven't had time to give it much thought. But I think those are reasonable conclusions to draw."

"I'm glad to hear you say that." Woodmansee showed his relief by leaning back in a more easy attitude and stretching his feet toward the hearth. "I suppose traveling with Pirtle has made me jumpy. She's looked for a bandit to spring out at us from a tree or rock ever since we left Mexico City."

"I judged she was nervous," Rennert said, wondering if the young man weren't trying, by this specious assertion, to throw a smoke screen over the implications of his confidence of a few minutes before.

"Nervous as a cat. That is, outside her native habitat, the schoolroom. I imagine she's like a good hefty rock there." Woodmansee raised and flexed one of his long legs, himself not unlike a sleek cat luxuriating in warmth. "Sorry I answered you like I did when you asked me if she was a teacher," he remarked with a smile. "But she cautioned me not to tell you. You sort of took the wind out of her sails by noticing that university button."

"Why on earth shouldn't she want me to know?"

"Beyond me." Woodmansee shook his head. "I've given up trying to figure the old girl out. God, this has been a trip! We've talked about nothing but the soul and the beautiful things of life. As soon as I get back to—" he checked himself—"where I'm going I'll have to hunt up the lowest dive and recover."

"When did Miss Pirtle break her spectacles?"

"The other day in Mexico City. She didn't want to get another pair till she was back in Brownsville. Didn't seem to trust Mexican oculists. She'd been going to summer school at the university and was through with her work. She advertised in the paper for someone to drive her car back for her. I was—well, at loose ends, so I looked her up and got the job. I—" Woodmansee laid a hand on Rennert's knee, a tense hand whose long fingers dug with unconscious force.

Above the sounds of rain and fire, muted now by familiarity, came the noisy chugging of a car through the mire. It was approaching from the south and was but a short distance away.

Woodmansee took his hand away and felt for cigarettes. Automatically he held them out for Rennert to accept one. Rennert did so and struck a match. The white tube was motionless in Woodmansee's tight lips.

The automobile sputtered and popped and rattled, then with a creak which was like an expiring sigh of utter weariness came to a stop in front of the house.

Woodmansee's sculptured nostrils flared ever so slightly as he drew in his breath, and Rennert fell to speculating as to what business the fellow had had in Mexico City before he found himself "at loose ends."

Woodmansee rose. He stepped swiftly out of alignment with the fire and stood braced, trim hips thrust forward as he fastened the second button of his coat.

The knocker clanged as Rennert got to his feet and, after momentary hesitation, moved to the other side of the chimney. It seemed an uncalled-for precaution—this avoidance of a position where the flames would make one's body a target—but there was something contagious about such apprehension in a man who was certainly no alarmist.

Bohannon had closed the lid of the phonograph and was standing with his back and elbows propped against it, sucking his right thumb as he watched alternately the front door and the rear archway in which Kerwick was framed.

Kerwick was clearly undecided. He didn't budge until Mr. Smith came and talked to him for a few moments. Then he heaved his shoulders in a shrug and walked forward into the room.

His walk was odd. There was a self-consciousness in the way he set down his heavy feet which Rennert, puzzled, could only have characterized by the expression "walking on eggs." And his course took him, not to the door from which came a second and more prolonged pounding, but straight to the northeast corner. He was scowling, and his hands were thrust into his pockets.

Rennert's first thought was that he was headed for the chaise longue where Lurcott lay, perhaps to move the man to another room before answering the summons. Bohannon apparently expected something of the sort, for he doubled his fists defensively and looked about as if for support. But Kerwick gave him scarcely a glance, passed by and entered the east alcove, pulling his flashlight from his coat as he went.

Rennert could have taken one long step and been in a position to spy upon him. He decided, however, that it was the part of wisdom to keep his distance from gun and scowl, and so contented himself with listening. The sounds from within he identified as those of a piece of luggage being opened, then closed with a snap.

Kerwick returned, carrying in his left hand a pair of bedroom slippers of dark leather, in the other the lighted torch. He proceeded to the door, halted and without kneeling removed his shoes and put on the slippers. He placed the shoes carefully against the base of the wall and straightened. A swift glance about the room, as if he were fearful of being stalked, and he turned the key and lifted the bolt. Opening the door only wide enough to allow passage for his body, he edged through and closed it quickly behind him, so that Rennert saw only a segment of night cut by bright slivers of rain.

For an instant he was gripped by the sheer fantasy of the procedure. Donning bedroom slippers before stepping out into the rain! It was like some absurdity out of *Alice in Wonderland*. Surely now someone would inject a note of levity and dispel the grimness which had crept into a child's game played by grown-ups. . . .

Smith had been joined in the alcove door by his daughter, where their figures were dwarfed by the candle-lit interior behind them and by the lancet arch over their heads as effectively as they had been by the expanses of Kerwick's seersuckers.

The dominant form in that end of the room was now Jesse Elkins, who had planted himself on the hearth in an attitude much like Woodmansee's. He frowned at the chair in which his wife sat and brushed his palm downward through the air, as if suppressing word or action on her part. How poor Miss Pirtle was faring, Rennert couldn't see.

Woodmansee had moved with swift lithe steps to Rennert's side, his feet making no noise at all. They stood with elbows touching, and Rennert was surprised at the feeling which contact with that hard arm brought: that the two of them were linked by some common quality which was purely impersonal in its nature. He sensed the magnetism, not of congenial flesh and blood, but of tempered steel whose extrinsic worth he respected while knowing that its present immaculateness did not signify that it had never known blood or other fouling.

Woodmansee's eyes were agleam and keen as he surveyed the bare tiles. "Mr. Rennert,"—for the first time his voice was not bold—"there's something wrong with this floor. They've been watching it—Kerwick and Smith and the girl—all evening. As if they were afraid they'd see something crawling there. Have you noticed?"

Instinctively Rennert's eyes too fell, to rove over the dull red squares whose smooth surfaces and narrow interstices offered so little in the way of concealment.

"Yes," he said, "I've noticed."

"I was down in Taxco last week. That place is alive with scorpions. I killed two in my hotel room. Do they have them in this part of Mexico?" Woodmansee's breathing was sibilant in the stillness, as if tiny hairs were obstructing his nasal passages.

From outside came the sound of a starting motor and a renewed rattle and chugging as the car moved forward and turned the corner of the house in the direction of the garage.

Rennert was purposely slow in formulating his reply. So often had his friends professed to find in him a hankering after sensationalism that he had grown hesitant about expressing any theory such as the one which was plaguing him now. A theory which had first found lodgment in his mind when he saw Kerwick stoop with a forked stick and dig a small bright pin from between the tiles. And which had been given color, albeit a dubious color, by the sight of the Apizaco cane and the sound of driving rain.

"I know they do," Woodmansee forestalled him. "I read a newspaper account of the trouble they were having at some old *hacienda* up here in northern Mexico. A lot of people were dying mysteriously. They found that the fellow who'd owned the place before the Revolution had kept scorpions in the cells of his dungeons—hidden in pieces of decayed wood. At night they'd crawl out and bite a prisoner he wanted to dispose of without formality. Well, they'd been left there and had multiplied."

"Yes," Rennert said, "and they were drawn out by the strains of music and killed. And everybody lived happily ever after. I've heard the story. And it may very well be true. Because there are *alacranes*, scorpions, in this part of Mexico. But I doubt very much whether there'd be many at this altitude."

"We're almost on the Tropic of Cancer, aren't we? That ought to make a difference."

"It does." Rennert frowned and damned Woodmansee for arguing the subject. "It's a peculiar region we're in—a sort of crossroads of the animal and vegetable kingdoms. A few miles north of us is the desert, and a few miles south is tropical jungle. We have mountains on one side and the Gulf on the other. So a scientific expedition could find a wide variety of venomous insects here. But they'd have to hunt, I feel sure. Not a very satisfactory answer, is it?"

"No." Woodmansee smiled wryly and flapped a trouser leg. "One poisonous critter is one too many. What about snakes?"

"The same applies to them. Under ordinary conditions I wouldn't expect to be bothered by any."

"Aren't these ordinary conditions?"

"No. There's the *chipi-chipi*—the rain."

"Well, that ought to keep 'em in their holes." Woodmansee shot a rather quizzical glance in Rennert's direction, hesitated and asked: "When was the last time you were in this particular part of the country?"

"This," Rennert said, "is the first time. I've been all along the northern and western borders of Tamaulipas, but I've never had occasion to travel this highway before. So any information you get from me is secondhand."

From the way Woodmansee fell silent and compressed his lips, he doubtless thought that the sudden constraint in Rennert's manner was due to the fact that the latter was piqued by his failure to maintain the role of pundit. The truth was that Rennert's attention had been increasingly absorbed by Bohannon's actions.

For several moments after Kerwick's exit the fat man had stayed at his post by the phonograph, seemingly puzzled by the muddy black-and-white sport shoes which stood by the opposite wall. Then his eyes, narrowed, had begun to move systematically over the floor. He had lifted his own feet, stared at the soles then put them down much as Kerwick had done. Gingerly. Now, as the handle of the front door was turned, he leaned back against the cabinet, his left hand fell to his side and surreptitiously rapped again and again on the wood.

It was an instinctive act which betrayed the superstitious nature of the man. What was vastly more important, Rennert thought as he shifted his gaze to the stranger on the threshold, it implied the actuality of some menace. Bohannon knew why that floor had been swept, why Kerwick had searched among the dry logs and why he had walked with such wariness over the tiles. . . .

"What's that? What's that?" the words came from behind a large black umbrella which was partly closed and tilted in Rennert's direction.

Kerwick stepped inside and closed the door. "Stay right there," he ordered. "Here. Hold these things."

The umbrella was lowered, and Rennert saw the pith sun helmet. That first glance of his must have been more comprehensive, for he was aware that the dumpy newcomer wore as well a khaki shirt with a black four-in-hand tie, flaring whipcord breeches and high laced boots. But these were incidentals which couldn't, for the moment, vie for interest with the sun helmet. Rennert grinned and stared (as he would have stared at a turban, a fez or a feather headdress) while the man started to put down a bulging briefcase in order to take the Gladstone bag, the kodak and the portable typewriter which Kerwick was thrusting at him.

"Don't set that on the floor!" Kerwick roared. "Hold all these or leave 'em outside!"

"But, my dear fellow—"

The protest was cut short as bag, kodak and typewriter were piled upon his short outstretched arms.

Hastily Kerwick removed his slippers, jammed his feet into his shoes and knotted the strings. Tucking the slippers under one arm, he relieved his open-mouthed guest of his burden and beckoned with his head. "Straight across the room. Open that door for me."

As he followed Kerwick the stranger took off the helmet, revealing a bald head that must have put all who saw it in mind of an egg. He had a rather flouncing walk, which was probably accounted for in part by the heaviness of his boots, and he swung the pith head-gear as if he were marking time. He held the door open for Kerwick and watched the latter deposit the luggage upon the floor of the passage without stepping over the threshold.

"I must say," he began as he handed over the brief-case, "that I don't understand just what—"

"That's all right," Kerwick interrupted him. "Now come on. The man's over here."

He led the way toward the chaise longue, saying to Bohannon as he passed: "This is Dr. Damson. He's going to have a look at your partner."

Damson wasn't young, yet he had a chubby-cheeked face, badly sunburned, which struck Rennert as being the most callow he had ever seen on an adult. He shoved the helmet toward Rennert with the words, "Hold this, my good man," and went to bend over Lurcott.

Since a rear almost as ample as Kerwick's precluded his view of the examination, Rennert lifted the helmet on one finger and cocked a critical eye at it. He had often wondered what these things felt like, looked like at close range. The man is very innocent and very trusting who will wear this particular bit of falderal into Mexico: innocent of the jokes which have it as their butt, trusting as to the poor marksmanship of small boys—and others. Only an American who has grown old and grizzled and tough south of the Rio Grande—an American who quite obviously is *un hombre de pelo en pecho*, hirsute in the proper places—has immunity while thus hatted.

Rennert exchanged a glance with Woodmansee, who was smiling openly.

"Know what they use those for down here?" Woodmansee asked, sotto voce.

Rennert nodded. "Once upon a time an Englishman wore one to a bullfight—" He stopped and glanced sharply at the owner of the offending article.

Dr Damson had straightened and turned and was regarding Kerwick severely. "Young man,"—his voice, Rennert would have described as fruity—"if this is your idea of a joke, I must say it is in very poor taste. Very poor taste, to say the least."

"A joke?" Kerwick stared at him. "It isn't a joke. What's the matter?"

"Why, the man's dead. Anyone can tell that."

10
EXIT WITHOUT SHOES

"DEAD!" KERWICK REPEATED. "He can't be! He was alive a few minutes ago."

Dr. Damson hitched at his ill-fitting breeches. "See for yourself."

Kerwick seemed altogether witless as he stooped, lifted Lurcott's left hand, let it fall quickly and rubbed his own palm upon his sleeve. Just as witlessly he directed his stare at the other end of the room, where Mr. Smith and his daughter still stood in the archway.

They had heard, for the former started forward, to be checked by the girl. "Don't, Father! Let Keith handle this."

She might have meant the words for Kerwick as well, for they were spoken clearly and produced an immediate effect on the young man. He threw back his shoulders, whipped out the automatic and, with a gesture which in other circumstances would have bordered on the melodramatic, waved it at Rennert, Woodmansee, Damson and Bohannon. "Get over by the door, all of you."

All of them moved to obey except Bohannon. His face had been hidden as he bent over Lurcott and tested pulse, heart and eyes in a more efficient manner, it seemed to Rennert, than Dr. Damson could have done. He crossed his former companion's hands over his breast, gazed down at him for a moment, then turned to Kerwick.

"Not so fast!" he gasped, his face twitching more violently than before. "Not so fast. What're you goin' to do about Tom here? Just forget him? Play like this never happened?"

Kerwick was breathing heavily. "I'm sorry." He released words in short phrases. "Awfully sorry. I'll talk to you about that. After a while. Not now. Something's happened. You've all got to get out of this room."

"So you can make a getaway? Take Tom with you and dump him down some ravine?" Bohannon's eyes rested uneasily on the gun. "Oh no, you don't, buddy. I'm stayin' with Tom. And I'm goin' to see that this thing ain't hushed up, neither. Too bad all these people are here, ain't it? If they weren't, you could just bump me off too and throw me away along with Tom. And nobody be any the wiser."

"All right! All right!" Kerwick sounded frantic. "Stay here and I'll talk to you."

Damson had stopped halfway to the door at the rear, where Rennert and Woodmansee were standing.

"I don't know your name," he addressed Bohannon, "but will you kindly tell me what is the meaning of all this? Have I entered a madhouse? Who is this dead man? Who killed him? Who is the owner of this place anyway?"

Bohannon pointed a thumb at Rennert. "Ask Mr. Rennert there. Let him tell you the whole story."

"Rennert?" Damson wheeled. "Who is Mr. Rennert? Which one of these men?"

"The one with your hat."

Rennert felt like some sort of unhappy specimen about to be transfixed by a pin as Damson came toward him, eyes bright and intent.

"You're not by any chance the detective chap?"

Rennert looked his dourest as he nodded and held out the sun helmet.

Far from being discouraged, the other took both the hat and Rennert's hand and began pumping energetically. "Very thoughtless of the young man not to have introduced us properly in the first place, Mr. Rennert. This is a most fortunate meeting. I am Gulliver Damson, as you know by this time. Do you have a few minutes to spare?"

"At the instant I'm scarcely a free agent, Dr. Damson." Rennert withdrew his hand.

"Oh, I didn't want to engage your services. No, no. Nothing like that." Damson slapped him lightly on the back and seemed to become interested in counting the vertebrae of Rennert's spinal column. "What I had in mind was an interview. If you can succeed in arousing my interest—and I think you can—I'm in the position to give you some excellent advertising. Quite free of charge, of course. Are you alone here?"

"Yes," Rennert said coldly, "but what I meant was that Mr. Kerwick there has something to say to us. Let's listen to him."

Kerwick was in the center of the room, in the attitude of a speaker momentarily at a loss for a means of coping with an unexpected heckler. Now that Damson was still, he turned to the group by the fireplace and called: "All of you come over here, please."

Mrs. Elkins was standing, her arm linked with her husband's. They exchanged a word or two in an undertone and started around the couch.

Miss Pirtle got to her feet as they came abreast of her and clutched at Jesse Elkins' free arm. "May I go with you? Oh, what is happening? Where is Mr. Woodmansee?"

"Here, Miss Pirtle." The young man stepped swiftly to her side and guided her to the wall.

The six of them stood in a row, facing Kerwick.

"Mad! Utterly mad!" The fierce whisper in Rennert's ear came from Damson, whom he was beginning to think of as a leech.

Wearily he nodded agreement. He felt an almost uncontrollable desire to laugh outright at the whole farcical procedure.

Kerwick cleared his throat and sent the beam of the torch wavering along the line. To Rennert he was more like a self-conscious football hero called on to make a speech between the glare of bonfires than like a man whose gun held the balance in some grim game of life and death. . . .

"I'm sorry about all of this. But it's not my fault. And there's no help for it now. All of you came here tonight wanting something to eat and a place to sleep. All right. You've had your suppers—"

"I haven't!" Damson reminded him tartly.

Kerwick scowled. "I'll bring you yours. Go on back to your rooms now. Nothing'll bother you. But first I want all of you to take off your shoes and leave them in here."

For five or six seconds no one spoke or moved, but audible breathing went like a rustle in and out of their rank.

"Would you mind saying that again?" Damson cupped a palm about his ear. "It sounded as if you were telling us to take off our *shoes.*"

"I did."

"Well, *I* certainly won't!" Mrs. Elkins' voice got a bit strident. "What's the matter? Do you think we're carrying bank notes in the soles?" She jerked a small purse from her pocket, opened it and tossed a handful of coins upon the tiles in front of Kerwick. "There! You have all my money. Are you satisfied?"

She started to turn to the door, but Jesse Elkins caught her wrist. After a glance of inquiry at Rennert, who had one shoe off and was unlacing the other, he spoke authoritatively: "Now, Vera, there's no use causing any more trouble. We don't know what this is all about. But let's take it as calmly as possible. The man has a gun, so what he says goes."

Frowning, she pulled off her black pumps and kicked them after the coins. "Any more orders, Mr. Kerwick?" she asked.

"That's all. Please, Mrs. Elkins, I'm sorry—I know how embarrassing this is—"

"Things are liable to be more embarrassing for you before this is over with. Ready to go, Jesse?"

Her feet were small and graceful, seen to advantage in sheer silk hose, and she managed to depart in stately enough fashion. Her husband didn't fare so well. He had an ungainly walk, which seemed due to a loss of self-possession as much as to the size of his feet. When he had held the door open for Mrs. Elkins he paused briefly, bunching his toes against the chill of the tiles. His eyes met Rennert's, and he said, "*Hasta luego*" in a low voice.

"*Hasta luego.*" Rennert, in his socks, was easing his weight off his right foot which felt sore now to the bone.

"Wait, Rennert! Wait!" Damson blocked his way to the door as he swayed back and forth in his struggle with the laces of the high tight boots. "You and I are bunking together tonight."

"You're mistaken," Woodmansee put in evenly. "I'm sharing Mr. Rennert's room with him. You can have the one on the east side of the patio. I'll get my things out right away." He stood at ease, his well-shaped feet snugly clad in dark silk socks with magenta clocks.

Damson glanced at him inimically and rested his rump against the wall. "I don't know who you are, but you're being very forward. Rennert and I have already made our arrangements."

"Think so?" Woodmansee smiled. "Ask him."

"Say!" Kerwick burst out. "What is this, anyway?"

"I'm not quite sure myself," Rennert told him and turned to Damson with scant politeness. "Mr. Woodmansee is right, Doctor. He and I have agreed to share quarters."

"Well, he can stay out until you and I've had a talk." Mumbling unintelligibly to himself, Damson set to work on the boots again.

"I'll be in as soon as I take Miss Pirtle to her room, Mr. Rennert," Woodmansee called as he went out. Miss Pirtle wore black stockings which showed the protuberances of corns. She stumbled over the luggage in the passage, and Woodmansee had to put an arm about her waist to prevent her from falling.

"Which is your room, Mr. Rennert?" Bohannon inquired softly from his place at the foot of the chaise longue.

"The one next to this."

"Good! There won't be any funny business, then, with you on the other side of this wall. No danger of the nice old gentleman tryin' to kill me with that cane the way he did Tom."

Rennert's eyes followed his. Smith was in the chair by the fire which Mrs. Elkins had vacated. He was bent forward, and both hands were pressed against his temples. His daughter sat on the chair arm, her shoulder touching his. She was staring, doubtless by chance, straight at Rennert. He smiled at her, she looked so young and helpless, but her eyes were cold and unseeing.

"Well, well!" Dr. Damson, the boots off at last, wriggled his toes in gray woolen socks and inspected the Smiths with avid interest. "So *that's* the murderer! Well!"

He grasped Rennert's arm companionably. "Come, Rennert. I expect you find this affair rather uninteresting, don't you? No mystery about who the murderer is."

PART TWO

Hugh Rennert was limping as he went out the door, so I had to slow my steps. He took my arm and spoke in his soft Texas drawl: "By Jove, I'm glad you're here, Damson! There's more in this than meets the eye. Something sinister that I don't like. You'll stand by, won't you?"

I assured him I would be only too glad to do so, and we looked past the flickering lamp into the Mexican darkness at the end of the passage. I knew he was on tenterhooks, so I said lightly: "Suppose you be the Limping Imp and we'll soon see what's going on here."

"The Limping Imp?" He was all ears.

"Yes. The Spanish tell of a Limping Imp who whisked off all the rooftops of Madrid so he could peek in each room and catch the people at their secrets. . . ."

> —*Heigh-ho Mexico!*
> by Gulliver Damson, Ph.D.

11
PRAYER FOR A STRANGER

WILMA SMITH STOOD in the archway and stared at the muddy shoes which Mr. Rennert had left behind him.

She wished Keith had let Mr. Rennert stay. He was the only one of these strangers who seemed, somehow, real and solid, the sort of person you pass on the street every day and never notice unless you're acquainted with him. She was sorry she had snubbed him so rudely when he smiled at her. Poor man, he was only trying in his friendly way to cheer her up. He supposed she was frightened or shocked or grieved because her father had hit that thief a little too hard and he had died. Mr. Rennert lived snug and safe somewhere with his wife and children and didn't know how easily men died—of the slightest rap on the head. . . .

It didn't matter. She was only looking at Mr. Rennert's shoes and thinking about Mr. Rennert to keep from looking at the shadow on the wall above them. A fat shadow that only stirred when some fragment of log in the east fireplace broke and dropped into a nest of embers. Then it seemed that the fat man whom she couldn't see was lurching toward her, leaving his voice behind to hold Keith and her father. . . .

"We're helpless," she heard Keith say. "There's not a damn thing we can do. Except wait and be careful."

For a long time the shadow didn't move. She was staring at it again, unwillingly, and listening to a faint sound that must have been the man's wheezing breath. Bohannon, was that his name?

"How long?" he asked.

"God only knows!" Keith wouldn't curse before her father unless he were boiling with rage. "Morning maybe. It depends on how
long the rain lasts."

"Mornin' will do." Bohannon laughed.

Wilma turned back into the dining room and walked to a chair
against the west wall, where candlelight fell. She felt as if Keith's
voice had come to her rescue, releasing her with its thickness from
the nightmare of watching that shadow. Funny about Keith's voice.
It irritated you because, although it was very pleasant, he never
took the trouble to talk distinctly. But it made you listen and expect him to say something more important than he ever did.

She sat down and, remembering what Keith had told her,
hooked her heels about the lower rung so that her feet were off the
floor. She wondered if he wasn't exaggerating, just a little, about
the danger.

She folded her arms tightly to keep from shivering. It was cold
in this drafty place, and she had brought no clothes for such
weather. The rain made her nervous, falling so steadily from a
silent sky, without wind or thunder or lightning. More like snow
than rain, until it struck the roof.

She heard Bohannon's far-away laugh and his words, "I'll be
back for my answer as soon as I put Tom to bed. Poor old Tom!
Last night he sleeps in a decent bed. Tomorrow he'll be 'way down
under the ground. Where it's cold and wet and things won't let him
sleep. . . ."

Why didn't Keith make him stop?

The door closed, and she knew he had gone.

She watched the flame of the candle sag in the current of air
which she could feel rising about her ankles. She saw the dishes
and the remnants of the food and thought she might as well carry
them back to the kitchen. It wouldn't be helping, of course, but
anything was better than sitting there and getting jittery about
what was going to happen.

Keith came in. He stood just inside the door for a moment and
didn't say anything. His face frightened her a little. In the gymna-
sium at school a girl used to show the rest of them how long she

could hang by her toes from a bar. Sometimes, after minutes and minutes had passed, her face would begin to look like Keith's and they would make her quit. Dark, screwed into knots, with bulging eyes. Some change had come over Keith this evening that she didn't understand. She had noticed it first after he brought Mr. Rennert in. And his feet had been muddy, too, just like Mr. Rennert's. . . .

He said, "Leave those dishes where they are, Wilma."

That tone of his always made her furiously angry, and it was a moment before she could trust herself to answer naturally:

"I'm going to take them to the kitchen and wash them, Keith. They look so untidy."

"Don't be silly. Your father's bringing you a pair of slippers. Put those on and go out in the kitchen. There's a cot, and you can lie down and rest. There'll be time enough to get some sleep."

"I'm not tired. I'd much rather do these dishes."

"Of course you're tired, Wilma. This has been a hard day for you." He took her wrist and removed a bowl from her fingers as if she had been a child.

She was so surprised that all she could do for an instant was look at his hands. It was the first time, as far as she could remember, that she had known the feel of them. They were rough and calloused and were hurting her a little.

"Let me go, Keith. I'm neither tired nor sleepy. Do you understand? I'm the one who ought to know." She hadn't intended to speak so sharply.

He put his hands in his pockets and stared at the floor by the west end of the table, where the pots of cactus had been broken. "I'm sorry, Wilma. I was only trying—not to worry you. You see, if you walk around here it'll be that much harder for us. And, God, it's dangerous!"

"Oh." It was the same old story. Keith always left her feeling flat when he explained the reason for his actions. He was usually right in practical matters, she was willing to concede, but he made the mistake of assuming that she and everyone else were going to yield to his judgment without question. Somebody ought to point that out to him. . . .

But this was no time.

"I was forgetting, Keith. I'll go to the kitchen and stay." And then, because she too was looking at the floor and because she had been thinking about Mr. Rennert and his shoes, she remembered how he had stopped when he was walking away with those two plates of food. Her throat seemed to have gone dry, so that her voice sounded strangely unlike her own: "Keith!"

"Yes?"

"Mr. Rennert stepped on something during supper, didn't he? And hurt his foot?"

Keith nodded. "A cactus spine, that's all."

"But it was there on the floor. And if it's dangerous for me to walk around with whole soles on my shoes, what about him? If it drew blood—" She wished Keith would turn his head so that she could see his face by the full light of the candle. His eyes particularly. They looked feverish, and he had stared so long without blinking at the dark tiles. . . .

"Listen, Wilma." She had never heard his voice so thick. "If anything happened to Mr. Rennert, then there's nothing to be done about it. Nothing."

"That doctor could look at his foot."

"The doctor wouldn't find anything wrong—yet. And if he did he'd be helpless. There's no antidote or cure. That's why I've been so worried about you—and your father."

"But these other people, Keith! Oughtn't you to have warned them?"

"I couldn't, without telling them everything. About this house. And then I'd have to hold 'em here by main force, so they wouldn't go to the police. But they're safe enough now."

"Are you sure?" She had given up trying to read his face.

"Of course I'm sure." He had hesitated, however, just a fraction of a second before he said it. "But I came to talk to you about your father," he hurried on. "Did you hear Bohannon's offer?"

"Yes."

"He'll hush up that man's death if we agree. He'll bury the body out in the mountains, and no one will ever know."

"But these strangers—they'll tell."

"Listen." He stood close to her. "If the car gets back tonight, you and your father can be across the border at Matamoros or close to it before these folks wake up in the morning. If it doesn't come until after daylight, you and he can leave, and I'll see that everybody stays here until you're safe. In the United States."

"But what about you?"

"Oh, I'll be all right. There won't be any charges against me to amount to anything. These people will all want to get back to the States as soon as they can. If any of them do take the trouble to go to the authorities, there won't be any—what do you call it?—*corpus delicti*. It'll be their word against mine. The whole thing will blow over in no time: What's wrong about that plan?"

"Well, it's asking a lot of you."

"No, it isn't. It's the first time I've ever been able to do anything for your father. I want you to talk to him and make him agree."

"He doesn't want to?"

"I'm not sure. He hasn't said much. He's sitting in there now thinking. I'm afraid his idea is to go down to Victoria and give himself up. Plead self-defense. That's what it was, of course, but you never know about a Mexican court. There's no telling what they'd do. At least he'd be in prison for a long time. And Mexican prisons are bad places to be. Especially for a man in his health—"

"Don't go on, Keith. You're right. It's the only thing to do. Tell Father to come in here. I'll make him agree. And Keith—" He had already started away.

"Yes?"

"If it weren't for Father I wouldn't let you do this. As it is, well— all I can say is, 'Thank you.'"

He jammed his hands into his pockets again and blinked at one of the candles. "That's all right." He put his chin up as he spoke. "I'd do a lot more if I could." His right hand came slowly out of his trousers pocket, and he laid on the table a long string of illuminated beads with a crucifix.

She recognized them at once, picked them up and ran them through her fingers. They were moist, and some of the perforations were clogged by black mud like that on his shoes.

"They're ours, Keith."

He nodded. "I found 'em this evening. I thought you might like to keep 'em. And maybe say a prayer if you feel like it. They'd come to pieces in my hands if I tried." He swung around and went from the room awkwardly, his big shoulders swaying from side to side as if he expected to have to smash his way through the door.

A prayer. Wilma wouldn't have been more astonished if he had burst out crying. She had heard him so often joking about objects of worship; had seen him standing images of saints on their heads, putting boxing gloves on their hands and cigars in their mouths. But then she had realized this summer what an utter stranger to her Keith was, although for years their house in San Luis had been his home, the only one she had ever known him to speak of. She had been away at school when her father gave him a job, and in the short vacations he had always been busy with his affairs and a little aloof when she was near. Perhaps it had taken a happening like tonight's to get them acquainted.

Mechanically she pushed the beads along the string and decided that Keith must have been with Mr. Rennert when he found them. Mr. Rennert. She remembered exactly what his face had looked like when he leaned there with one hand on the table and worked that cactus spine out of his foot. It must have hurt. It must have gone deep into the flesh. . . .

As her father came slowly from the living room into the candle-light she put the beads away and stilled the motion of her lips. It wouldn't do to let him think she was frightened.

"Well, Wilma!" His attempt at jauntiness was a failure, and both of them knew it. Her eyes were suddenly keen, seeing for the first time the grayness and thinness of his hair, the lax muscles below his eyes, the lines in cheeks which at a distance seemed so plump. Surely he hadn't looked so old when they left Brownsville that morning!

He laid her slippers on a chair and came toward her. "I know what you're going to say. So save your breath. Keith's been talking to you, and both of you are going to try to make me go off and leave him here to face the music. Well, I'm not going! When the car comes, you and the chauffeur are going to Brownsville. You'll stay there until this business is settled." He put an arm about her. "And you're not to worry, Pill. Everything will be all right."

Pill! He hadn't used that nickname since she wore pigtails. It brought memories crowding: the huge old house in San Luis where a pampered little girl had queened it over a succession of fat and adoring Mexican governesses; champagne bubbling in tall glasses and the rich odor of Cuban cigars during long dinner parties; the hearty sound of men's laughter and the softer tinkle of women's that came up to her ears when, late at night, she used to creep to the head of the stairs; her father's face flushed with food and drink and the joy of living and (even then) his chuckles at the doctor's warnings. . . .

"But a Mexican prison—"

"Nonsense!" He hugged her. "That's more of Keith's talk. The young rascal is making the whole thing more serious than it is. Trying to scare me into running away. Why, I feel like tanning his hide." And he swished the snake cane through the air. She had always hated that cane but knew he carried it because Keith had given it to him.

"But Keith says—"

"Now, now, forget what Keith says. You must try to get some sleep. We'll talk things over in the morning and they won't look so black. I'm going to have that doctor examine Lurcott. Maybe he had a weak heart or something. I still don't think I hit him hard enough to kill him if he'd been healthy." The words had been coming more and more slowly, as if he were running out of breath. He paused and said brusquely, "Take off your shoes now and toddle on to bed."

"I hate to leave you out here. You'll be careful?"

"Has Keith been scaring you about the danger?"

"Well, he said there was some."

"Fiddlesticks! He doesn't know what he's talking about. There's not a chance in a thousand of any of us being harmed."

"Are you sure?"

"Of course I'm sure."

"But just the same you'll be careful—and make Keith be careful?"

He looked straight at her, his eyes bright and alert and full of understanding as ever. "You care, Wilma? About Keith?"

She nodded and amended quickly, "I care because he's so loyal to you. You can't let anything happen to him."

Suddenly she was in his arms, her head nestled against his shoulder, his voice low in her ear: "The boy's all right, Wilma. Nothing's going to hurt him. What do you say we take a cruise down in the Caribbean in a week or so? You and Keith and I. Find the sun and forget all this—"

But the dead weight which dragged at the syllables told her he would never be able to forget the word that horrid doctor in the sun helmet had used:

Murderer.

12
OLD MAN OF THE SEA

"THEN YOU CAME IN, Dr. Damson, and told us Lurcott was dead. You know the rest."

Acquaintances who thought of Rennert as a man of equable temperament, too phlegmatic or self-possessed to be responsive to anything as intangible as atmosphere, would have known him better had they seen him ranging haltingly, in loose bedroom slippers, over the quarters which were his for the night. One hand was in a pocket, fiddling with coins. The other kept shooting up from his side to perform some altogether purposeless action. He took books from the shelves, put them back unopened and evened the rows. He turned pottery this way and that, as if studying the effectiveness of the designs. He punched and replaced the pillows on which Mrs. Elkins had leaned. He worried for some time at the lock of the empty gun case.

He was acting, it occurred to him, not unlike a dog or cat that goes about sniffing to familiarize itself with new surroundings. That, in a way, was what he had been doing while he talked. But it was his subconscious which was on the alert, trying to find some association with an object or a bit of his narrative that would start a train of thought. Until now he hadn't realized how tense he had become during the few but crowded minutes since he knocked at the door of this house. Now that he was relegated to these four walls and told to go to bed while some drama of which he had been accorded but a glimpse moved toward its end . . .

He paused, his right foot lifted off the floor, and spent a moment in deciphering the letters on the tile mosaic before the empty fireplace. Breathing was easier here, although the flutter of rain-drops in soot made him think of the chimney as an air hole which was being choked by the slow fall of feathers.

"Come, come, old man!" Dr. Damson chided him. "Play fair. You're holding too much back."

Rennert turned. There had been growing in him a feeling of impotence—against the elements and against whatever it was they had hatched here tonight. This combined with the soreness of his foot and his general physical discomfort to set up an intense irri-tability which was gradually focusing upon Dr. Damson as a target.

Yet so far Damson had been innocuous enough. He had accom-panied Rennert from the living room, bringing his luggage with him, then quite naturally had wanted to know of the events pre-ceding his arrival. He had listened attentively and without com-ment to Rennert's incomplete version, sitting upright in a chair and consuming with relish the plate of food which Kerwick had handed in at the door. Now the emptied plate was on the table, and he was leaning forward with his hands folded across his stom-ach and one Oaxaca sandal laid upon the other.

His hands were overlarge, smooth and seemingly devoid of hair. He looked, Rennert thought, more like a big, solemn, well-fed baby than anything else, although there was nothing innocent about his eyes. They were always still and possumlike when you glanced their way, but they gave you the uncomfortable feeling that the instant before they had been very busy taking in little details of your per-son which didn't call for scrutiny.

"I've told you," Rennert said with quiet emphasis, "all there is to tell."

"Don't forget I'm Watson."

"You're what?"

"Dr. Watson. Your confidant and chronicler." Damson jumped from the chair and came over the tiles, to the accompaniment of the clicking of his breeches laces. He rammed a hand into each of Rennert's armpits and made as if to heave him off the floor.

"This is excellent!" he exclaimed exuberantly. "Much better than I thought it was going to be. There is a mystery attached to the affair. I've just decided on the procedure we'll follow. We'll do exactly as if this were a detective story. You go about your work, and I'll be right at your heels, asking leading questions now and then. And I'll put things down as they happen. But you must be frank with me. Up to a point. I shan't object if you withhold your deductions until the last. But you must make your own position clear. You must tell me who's hiring you and for what reason—"

"Just a moment!" Rennert, shaken, bewildered and angry, tried to draw away.

But Damson only put an arm about his shoulders and hugged him while he chatted. "Your yarn about being on a business trip and stopping here by accident is a plausible one, but it didn't fool me for a minute. I saw through your masquerade at once. Why, I may be able to build you up enough to fill my entire last chapter, Rennert! Though you aren't to consider that as a promise. Now begin your story at the beginning, and we'll see what possibilities it has." He whacked Rennert on the small of the back and let him go. "Sherlock."

Those same acquaintances who would have remarked on Rennert's nervousness a few moments before could now have read, although seeing them for the first time, the storm signals on his face. Spots of color brought his strongly defined cheekbones into greater prominence while the whiteness that came from tightening muscles did the same for his mouth. His eyes were bleak as he said evenly: "Sit down, Dr. Damson. Let's get a few things straight. This farce has gone far enough as far as I'm concerned."

Storm signals flew without the slightest effect on Damson, for with an excited "Wait a minute before you begin talking!" he padded over to the luggage which he had left on the other side of the room. He laid the briefcase on the studio couch, unbuckled it and produced a loose-leaf notebook and a fountain pen. He came back and stood by the candle while he opened the book and consulted the lettered tabs.

"It won't do to lose any of your pearls of wisdom, Rennert. Here we are! R for Rennert." He turned pages and read aloud: "'Railways, ranches, Real del Monte, Conde de Regla, Virgen de los Remedios, restaurants.'" He inserted a blank page from the rear.

"I'm putting you between the Virgin of the Remedies and restaurants."

"*Sit down, please.*"

"All right. Don't be impatient." Damson plunked himself into a chair and watched Rennert pull another around from its position in front of the fireplace so as to face him.

"Oh, I say!" he spoke up eagerly. "What's the matter with your foot? I've noticed you limping."

"I merely ran a cactus spine into it."

With a clucking sound of the tongue Damson was up and on his way across the room. "We must do something about that. Danger of infection, you know. I always carry a first-aid kit. I'll bandage you up in no time." He squatted down by the Gladstone from which he had taken his sandals and began to transfer layers of its contents to the couch.

"Don't bother, Doctor. It's not serious." Rennert was sensible enough to make his protest a halfhearted one.

"How do you know?"

"I've stepped on dozens of the things."

"The graveyards," Damson retorted darkly, "are full of men like you. And of men who've monkeyed with unloaded guns."

Rennert's eyes had brightened as they fell on two articles which the other was putting back into place, and he regretted that he had been so near to losing his temper over a bit of shoulder slapping.

"I'd like to glance over your guidebook a moment, Doctor. And I see you have a carton of cigarettes. My favorite brand. I wonder if I might have one? I neglected to bring enough."

"Very well." Damson didn't sound particularly gracious, although he was smiling with what looked like satisfaction as he returned carrying a large aluminum case, a package of cigarettes and the book which Rennert desired. This was the fat little volume of encyclopedic proportions which, although unleavened by wit, is a standing reproach to the titbits of Mexicana fed to gullible tourists by precious lady writers.

"That," Damson said as he handed it to Rennert, "is a most dull book. No pictures at all to appeal to the eye. A month ago I could have furnished you with a number of other guidebooks. Unfortunately Mexican weather and traveling wore them out. That's the only one left. Sit down, please!" he ordered, and Rennert, as he obeyed, wondered if there weren't in the tone a faint mimicry of his own.

Very carefully Damson loosed cellophane and revenue stamp from the cigarettes, shook one out for Rennert, then folded the broken seal into place and put the package into a shirt pocket.

"Thanks." Rennert blew smoke from his nose. "Why don't you let me buy that package from you?"

Damson drew a low stool in front of Rennert's chair, perched himself on it and caught up Rennert's right heel. "I can see you're inexperienced in roughing it," he scolded while he propped the foot on his knee, rolled up the cuff of Rennert's trousers, unclasped his supporter and stripped off his sock. "I don't suppose you have any quinine or serum or mosquito netting or ammonia water or anything?"

"No," Rennert admitted meekly, "I don't." He had to grasp the arms of the chair as Damson raised the injured member toward the candlelight and frowned at it judicially.

"A tenderfoot like you wouldn't last a week in the wilds I've been in this summer, Rennert. Let this be a lesson to you." Damson lowered the foot and began puttering about in the kit.

Rennert made an examination of his own and found on the ball of his foot only a slight puncture with a little swelling around the edges. He settled back then, smoked and opened the guidebook to the index. Under the letter S he ascertained the number of the page he wanted. He turned to this and almost at once had to repress a whistle of surprise. He reread the two and a half lines of fine print; his eyes became bemused, and a frown puckered his forehead.

He started as cold liquid drenched his foot and ankle and ran down his shin.

"Hold steady," Damson soothed him. "This isn't going to hurt you. I just spilled a little alcohol."

Detachedly Rennert watched the manipulation of bottle and gauze and gazed at the hinged kit which lay open on the floor. It was one of those well-stocked, efficiently arranged, expensive outfits sold by drug and department stores to—well, he didn't know to whom they sold them. He'd never seen them except in windows and on display counters. This one showed no appearance of having been used.

"About those cigarettes, Doctor," he reminded. "I'm serious about wanting to buy that package. Or two, if you can spare them."

Damson swabbed away, and his voice became significant: "Oh yes, the cigarettes. It's not my policy to sell any of my supplies, Rennert. But I'm near the end of my trip, and I might make an exception in your case—since it looks as if you and I were going to be congenial."

"Oh yes," Rennert agreed with excessive politeness.

"You smoke a great deal, I take it?"

"A great deal."

"And you're more sociable and talk more freely while smoking?"

"Yes."

"Men frequently do. That's why I carry cigarettes. I seldom smoke myself, but many of the people I interview prove more easily handled with nicotine. Now I know you're wanting to talk, so I'll keep still and listen." Damson poured more alcohol and continued to bathe the foot, without much regard for the location of the wound. "Are you here in an official capacity or as a private detective?" he prompted with a cherubic smile for Rennert.

Rennert pulled his foot away and crossed it over his knee. He took one more draw on the cigarette and threw the butt into the fireplace. "Do you have any glass beads?" he asked.

"Beads?"

"Yes, or other trade goods. I might barter you a native wife or a piece of ivory for them."

Damson sat back, arms akimbo, and surveyed him for a moment in silence. "Are you by any chance trying to be facetious?" he inquired cuttingly. "If so, it's not one of your strong points. And you needn't swell up like that, either, Rennert. I'm not as much impressed by your importance as you think. I've a good mind to leave you here twiddling your thumbs. Do you know that you have a large bean decorating the front of your necktie?"

At the smart rapping of knuckles on the bathroom door he glanced in that direction and admonished in a whisper: "Don't answer it!"

"Come in!" Rennert fairly shouted and with his handkerchief removed from the fold of his tie the souvenir of his scratch meal in semidarkness.

Damson snorted at him. "Maybe someone else will listen to your fussing about a sore foot," he flung over his shoulder as he moved back to his chair.

Woodmansee came in rather buoyantly, despite his burden of two large raglan-style Gladstones of russet cowhide and a bulging duffel bag. On one side of his head was cocked a snap-brim felt hat, and on one shoulder was draped a long tan topcoat. The socks which he still wore and the cuffs of his trousers were by this time soaked.

He grinned impudently at Damson and greeted Rennert with a cheery "Hello, roommate! *We* have company, I see." He deposited his belongings by the couch and got out a pair of shoes and dry socks. "I thought I never would escape from Pirtle. Why, what's wrong?" he asked a little sharply as he came to join them.

Without so much as a by-your-leave to Damson, Rennert had helped himself to the latter's kit, touched the wound on his foot with a standard disinfectant and affixed a small neat bandage. "I stepped on a cactus," he told Woodmansee, "and I made such a fuss about my injury that the good doctor here got disgusted with me. But draw up a chair. I was about to make a speech. You've already heard it, but Dr. Damson hasn't."

Rennert put his foot into its slipper, sat straight in his chair and fixed Damson with what he hoped was a silencing gaze.

"You wanted me to talk about myself, Doctor, so that's what I'm going to do. Several times in my life I've been involved in criminal cases in Mexico or along the border. In most of them I've butted in where I wasn't needed and made a busybody out of myself. There was a certain fascination in it for me, I grant, and in a few instances I was able to hasten a solution that others would have arrived at sooner or later. As long as I was in the customs service, a little fretful at routine, that sort of thing threatened to become a hobby of mine. I quit it, though, when I quit the service. Only once have I broken over since, and that was when I felt I could be of assistance to friends of mine. But I am not now and I never have been a professional detective. I have nothing at all to sell to anyone except grapefruit and lemons. I'm a farmer. Is that clear, Dr. Damson?"

Damson was staring at him with parted lips. "But, Rennert, you led me to think—"

"I led you to think nothing. You jumped to the conclusion that I was here for some melodramatic purpose—on the trail of a supercriminal or secret documents—God only knows what you thought. Both of you men know just as much as I do about what's going on in this house. Maybe more. Both of you have just as much reason as I have to find out the truth. I'm interested, I admit, but so are you. Please get it through your heads that I'm just an ordinary traveler who's going to get a night's rest if it's at all possible." Rennert drew breath. "I've gathered, Dr. Damson, that you're writing some kind of a book and that you want to include tonight's events. But will you tell me why, in heaven's name, you—"

A stifled ejaculation from Damson interrupted him. Damson's eyes got big and round with astonishment. "And am I to gather from your words, Rennert, that you don't know who I am?"

"I'm very sorry, Doctor, but I might as well be frank. I haven't the faintest idea who you are."

Damson sighed profoundly, sank back and shook his head. "It was my fault in taking too much for granted in a Texan. I was aware you had been buried in little border towns most of your life, Rennert, but I supposed you kept in touch with the outside world. They told me in Greenwich Village I'd run up against this, but really I didn't credit it. It seems—"

"I thought," Woodmansee put in suddenly, "that you were a doctor?"

"I am."

"Then what are you doing writing books?"

"I think," Rennert said, "that this is getting to be a comedy of errors. I was about to ask our friend here if he isn't a doctor of philosophy, not of medicine."

"Of course," Damson sighed again, "my degree is a Ph.D."

Woodmansee's eyes had narrowed. "Then you don't know any more about a dead man than we do."

Damson gave him a brief but withering glance. "You forget, young man, that a traveler learns to deal with emergencies. I carry a full first-aid kit—"

"So does a Boy Scout. But Kerwick thought you were a real doctor, didn't he?"

"A real doctor?"

"You know what I mean. A physician."

"I can't say what Mr. Kerwick thought. I introduced myself as Dr. Gulliver Damson. I assumed that was sufficient. However, I can set your minds at rest on one point: the man whom I examined was most certainly dead." He dismissed Woodmansee with a nod and turned back to Rennert.

"But in reply to your question" (What question? Rennert tried to think), "I'll tell you a few facts about myself. The Gulliver is a nom de plume. That's French for 'pen name.' My real name is G. Oliver, but long ago my cronies changed it to Gulliver. So when I began to write I decided to use that. I have done quite a bit of poetry and book reviewing for various magazines. One of my poems was translated into Japanese. But I've always wanted to try my hand at a travel book. So I came to Mexico. I got several inches in the literary sections of the New York papers when I left. I'll show you the clippings later. I've spent the last month here taking notes. *Heigh-ho, Mexico!* is my tentative title. But in one respect the country has disappointed me. Except for having my pocketbook stolen in a Mexico City market, I've met with little in the way of adventure. Hence my interest when I walked into this house—a first-rate setting for a mystery, by the way—and was introduced to a corpse and to a man whom the newspapers had termed a detective—"

Woodmansee made a peculiar noise in his throat, exchanged a glance with Rennert, and both of them got up.

"Excuse us a moment, Doctor," Rennert murmured.

They walked hurriedly to the door and into the passage, where the lamp was flickering and burning low as its supply of fuel approached exhaustion.

Woodmansee was the first to find voice. "Am I nuts?" he asked Rennert anxiously. "Or is that something real you've got in there?"

"Ever hear of the Old Man of the Sea? Well, that's what I have on my back. A composite of all the tourists, all the writers, all the lecturers I've helped enter Mexico. The ancient gods are abroad tonight and are punishing me for the plague I've been instrumental in letting into their country."

"Why don't you boot him out?"

"How many cigarettes do you have?"

"Cigarettes? Only a few. But you're welcome—"

"No," Rennert said as the other's hand moved toward his pocket. "I'm going to try a little guile. Like Sinbad. Damson has a whole carton. He told me in so many words that he'd sell me some if I furnished him material for his book. I don't see any reason why I shouldn't give him a cock-and-bull story, pose as a detective if that's what he wants. His book will never see print. And it'll be twelve hours at the very least before either of us has a chance to get any more cigarettes."

Woodmansee chuckled. "Go to it. And buy me some if you can. Then we'll send him out on his bald head and have the place to ourselves." He glanced at the opposite door and lowered his voice. "We could do with some wood for that fireplace, couldn't we? I think there's someone in the kitchen. My guess is it's Miss Smith. I'll venture in and see what sort of a reception I get. Make wood my excuse. I may be able to get some information out of her. I'd sleep better if I knew what it is that's loose in this house."

"I want you to verify something for me, if you can. I looked in the San Luis Potosí section of a guidebook a few moments ago. I found a C. C. Smith listed there right enough. But it was his occupation that interested me. He owns one of the largest plants in Mexico for the manufacture of religious articles—images of saints, crucifixes, rosaries."

Woodmansee whistled. "That sounds screwy.

"Yes," Rennert told him, "it sounds very screwy."

13
SLAYER OF DRAGONS

THE KITCHEN WAS TWICE as large as the room which had been Wilma's in the dormitory at St. Cecilia's. It was the only part of the house that had anything in common with St. Cecilia's or with home in San Luis or with everyday life anywhere. If people ever lived in the rest of the lodge, one felt they would be queer story-book people, here for the queerest of reasons.

But somebody with good solid strength and a passion for cleanliness had scoured the pots and pans on the shelf over the sink in the west wall. It couldn't be a very sinister cook who used the large spick-and-span kerosene range by the entrance of the dining room. All the burners were lighted, and warm billows from the open oven had already taken the chill from the southeast corner, where Wilma sat, with feet tucked under her, on an iron cot.

If she had been able to secure the north door, Wilma thought that she would have taken her father's advice and tried to get a cat nap. But the bolt was on the other side, in the bath that connected with the room to which Bohannon had carried the dead man. A few minutes ago she had heard running water and the soft, animal-like pad of Bohannon's slippers; although she believed he had gone now, back to get his answer from Keith and her father, she couldn't nerve herself to venture in and bar his access to the bath. He might still be there, sounds of his presence drowned by the monotonous beat of the rain, by the purr of the stove and by the minor irritating note of water dripping from a tap in the sink. A meeting in such a place . . .

She sat up, her heart pounding, as someone rapped on the door nearest the cot. This was the door to the passage, and a glance told her that, in her preoccupation with Bohannon's whereabouts, she had neglected to fasten it.

Before she could make up her mind whether it would be wiser to remain where she was and trust that the person would go away or to tiptoe across the tiles and lock herself in, the door was swung open and a man thrust head and shoulders through. A candle was on the floor between them and threw its light directly into his face. Relief flooded over her as she saw it wasn't Bohannon but the tall, straight young man in the tan suit.

He smiled, said "Hello, there!" in a cheerful matter-of-fact way, came in and closed the door.

Wilma didn't know his name, but he had attracted her attention in the dining room, he was so very handsome and sleek, with hardness and egoism written all over him. He didn't look so hard now, as his smile widened and became more pleasant, but suddenly and unaccountably panic took hold of her. She remembered the floor and started to her feet.

"You can't come in here!" She was vexed at herself for sounding so weak and schoolgirlish.

His eyes moved swiftly about the room and came back to hers. Like everything else about him, they were arresting eyes, cool and searching and at the same time a little amused.

"I'm already in," he said. "You don't really mind, do you?"

"Yes. Please. You mustn't come any farther."

He stopped, and she glanced down at his shoes. They were exactly like those which he had taken off, large but cut on lines that gave them the effect of grace and strength.

"I won't track in any, mud, if that's what you're afraid of. Is it?"

"No. But please do what I ask."

"I will. But look at me first. Me, not my shoes."

She did so and had to smile back, nervously because she couldn't get rid of that panic for which his nearness seemed to be responsible. Yet there was no longer anything hard about his face, but rather warmth and the even tan that could come only from a healthy outdoor life. His wide mouth with little good-humored crinkles at the corners and his eyes (slate blue, she thought they were) invited inspection and appeared to be trying to give her confidence.

"You see," he said, "I'm not the big bad wolf, am I? Your father introduced us, though he didn't give my name. It's Woodmansee. George Woodmansee. I'm staying across the hall with Mr. Rennert. We have a fireplace there but no wood. I thought I'd come in and get some. Now that I'm here I'd like to sit down and talk to you awhile. You'll let me, won't you? I promise"—he hesitated slightly—"to be careful where I walk."

Wilma sank back on the cot, too confused to make any reply at once. This was an awkward way to make anyone's acquaintance, but her father had pooh-poohed Keith's warnings about the danger, and she *did* want to know more about George Woodmansee. She liked his name. . . .

He took her permission for granted and came toward her, moving with an easy balanced stride that she couldn't help contrasting with Keith's heavy lumbering one. He sat down, giving a little upward jerk to the knees of his trousers, and held his feet straight out in front of him as he looked at her a little sharply.

"Is it safe to put my feet on the floor?"

She nodded, wondering if he could possibly know. He didn't take his eyes from her face, but studied it with a sort of remote puzzlement.

"You're sure?"

"Yes, I'm sure."

"You'll put yours down?"

She realized then that without thinking she had curled up as she had been before he knocked. She felt herself blushing like a simpleton as she straightened.

One of his shoes touched hers as he lowered them. He crossed his legs and turned his head sideways so that he could look down at her. The springs of the light cot sagged with his weight, making an incline down which she slipped nearer to his side. He was a larger and a heavier man than she had judged from his walk, and her sudden awareness of this impelled her to draw away from him in distrust.

"Do you know why I asked that?" His voice was low, and she couldn't decide whether it was bantering or serious. "I noticed Kerwick looking for something on the floor. And when he made us take our shoes off I wondered if he was afraid we'd stepped on whatever it was. What was it?"

She tried to brace herself, but when she put her hand down she felt against it the rough tweed over, his thigh and hastily withdrew it.

"Let's not talk about that—please. I know you must have thought we were crazy. But we had to, really. I'll —I'll explain all about it in the morning."

"Why not now?"

"I can't." She shook her head decisively.

He was silent for a moment, then laughed and said: "You know, you've got a very nice chin. A nice chin to look at, but not one to argue with. How about a cigarette while we think of a topic that isn't for bidden?"

"All right." It was ridiculous of her to act so flustered, he'd think she was being coy. She liked him better since he had laughed. And if he was staying with Mr. Rennert . . .

"How's Mr. Rennert's foot?" she asked. "The one he hurt on the cactus."

"I didn't pay much attention to it. Why?" As he brought out a package of cigarettes and held a match for her, she observed his hands again, finely shaped and pliant and suggesting such easily used strength, and compared them with Keith's.

"I just hoped the spine didn't go very deep." She leaned back, came into contact with his arm and, after only a second's hesitation, settled comfortably into the crook of it. The cigarette seemed to have steadied her.

"Now what's wrong with this?" he asked.

"This is great. It's just like being back at St Cecilia's. We used to slip down in the kitchen there and smoke."

"St Cecilia's?"

"Yes, that's the school up in Virginia I've been going to. Smoking was against the rules."

"St Cecilia's. Yes, I've heard of it. That's right, this is vacation time, isn't it? I suppose you're on your way back there now?"

"No, I'm living in San Luis with Father now. I graduated last June."

"I certainly like your father. He seems very jolly."

"He is. He's the best sport in the world. I've had a hard time with him lately. He's suffering from the gout, and the doctors have put him on a diet. He's always eaten and drunk what he wanted to."

"He manufactures religious articles, doesn't he?"

"Yes." Something about Woodmansee's tone made Wilma pause. It wasn't what you would call conversational. Rather exacting, it seemed to her. "How did you know that?" she asked him, turning her head.

She could see only his firm chin and his slightly puckered lower lip, but if she didn't succeed in reading his thoughts, she had immediate and very intimate knowledge of him physically. His face was freshly shaved and gave off a faint but tingling odor of lilac toilet water. The tweed that was brushing her cheek had the cleanly smell of tobacco and motor oil and hot, baking sunlight. Somewhere about him leather kept creaking, barely audible. She heard it more distinctly when he laughed.

"I read the guidebook. Lot of information there. But not quite enough always. Who's Kerwick?" "He has charge of the factory."

"Rather hotheaded, isn't he?" Woodmansee laughed again to the accompaniment of creaking leather. "That chin's going up. Did I speak out of turn?"

"What makes you think Keith's hotheaded?"

"Red hair. The way he waves that gun around. He's got your father into some trouble, hasn't he?"

She tossed away her cigarette, not caring where it fell, and tried to sit up. But his arm wouldn't let her. Nor his voice, which was quietly imperative, half bantering, half urgent.

"Now listen, Wilma. Whether Kerwick's responsible or not, I know you folks are in trouble. And I want to help you. Why, this is just like a fairy story. Here I come to a dark castle 'way out in the wilderness, and I find a girl who needs help. There's a big dragon or giant or something scaring her. I take out my sword and— *swish!*—I cut off its head. Just as easy as that. Don't forget another fellow named George killed a dragon once. Maybe he was my ancestor. Now tell me what's happened, and I'll prove I'm as good as the man they made a saint out of. It's the only chance I'll ever have to be one."

Wilma wished she could be alone for a minute or so, to think this over clearly and sanely. She wasn't at all sure whether she ought to listen to her father or to Keith. Each was influenced by his affection for the other. Keith was hotheaded and impulsive, it was perfectly true, and her father had never been of much practical assistance in an emergency. A disinterested party might advise her to which of the two she should turn. . . .

"Really and truly, I am something like a knight," Woodmansee went on unhurriedly, as if he were giving her time to think while he talked. "They call 'em soldiers of fortune nowadays. I found Miss Pirtle in Mexico City, helpless because she'd broken her specs. I'm driving her back to Texas. You saw her, didn't you?"

"Yes."

"Then you know what a very respectable schoolteacher she must be. If she thought it was safe to ride with me half across Mexico, you oughtn't to be suspicious of me."

"I'm not suspicious of you, Mr—"

"George!"

"George, then. I *do* want to ask your advice. It's about Father— and the man he killed tonight. What do you think the Mexican authorities would do to him if he went down to Victoria and gave himself up—explained how everything happened?"

"Well, Wilma, I can't very well say until I know how everything *did* happen."

"You know that Lurcott was trying to rob Father, don't you?"

"Yes, but some of these people here are saying that this isn't really your house. Is that true?"

"Yes, that's true. We don't even know whose house it is. But does that make so much difference? We can explain how we came to be here. We'll make it all right with the owner."

"Then why don't you tell me? The Mexican police are going to pay more attention to what the witnesses have to say, Wilma, than to your story. At least at first. And the way Kerwick has acted, I don't think many of these folks are very well disposed toward your father. I am because I feel sure he must have been in the right. I'll be glad to testify in his favor. But I think it's due me to know just what I'm getting into. Don't you agree with me?"

Wilma felt a hard cool hand close over hers. "Yes," she said, "I do. I'm going to tell you. . . ."

14
SWAN SONG

VERA ELKINS SPREAD cold cream over her face and wondered if men followed this back-to-nature craze because they really liked it or because they had fooled themselves into thinking they did. It struck her as exactly the same urge that sent small boys out into vacant lots to put up tents and play the parts of the big shaggy woodsmen they read about in books and saw in the movies. As soon as they outgrew that, unconsciously they made big game hunters and explorers their heroes and felt they had to assert their masculinity every so often by dashing off to some God-forsaken spot like this.

Snorre's ancestors had been Vikings, so he'd bought a yacht and built this mountain lodge—and never used either except for parties that could have been held a lot more conveniently in a city apartment.

Jesse had been unusually tiresome this afternoon as he held forth on his relief at getting away from civilization and having an open road ahead. Yet she would wager that right now he'd trade all this scenery for an easy chair and an electric lamp, the evening paper and the adventures of Flash Gordon and Jungle Jim. He had fussed like an infant because his leg smarted from those cactus spines. He'd fuss again in the morning when he found there wasn't any hot water to shave with.

Jesse was sitting on one of the two single beds against the north wall, playing his everlasting solitaire. She had the only candle on her dressing table by the east window, so that he had to hunch over to see the cards. She watched him in the mirror.

Jesse had something on his mind—she hadn't been able to decide what. He didn't play in the slow methodical way that so often set her nerves on edge, but with quick flicks of the fingers and wrist. He hummed snatches of tunes that she didn't recognize but took to be Mexican, and he kept jerking his head toward the door. He had acted excited ever since they came back to this room and, she remembered now, had put on a mysterious manner when she opened the subject of Kerwick and the Smiths. "We'll see, we'll see," was all he would say. Jesse being mysterious about anything was highly comical.

"Jesse," she asked, "do they have beauty parlors in Tampico?"

He scooped up the cards and began to shuffle them, but with rare maladroitness let one slip to the floor.

"Beauty parlors!" He grunted, and she knew that for some reason the introduction of the topic pleased him. "I suppose so. I wouldn't be surprised if we'd find one on every block—along with movies and night clubs, and all that stuff. There'll be traffic cops and a Chamber of Commerce and churches. 'Oh, yes,' they'll say, 'we're nice and law-abiding here in Tampico.' Their eyes'd pop out of their heads if I told 'em a few things about the old days. It was every man for himself then, and you carried your own law on your hip. And, let me tell you, V., you had to be quick on the draw. Why, I remember one night . . ."

"Oh God," she sighed to herself, "I've got him started again!" That was the reason she had encouraged Jesse to make this trip. She wanted him to get Tampico out of his system. When they were first married he would scarcely ever mention the place. Now, as the years went by and he got more restless, it was threatening to become a monomania with him. She knew by heart all his exploits, the location of all the wells he'd brought in, the names of the young hellions he'd been associated with. Maybe, she had thought, if he went back and saw how everything had changed he would drop that period of his life into the limbo where it belonged.

Vera's eyes left him and began to wander about the room. Everything was as she remembered it, save that the whitewash on the walls had begun to peel a little. It was probably silly and sentimental of her, but she wished she could be alone there for a while, just day-dreaming as she had been doing in the gun room when that Mr. Rennert walked in. She was getting over her resentment at finding strangers in Snorre's house and, although she was still puzzled as to what they were up to, she was beginning to see the humorous side of the situation. Snorre would guffaw when she told him how she and Jesse had stopped and she had had to pretend she didn't like the looks of the lodge. Mr. Rennert had caught on at once, but Jesse, of course, would never suspect. Rennert was nobody's fool. . . .

The heater, on the floor between her and the bed, was smoking, and she hoped it wasn't going out. There wasn't much kerosene in it, but they had thought it would last until bedtime. Jesse would be wanting to turn in soon, but she was considering sitting up all night. She couldn't sleep, she felt sure, as long as Kerwick had the key to the door and they couldn't lock themselves in. And as long as the rain kept up that damnable steady tapping on the hollow tiles right over her head. In time, if you let it, that rain would be tapping on your skull like the Chinese water torture. . . .

Jesse had stopped his game and turned his face toward the door again.

"What are you listening for?" she asked curiously. There was nothing to hear except the rain.

"I thought somebody was coming. I guess I was mistaken." He went back to his cards and didn't say anything more for a time. "I was sort of expecting Mr. Rennert to call," he said in an offhand manner.

Interested, Vera slid around on the bench and held her red silk mules to the fire. Maybe she'd better get that cold cream off and make her face more presentable. Rennert was a bachelor, middle-aged, a little stiff and starchy, she thought, and he'd probably be embarrassed at stepping into a bedroom and finding her engaged in the intimacies of her toilet. Or perhaps not. He had treated the matter of her previous visits to this house matter-of-factly enough, although he surely understood. God, he certainly wasn't one of these hypocrites who would feel called on to tell Jesse!

"Did he say he was going to call?" She paid attention to Jesse's face. "I didn't know you'd got acquainted with him."

Jesse studied a card as if it were a matter of life or death where he placed it.

"Oh yes, I made a point to get acquainted with him. I only talked to him a short time, though. I saw he didn't like it because that fool schoolmarm blurted out that he was a detective. So I just told him to count on me if he needed any help. He knows where the room is. I expect he'll be along any minute now."

"But did he say definitely that he was coming?"

"Well, not definitely." Jesse's voice was gruff. "I told you we couldn't talk with everybody listening. But as I was leaving I said '*Hasta luego*' to him. That means, 'I'll see you later.' He answered '*Hasta luego*' so I know he means to come as soon as he can."

Vera got up and started to the bathroom. She was wearing a silk dressing gown which, she decided, was safe, whatever Rennert's ideas of convention might be. It matched her mules and went well with her loose black hair.

"You're sure Mr. Rennert's working on a job here tonight?" The fellow must be more foxy than she had thought. No wonder he had agreed with her so readily that the Smiths didn't own the house! He knew it just as well as she did.

"Sure! A detective like Rennert doesn't show up by accident when there's something queer going on in an out-of-the-way place such as this. You mark my word, it's a big case or he wouldn't be handling it." Jesse laughed and said grudgingly, "You were right, V., about these people who claim the house. Smart girl! I don't mind telling you now that I had some doubts about them myself. I didn't want to let on to you, though, for fear it'd worry you. They used to say of me that I could size a man up at one glance. Believe me, you couldn't trust anybody's credentials down in Tampico . . ."

She left him talking and went to moisten a washcloth at the tap. Although she had learned to take everything Jesse said with a grain of salt, she couldn't help being impressed by the enthusiasm he was showing about this Rennert. What in the hell was a detective like, anyhow? In real life, that is, not in books.

That good-looking, hard-boiled Woodmansee was the type she would have picked as more likely to be following such a profession. Or (she slapped the cloth against the side of the basin) just as likely to have a detective on his trail. A slippery customer, that young fellow. All he had been interested in while they ate supper together was quizzing her about Jesse. He might very well be a confidence man. If so, she'd better watch him or Jesse would be buying another gold brick.

Rennert was a different proposition, although she sensed the presence of a shell of reserve about him as well as about Woodmansee. She wasn't quite sure what one would find within. Physically he was attractive enough—well built, with a muscular springiness that was toned down by a sound quality which she could think of only as ripeness. He was probably quiet and a little diffident, but judging by the effect that music had had on him he'd pour out all his thoughts and feelings once he was sure of a sympathetic listener.

And (Vera had to smile as she returned to the dressing table and opened a powder box) once you'd plumbed him he'd doubtless be an intolerable bore. Just like Jesse. And if you were unlucky enough to be married to him—and fool enough to stay married to him until he appealed to your heart—well, you were in for a hell of a life unless you were smart.

"Jesse,"—she felt exactly as if she were releasing the catch of a phonograph—"who is this Rennert? I never heard of him before."

Jesse laid down his cards and sat on the edge of the bed, tapping the soles of his shoes on the tiles. They were new shoes that he hadn't yet broken in.

"Why, V.," he said reprovingly, "I thought everybody knew about Hugh Rennert. He used to be with the U. S. customs. Did a lot of first-class jobs in the detective line. He got quite a reputation and quit the service to go into private practice, or so I heard. At least he seemed to drop out of the picture. I guess he keeps this farm for a front. There's nobody in Mexico I'd rather have met on this trip than him. We've got a lot in common, I know. He's a man who's done things, and I can talk his language. We'll probably talk all night, once we get started. There won't be anything in it to interest you, V., but be nice to him, won't you?"

"All right." Jesse had leaned over and pulled up his trouser leg and was examining the rash which the cactus had left on his ankle.

"Don't scratch that, or you'll only make it worse," she said. "Why don't you ask Mr. Rennert to go down to Tampico with us?"

He looked up quickly, his face a little flushed from the blood which had run into it. He let the trousers fall about his ankles and stared at her. "By George, V.! That's an idea. Would you mind?"

"Not at all. There'll be plenty of room in the house that man's loaning you. And I thought Mr. Rennert might be company for you."

Although Vera had never been to Tampico, she saw it quite clearly, thanks to years of listening to Jesse. There was a private beach by that cottage, and on it she was placing now two persons. Not Jesse, who after those girls had snickered at him in Miami would never again put on a bathing suit, but herself and Rennert. They were drenched by sun and baked by sand; the shell which she knew was about Rennert melted slowly while she watched the result and decided whether or not she wanted to explore further.

Jesse was on his feet, warming his hands over the stove, bringing their palms together as if he were clapping.

"I'm going to do it, V.! I've been thinking I'd like to have somebody to pal around with down there. All the old-timers will be gone, I expect. And I don't want to be bothered by any of these young sprouts who think they know about Mexican oil. Rennert and I can make a trip up the Pánuco a ways, and I can show him some of my old stamping grounds. I can tell him things even he doesn't know about." He was silent for a moment. "He might not be interested, though. Or else he'll be too busy. The kind of life he leads, bumming around with me might seem tame."

She gave him the encouragement he wanted: "It won't do any harm to ask him. He seemed interested enough when he found out who you were."

"He did? He remembered me?"

When she nodded, Jesse came and stood beside her, so that she couldn't see his face.

"I'm glad you told me that, V." There was a huskiness in his voice that she scarcely knew. "I was beginning to think that he'd forgotten about me—or maybe hadn't even heard about me. He wasn't any too cordial when I shook hands with him. Or I may have imagined that. It's been a long time since I was in Mexico. A long time. And, naturally, it was only in the oil camps that I was well known. V., he—"

"Yes?"

"Rennert isn't very well dressed, is he?"

"You wouldn't expect him to be on a trip like this. What's that got to do with it?"

"Well, I was just thinking. I've been wondering why he bothered with farming. Everybody knows he's a detective. You don't suppose, do you, that he has to farm to help make a living?"

"I shouldn't think so. He must have known what he was doing when he gave up his job with the customs."

"Maybe he thought there was more money in the detective business than there is. If that's it, I might help him out."

Vera frowned and lighted a cigarette. She drew her feet up on the bench and hugged her knees.

"Listen, Jesse. Let me give you some advice. Don't go offering Mr. Rennert any money. Let's find out first if he needs it. You'd probably insult him. And why worry about his finances, anyway? Farming may be a hobby with him. Pay all his expenses at Tampico if you want to, but let it go at that. At least for the present."

"Oh, I wasn't thinking of coming right out and offering to give him money. I had something else in mind."

"What?"

"You'll think it sounds foolish."

"What is it?"

"Well, I was wondering if he'd let me go into a sort of partnership with him. Of course I wouldn't expect to do anything except stand on the side lines and watch—at first, anyway. I'd set him up in fine style, with an office wherever he wanted it and—well, laboratories or whatever you need in that business. I'd fix it so he wouldn't have to worry about money—just take the cases that promised to be exciting. And I might be able to give him a few pointers on his clients: whether they were telling the truth or not. I'd be good at that, with my experience. He ought to go to some bigger place than Brownsville. We could talk it over and let him decide. You aren't keen on staying in a little burg in Kansas, are you?"

Vera shook her head. It was hard to believe her ears—Jesse calling Acropolis a "burg." He'd got very angry once when she used the same word.

"You don't understand why I want to do this, do you, V.?" Jesse's hands were on her shoulders, very tenderly, but she was sure he didn't know it.

"I understand, Jesse. Better than you think I do."

"Do you think I'd look ridiculous to Rennert if I went right now and put the proposition up to him?"

She passed one of her hands over his, considering.

"I'd go a little slow, Jesse. Remember, you only know of him by hearsay."

"I've met him, V. That's enough. He's all right."

"I don't doubt that. But you can't expect him to make a decision tonight. Let's take him down to Tampico with us and feel him out. I'll help you. Why don't you go see him now and bring him in here? We can get better acquainted and invite him to be our guest for the next two weeks. We don't want him to think this is just a business relationship, do we?"

"Oh no, that's right. He might get that idea. V., I'd sort of like to have him live with us. It'll be more convenient, because he and I will be dashing in and out at all hours of the night. Would you object?"

"I don't think so."

"V.,"—he kissed her—"you're a swell girl! This is what the Mexicans call *vacilada*: me coming down here hunting for—well, for what I left here. And finding it just by accident. Because a landslide made Rennert and me stop at the same house. That shows Mexico hasn't forgotten me—if all the people have. I'll go get Rennert now, and we'll have a celebration."

He slammed the door behind him and, as he went past the window, began singing.

Vera sat very still, batting her eyes determinedly. It was the first time she had ever heard Jesse sing.

15
TAINTED WATERS

ON THE TILES of Miss Pirtle's room was a memento of Mr. Wood-mansee's brief visit: the prints of his damp socks just inside the door, where he had stood very stiff and formal and inquired if he could be of further assistance; the sketchy trace of his long strides to the heater; the heavier triangular blobs made by his toes and the balls of his feet when he got down to examine the empty reservoir.

Miss Pirtle sat in a hard wooden chair and, since so little else came within her range of vision, stared with a slight feeling of impropriety at these reminders of the urgency of her predicament. They exemplified so well the hymn that "every prospect pleases and only man is vile." Mr. Woodmansee had laughed as he waded through the patio and said he felt like a kid again. But the whole-some rain water which he had tracked in had become, on a man-made floor, slime.

This was the fitting crash to a summer which had been full of disappointments and vexations for Miss Pirtle. She blamed Edith, rather bitterly, for most of them. Edith, the new history teacher, had talked her into attending summer school in Mexico City rather than in Austin, as she had always done. It was Edith's suggestion, too, that she put a large part of her savings into a car on which they would share expenses during the trip. Edith had turned out to be a scheming little flibbertigibbet, there was no use mincing words. She had never evened up her account but had had the brass to insinuate that Miss Pirtle was padding it. Then, at the last, with Miss Pirtle practically helpless on account of the broken spectacles, she had deliberately picked a quarrel in order to have an excuse to return on the same train with a young American professor from the university whom she had pursued shamelessly all summer. Miss Pirtle had told Mr. Woodmansee all about it, and he had agreed that she should "have it out" with Edith the moment she set foot in Brownsville.

The difficulties with Edith and her eyes and last-minute packing had been responsible for her failure to take into consideration the misinterpretation which evil-minded persons might put upon her association with Mr. Woodmansee. She had never thought of him as a chauffeur, of course, but rather as a chivalrous young man who had come providentially to her aid. Yesterday's travel, listening to his descriptions of a beautiful landscape which she couldn't see, almost made up for seven weeks of tribulations. It wasn't until last night in Ciudad Juárez, when the despicable little hotel clerk leered at her over the register, that the world's ugliness was brought home to her. She had said nothing then or since to Mr. Woodmansee about the matter, and he had passed it over in like silence. It had probably made no impress on his clean, healthy mind. But as every mile brought them nearer to Texas and conventionality the danger of her position had loomed larger and blacker before her.

And like a materialization of her fears the mist that the Mexicans call *chipi-chipi* had closed in on them, imprisoning her by the side of a road which was bound to be frequented by citizens of Brownsville. She had met only one, but, as luck would have it, this was a man who by a word could destroy all she had accomplished by fifteen years of faithful duty in one school system. And, as if that weren't enough, somebody (she hadn't yet been able to find out who) had chosen this house to get killed in. The newspapers, Mexican and American, would get wind of the affair. They would all be held for questioning. She saw the headline: *Brownsville Teacher in Mexican Murder Quiz!* Reporters would ferret out the fact that she and Mr. Woodmansee were traveling together. Brownsville tongues would wag, with Edith venting her spite by spreading the story, and the school board would be forced to take action.

Anger at the injustice of it stiffened Miss Pirtle's back, and she got up with determination. She had never been one to vacillate in a crisis, and she wasn't going to start now. Mr. Rennert was going to listen to her.

She went to the door and looked with a slight qualm into the patio. The rain hadn't slackened and she could barely distinguish the blur of light on the other side that told her where the corridor and Mr. Rennert's room were. (Mr. Woodmansee had spoken of errands, and she hoped he wouldn't be with Mr. Rennert yet. If possible she preferred not to worry him.) A fit of sneezing seized her, and she pulled the coat collar about her throat, which had been bothering her all summer. She remembered the injunction in the guidebook: "To prevent taking cold on the Mexican highlands breathe through the nostrils, not the mouth." She drew in a deep breath through her nostrils and felt the constriction of the woolen band about her stomach. That stomach band hadn't been a great success, in several ways, although she was willing to concede that the trouble might lie in the food which they served at the boarding house on Serapio Rendón.

She set out, running one hand with a feeling of repulsion along the slimy adobe wall. As she turned the corner something reached out (or so it seemed) and caught her skirt. She almost screamed in terror, but it was only a trailing cactus. When she arrived in the passage her lungs ached, and she had to open her mouth to regain a degree of composure before meeting Mr. Rennert. It struck her for the first time how very bold she was, knocking at his door at an hour of the night when he might have gone to bed or be undressed. But she had got a good look at his face in the living room and had thought then that he resembled Mr. Pettigrew. Mr. Pettigrew was the superintendent of a school in which she had taught. . . .

She tapped lightly, so as not to disturb anyone else, and wondered if Mr. Rennert hadn't once been a schoolman. One came to recognize them in time, men whose lives were passed in the classroom. There was such wholesomeness and zeal on their faces.

The door was open, and Mr. Rennert was standing there looking at her over the flame of a candle. "Why, Miss Pirtle! Come in."

She stepped inside, confused by the stirring of a third person, whom she couldn't identify, in the center of the room. "Are you a schoolman, Mr. Rennert?" she heard herself asking. What had possessed her to say that?

He laughed. "No, I'm not, but I take it as a compliment. This is the first time anyone ever made that mistake. Won't you sit down?"

"You aren't alone?"

"Dr. Damson is with me. Miss Pirtle, may I present Dr. Gulliver Damson, the well-known author?"

She nodded and thought the man was doing likewise, although she could see nothing but the top of his bald head as he turned around in his chair.

"I wonder, Mr. Rennert, if it would be asking too much of you to come to my room for a few minutes? I may not have a chance in the morning, and I *must* see you. In private," she added hastily for the benefit of the author, whose name she couldn't for the life of her place. "It will be quite all right. There's a married couple, the Elkinses, in the same suite."

"Oh!" Mr. Rennert said it in the oddest way, probably on account of his relief. "Why, yes, of course. I'm sure it'll be all right. Dr. Damson and I are through with our interview, aren't we, Doctor?"

Dr. Damson had the most disagreeable voice Miss Pirtle had ever heard: "By no means, Hugh. Do you have any scientific basis for your statement about the effect of the rain or are you relying on native superstition?"

Mr. Rennert's voice changed and became very dry and precise, as if he were lecturing: "We shall have to define terms, Doctor, before I can answer that. After all, what you would call superstition might have an altogether different meaning for another person. And don't forget that native belief is the result of centuries of living close to nature, of first-hand observation and experimentation. There may be only a kernel of truth in it, but that kernel, I maintain, has been scientifically arrived at. Think that over and see if you don't agree with me." He cleared his throat. "Has our session been satisfactory, Doctor?"

"Well, yes—"

"Does it warrant your parting with some of your supplies? Two packages of cigarettes, to be exact?"

Dimly Miss Pirtle watched Dr. Damson get up and move across the room.

"I shall spare you one package," he said. "You are presenting some interesting possibilities, I admit. Rather disturbing ones, too. I'm not sure I shall sleep well as long as it's raining."

"Why, Doctor! I was expecting *you* to bolster up my courage. If a hardened traveler can't sleep, what's a tenderfoot like myself to do?"

"I meant the scientific aspect of your theories would keep me awake thinking. That will be eighteen cents. The sales tax, you know."

"Death and taxes." Mr. Rennert took some money out of his pocket and gave it to the man. "What's that you're getting out of your kit? More first aid?"

"Serum." Dr. Damson fairly hissed the word. "I thought I'd better check over my supplies. I have an airtight bottle of ammonia and the makings of tourniquets. So you aren't to worry, Hugh."

"Thanks. I shan't. I don't want to seem to hasten your departure, Doctor, but I'm going to turn in as soon as I return. So I'll say good night now."

"Hugh, we can't stop at this point!"

"I'm sorry, Doctor, but I don't feel up to further discussion. Shall we go, Miss Pirtle? I shouldn't have kept you waiting."

It was on the tip of Miss Pirtle's tongue, as Mr. Rennert took her arm and conducted her down the passage, to ask him what they had been talking about. But she decided he would want to breathe through *his* nostrils and not talk, so kept silent.

He didn't seem to fear the dangers of oral breathing, however, for he spoke in what sounded to her like a bubbling voice: "Glad you called when you did, Miss Pirtle. I needed to come up for air."

"The air in this house *is* bad, isn't it? I don't know when my room can have been ventilated."

Mr. Rennert turned his head as a man went along the opposite side of the patio, in the direction from which they had come, singing in a voice which had no regard for others' slumbers. Miss Pirtle judged that he had been drinking, for his song had no meaning at all. Simply: "*Son, son, son los E-na-nos*" over and over again.

"Oh yes, the air." Mr. Rennert seemed to have been diverted by the lusty singer. "Poor ventilation isn't altogether responsible. We're feeling the effects of the *chipi-chipi*. The clouds are pressing down on us—rather like a feather mattress—and the results are almost as suffocating. It'll take a good strong wind from the Gulf to blow them away. This is your room, isn't it?"

He held the door open for her, and they went in.

"Sit down, Mr. Rennert. I expect you'll find it cold in here, but there isn't any oil in the stove. Mr. Woodmansee said he'd try to find some, but I don't suppose he's been able to." She stopped, wishing she hadn't brought Mr. Woodmansee's name in just yet.

Mr. Rennert dropped onto the bench before the dressing table and rather stiffly put his right knee over his left. She saw for the first time that he was wearing bedroom slippers.

"Oh, Mr. Rennert," she cautioned him, "you oughtn't to be walking around in your slippers. You'll catch your death of cold."

He had a very nice laugh. "Let's be more optimistic, Miss Pirtle. Because this is all the footwear I have. I brought only one pair of shoes, those I had to leave behind me in the front room."

"You must tell Mr. Kerwick that at once, so he can make his tests on your shoes first and give them back to you."

"His tests?"

"Yes, Mr. Woodmansee said that must be the reason we had to take off our shoes. Something to do with footprints. On the scene of a robbery, perhaps. And the young man wanted to make comparisons with the shoes of everyone present. It isn't very clear just what has happened."

"No, it isn't, is it? But I daresay Mr. Woodmansee is right. Do you mind if I smoke?"

"Why, no, go right ahead. I'm very fond"—Miss Pirtle, in the single rocker, leaned forward to see what he had—"of the odor of good cigarettes." That's what she had told Mr. Woodmansee as they were leaving Mexico City. And during the long hours that she had sat by his side, unable to gaze at anything except the interior of the car and his knees and hands, nicotine *had* become less offensive to her. She would always, she thought, associate it with Mr. Woodmansee.

She watched Mr. Rennert light his cigarette and couldn't help thinking of Mr. Woodmansee's hands. She knew every detail of them: the play of tendons and muscles as he gripped the wheel, the way the nails grew, the silky texture the sunlight gave to the hairs on the backs. . . .

She was sure Mr. Rennert glanced at the prints of Mr. Woodmansee's wet socks as he said: "Mr. Woodmansee and I smoke the same brand. You haven't any idea how lost a slave to Lady Nicotine is when she suddenly fails him."

"I suppose not. Have you gotten to know Mr. Woodmansee well, Mr. Rennert?"

"As well as is possible with such short acquaintance. He told me of the way you folks met in Mexico City. A fortunate arrangement for both of you. Was he merely traveling or did he have some business down there?"

"Why,"—Miss Pirtle tried to remember; she had been so rattled the morning Mr. Woodmansee came to the boarding house—"I think, Mr. Rennert, he had something to do with automobiles. He brought a shipment down from the United States or he was arranging for one, I'm not sure which. He told me when he offered to give references, but I didn't get it very clear. And Mr. Woodmansee isn't the kind to talk about himself—I suppose you've noticed that."

"Yes, I have. An admirable trait. It's so much better to let references speak for you. And I'm sure his were excellent."

"Yes, I'm sure they were. I couldn't read them, of course, without my glasses. And it was such a relief to have someone take charge of everything. Mr. Woodmansee was a regular dynamo of energy. Do you know, Mr. Rennert, that exactly one hour after he answered my advertisement we were driving out of Mexico City? As soon as he found I was ready to leave at once he changed all his plans to accommodate me. I was in such a terrible situation. Edith had gone off . . ."

Before she knew it she had told him all about Edith, even her suspicion that Edith had knocked the spectacles off the table one night when she came in late, acting in a noisy way which had led Miss Pirtle, lying awake in the dark, to feel certain that she had been drinking. Edith had denied it the next morning, but (Mr. Rennert was in strong agreement with her on this) the evidence was against her, even if it was only circumstantial.

Miss Pirtle felt very definitely that an entente had been established between her and Mr. Rennert. It wasn't so much what he said, for he spoke very little, as the manner in which he said it, letting the warmth of his sympathy flow out to encourage her. It was odd that she should find it so much easier to talk to him than to Mr. Woodmansee. Of course, he was nearer her age. . . .

As she concluded the account of the trip, he lighted another cigarette and leaned forward on the bench. "I wish you'd tell me exactly what happened when you drove up to this house."

His words were a bit disheartening, for she had tried to make it plain how very gentlemanly Mr. Woodmansee's conduct had been throughout and how innocent was their association.

"Mr. Woodmansee," she told him emphatically, "had been making every effort to reach Brownsville tonight. If it hadn't been for the rain and the detour he'd have driven straight on without stopping. He got some sandwiches in Victoria, and we ate those before dark. He was very much worried and put out when we had to turn off onto this road and when something began to go wrong with the engine. It was the first time, Mr. Rennert, that he seemed the least bit cross. And the only time he used any profanity at all was when he was putting on the chains. And he apologized at once. That will show you how anxious he was to spare me any more mortification like that in Ciudad Juárez. When we came to this house he stopped and looked at it, then laughed and said something about it being safer than a hotel. I agreed with him that it would be foolhardy to go on and begged him not to worry about me. So that's the reason you found us here, Mr. Rennert. I give you my word that both of us are absolutely blameless."

"Certainly. You don't need to assure me of that."

"I've convinced you that we've been guilty of no misconduct? You don't have any more doubts?"

She restrained an impulse to lay a hand on Mr. Rennert's knee. He was leaning back now, his shoulder blades resting on the dressing table, and smoke wreathed his face so that she couldn't see it plainly.

"No, Miss Pirtle," he said softly, "I have never had any doubts. I understand, and I'm sure everyone will, exactly how it came about that you and Mr. Woodmansee are here tonight. I think you are distressing yourself needlessly on that score."

"But if our names come out in the newspapers, Mr. Rennert? People in Brownsville will talk. And the school board will certainly ask me if it's true that I was traveling through Mexico with a man. I'll have to say 'yes.' And it will be so hard to make them see how it really was. You said Mr. Jester, the president of the board, was a friend of yours. I wanted to ask you if you wouldn't intercede for me, Mr. Rennert. Mr. Jester will listen to you if you say that you saw both Mr. Woodmansee and me here and that everything was perfectly proper. My job means so much to me—"

Mr. Rennert sat forward suddenly, his hands on his knees, and turned his head so that she could make out the pleasant grin on his lips.

"You don't know Mr. Jester, do you?"

"No, I don't. Only by sight."

"Isn't that enough?"

"Enough? I don't know what you mean, Mr. Rennert."

"To show you that he has a sense of humor. And a gift of combining wisdom with laughter that I don't have. Tomorrow I'm going to take you to him and introduce you. I want you to tell him the whole story about tonight. He'll enjoy it and have you laughing yourself before you're through. He'll probably make life miserable for you by his kidding, but by doing so he'll leave the atmosphere clear of any breath of scandal. Use a little discretion as to what you say about Mr. Woodmansee among your friends, and"—he spread his palms—"memories of the adventure will become more pleasant as time goes on."

"Do you really think so, Mr. Rennert?"

"I know it." He tamped out his cigarette. "Now let's forget all that. I was interested in your arrival here for another reason. Was anyone about the house or grounds when you drove up? I realize, of course, that your eye sight would prevent you from distinguishing a person in the darkness, but I thought perhaps you'd heard someone."

"There wasn't anyone, Mr. Rennert, so far as I know." It made so little difference now—what had happened or what was going to happen in this dreadful place—as long as she had Mr. Rennert's assurance. She took away her finger from her upper lip and let herself sneeze.

Mr. Rennert waited until she was through, then asked: "You and Mr. Woodmansee got out at the same time and came to the house?"

"No, he left me in the car while he found out if we could stay for the night. He came back in a few minutes, said it was all right and took me in. Then he and Mr. Kerwick went to put the car in the garage."

"Did Mr. Woodmansee stop to examine the car or the tires when he got out?"

"Why, yes, I believe he did kick one of the front tires. It was getting low, he'd said."

Mr. Rennert got up and looked at her for a moment.

She began to tell him how grateful she was, but he stopped her. "I'm the one to thank you, Miss Pirtle. But let's postpone that until morning. Do I need to tell you that you're taking cold?"

"I know it. This room is so chilly, and my feet got so wet walking through the patio. I wonder if I could ask one more favor of you, Mr. Rennert? You've been so very kind to me."

"Sure. What is it?"

"I have a little medicine kit in Mr. Woodmansee's duffel bag. He put it there when he helped me pack. There are some sleeping tablets in it. I'd like to take one before I go to bed. I didn't sleep well last night. Worrying. And I—really, I'm feeling pretty miserable now."

"I'll be back with it in a little moment, as the Mexicans say. And I'll bring you some blankets from the chest in my room."

"You're so thoughtful, Mr. Rennert. Do be careful yourself. Breathe through your nose while you're outdoors. And dry your feet as soon as you can. Wet feet are so very dangerous."

And as Mr. Rennert went to the door she noticed that he was limping.

16
NOCHE TRISTE

RENNERT WISHED, as he left Miss Pirtle and made his way through running water under the eaves, that he weren't so pervious to appeals to his sympathy. A glimpse at the unaired corners of a human being's life had the same depressing effect on him as this weather. Unless he shook it off quickly he was apt to fall prey to a gentle brooding sadness which was altogether futile and only fed on itself. (Miss Pirtle, bespectacled and safe in Brownsville, would be an altogether different individual, irksome and without nuances.) He envied at moments such as this the versatility of the Mexicans, who illuminate the drab grayness of *Weltschmerz* with the skyrockets of *vacilada*. That escape was denied, he firmly believed, to men of a single blood stream. They could appreciate the beauty of the sparks (drink helped here), but when they tried to send up rockets of their own they saw them fizzle out at the damp touch of Anglo-Saxon logic.

Tentatively Rennert whistled "Los Enanos" and thought of the man, Jesse Elkins undoubtedly, who had sung it without constraint, without regard for the first question to be asked by one of his compatriots: What does it mean? Rennert knew that, like "La Cucaracha," it didn't mean anything. The Midgets were angry and had pinched an old lady. But its very meaninglessness might make it a gesture for the singer, a sort of nose-thumbing at something outside or within his own little cosmos. A rocket in the night . . .

Rennert wondered.

He opened his door to find Damson standing, candle in hand, by the bookshelves at the end of the couch.

He chirruped a greeting and came toward Rennert. "Got the old sister quieted, did you, Hugh? Evidently she has had experience with schoolmen and wanted to make sure you weren't one before she trusted you into her room. I caught your meaning when you told me you were too tired to talk any more tonight. A gentle hint to her not to keep you. What I want now, Hugh, is some personal information about you. Not a long biographical sketch, but a list of your hobbies and idiosyncrasies. Something about your daily life—"

"Did I have a caller right after I went out?"

"Yes, a very bully sort of man came to see you. Elkins was his name. He seemed set on making himself at home here until you came back, but I told him you and I were in the midst of an appointment and he couldn't talk to you until we were through. I had him help carry my luggage into the next room, then gave him permission to cool his heels there. Let's sit down, Hugh."

But Rennert had turned his back on the insignificant Damson and was hastening to the connecting bath. After all these years to have met Jesse Elkins again and then, not only let him come more than halfway in a gesture toward friendship but subject him to a whippersnapper's impertinence . . .

Rennert's smile was at its widest as he threw open the door of the adjoining room and saw Jesse Elkins sitting in a rocker on the other side of the center table. In the candlelight his bald crown glistened with moisture.

"Well, Elkins—" he began and stopped, the smile gone from his face.

Elkins' right side was to him, his back to the patio door. His posture was that of a man who has fallen asleep. His left hand lay in his lap; the other rested on the arm of the chair. There was no stir, no sound of breathing as Rennert went closer, hesitated and caught the right shoulder. That hand slipped off and dangled limply while the metal pencil which had been in its fingers clattered on the tiles.

That he was close on the heels of death would have been mani-
fest to Rennert even without the support of his sureness that this
was the man who had gone singing through the patio—how long
had that damned woman kept him talking?—twenty, twenty-five
minutes ago.

With swift careful fingers he unbuttoned shirt and vest, then
buttoned them over the massy chest where his ear had found
warmth but no pulsation. He lowered heavy lids upon the eyes
which had been staring blankly, without fear or shock or pain, at
the whitewashed wall. He stood back and became a questing dog
again, senses sharpened against the presence in that room of another living thing. To the faintest vibration in discord with the
pervading leitmotif of fluent water his tense and susceptible body
would have reacted as to the flick of a whip. For Rennert's first
thought was that his ill-timed hoaxing of Dr. Damson was a boomerang, ready to hurtle back at him with deadly precision. . . .

"My good hardy fellow," he held stern communion with himself, "this is the nearest you've ever come to a womanlike surren-
der to nerves!"

It was a simply furnished room, slightly longer than Miss
Pirtle's, with single brass beds against the north wall and between
the two windows on the east. At the south end was the door to the
bath through which Rennert had come, with a dressing table and
bench in the corner on one side and on the other a shallow closet.
The closet door was ajar, and he could see that the interior was
empty save for Damson's sun helmet on a hook. Damson's brief-
case and kodak and first-aid kit were on the table by Elkins. The
rest of his luggage, the Gladstone and the typewriter, were on the
floor by the window to the left of the patio door.

A slat was missing from the shutter of this window, and through
the gap water from some leak in the eaves streamed down over the
lower panes and seeped beneath the sill to trickle darkly across
the whitewash. Backwater from the flooded flagstones outside was
making its way under the door and creeping steadily forward along
the interstices of the tiles.

But with the chill of the room and the dampness which numbed his feet there came to Rennert a strengthening sense of his aloneness there. He relaxed, lighted a cigarette and gave study to the figure in the chair.

Death had dealt gently with the Monk of Tampico's rowdy days. There was nothing about the bold Caesar's face inconsistent with sudden but painless cessation of the heart's activity. It was in no wise contorted; in fact (curious, this impression!) it seemed to have more vitality now than at the moment of Rennert's introduction. The lips were slightly parted in a smile; the skin between the jutting eyebrows was wrinkled as if by thought. Jesse Elkins had simply put his head back to rest—and died.

Well, Rennert wanted to know, why not? While Elkins couldn't be called old (Old! Why, his years weren't many more than Rennert's own!), his early manhood had been a strenuous one, spent in the most insalubrious spot in Mexico. Nobody, it used to be said, ever threw off entirely the malignant effects of Tampico's malaria. So what explanation could be more natural than that an organ had weakened and ceased its functioning in rarefied air which put a strain on the most healthy of men? And Damson had told him that Elkins had helped carry this luggage. The cigarette twitched in Rennert's lips. If it was that extra exertion which had proved too much . . .

He wouldn't face that thought now. He stooped to pick up the pencil which had dropped upon the floor and, in doing so, caught sight of the paper which must have accompanied it.

This was an empty envelope addressed to Elkins at Acropolis, Kansas, and on the back were penciled notations.

Rennert read them, then fixed the dead face with his stare, as if expecting to find there some vestige of expression which the man's will had left to complete the message to—himself. Some such expectation may have been at the back of Rennert's mind; he was never sure. Had he not been defensively thick-skinned against anything so easily imagined as tappings upon the exterior of the world where his senses had mastery, he might very well have ascribed his lightheadedness and quickened pulse to a Jesse Elkins who was actually in that little room, very close, very companionable in his appeal.

Rennert went so far as to lay a steady hand on Jesse Elkins' shoulder, and when he set about his examination of everything within those four walls it was with the manner of a man who is not alone but knows that another is watching him with critical friendliness and waiting on him. He timed himself and at the conclusion of his task found satisfaction in the knowledge that his eyes hadn't lost the alertness or his fingers the sandpapered lightness which customs training had given them. Although he had had only a candle for illumination, he was ready to take oath that floor, walls, furniture, Elkins' clothing held nothing animate which could have been responsible for death.

So much for that. Rennert stood for a moment on the west side of the room, running his fingers through his wet hair as he gazed at the dark water moving over the tiles. It came almost to the rear of the chair's rockers and, since there was a downward slope to the floor, it was collecting in the southwest corner, about the closet and the bathroom door. There was a drain in the bath, which would keep the place from being flooded—unless that became clogged.

He sneezed and went into the patio, pausing but briefly for contemplation of its dark, rain-washed desolation. The lamp in the passage was dimming down to extinction, like a night light carefully tended to mark the settling of sleep on sickrooms. But here (Rennert moved on) there would be no twilight halt short of utter blackness, just as there would be no acceptance of slumber, at least in the room to which he was going. Or would there? He had no romantic illusions as to what the married life of the Elkinses must have been. Bonds of interest, he guessed cynically, had held the woman to the man, and her emotions at news of his death would be oddly mixed ones.

He knocked at her door and waited to see.

She called almost immediately from the other side: "Jesse?"

"Mr. Rennert, Mrs. Elkins. May I come in?"

She opened the door. He was vaguely aware, as he stepped within, of a subtle change in her, a softening of her face, an absence of the brittle snapping quality from which before he had been on the point of recoil. Only a little less vaguely was he aware that she looked extraordinarily beautiful, with her loose smoky black hair just covering the collar of a Chinese-red dressing gown.

Before he could speak she had his hand, and hers was nestling snugly in his palm as her eyes went past him to the door which he had closed. "Jesse not coming?"

"Not right now, Mrs. Elkins. I had to see you alone." Seeing her quick smile, he realized with dismay the terrible irony which her misinterpretation of his words was lending to the situation. "Shall we sit down?" he said shortly.

"Of course. I was hoping you and I could have a little talk without Jesse butting in. You probably think he's cuckoo—" Her eyes had been on his face as she made her way to the rocker. They sharpened now, and she paused abruptly. "What's the matter?"

"Please sit down." Rennert drew the bench forward and looked at her steadily until she sank into the chair.

"What's the matter?" she demanded again impatiently. "What did Jesse say to you?"

"He hasn't said anything, Mrs. Elkins. I came across him only a few moments ago. He wasn't able to talk. There wasn't anything I could do for him."

She reached out and shook his knee. "What do you mean? Tell me. Is Jesse hurt? Oh!" She stared at him and withdrew her hand. "I see. Something's happened to him. You're trying to tell me he's— had an accident."

"Not an accident. I found him in the room next to this. He died very peacefully—without any pain or ugliness. It was his heart, I feel sure. If you wish me to, I'll bring him in here."

Her face had gone blank. "But, Mr. Rennert, you've made some mistake. What you say just isn't possible. Jesse can't have died like that. Where's the doctor?"

"Damson is a doctor of philosophy, Mrs. Elkins, not an M.D. It will do no good to call him."

She got up and held her hands over the heater in what seemed a purely automatic gesture, and he noticed that she wore now several diamond rings. "Then you're the only one who has seen Jesse?"

"Yes."

"And you got excited and thought he was dead," she laughed weakly. "Take me to him, Mr. Rennert."

"There's no need for you to go out. I'll bring him in."

"Yes, do." He left her talking away as if to herself. "I'll get the bed ready for him. You'll see he's all right. You don't know Jesse like I do—"

Someone was coming along the east side of the patio, joggling a flashlight, as Rennert emerged. He paused, saw it was Kerwick, then hastened his steps.

Kerwick knocked on the door of the room where Elkins was, heard Rennert and raised the light to his face. "Hullo!" he said. "What're you doing?"

"Visiting. Are you looking for someone?"

"That doctor. This is his room, isn't it?"

"Yes, but I'm using it at present. Damson's in mine." Anxious as he was to talk to Kerwick, Rennert didn't want his interference at this juncture. "I trust nothing else has happened?" he asked as he got between the fellow and the door.

"No." Kerwick was hesitant. "Mr. Smith and I wanted him to take another look at that man Lurcott. Mr. Smith doesn't think he hit him hard enough to kill him. He thought the doctor might find something wrong with his heart."

"Unfortunately, Kerwick, Damson can't help you. He's a doctor of philosophy, not of medicine."

Kerwick looked at him stupidly. "Oh," he said, "a college professor."

"A writer. But tell me—it's of vital importance to all of us—is there anything in that front room or anywhere in the house which might have killed Lurcott while he lay there unconscious?"

Kerwick's eyes wavered and followed the beam of the torch into the rain. "No,"—he swallowed—"not that quick." He was gone, splashing angrily through the pond that covered the stones.

17
DEATH IN TAMPICO

ANOTHER SIGHT of Jesse Elkins sitting with every semblance of deep and restful slumber, and the memory of his wife's refusal to accept the fact of death, almost tempted Rennert to repeat his examination.

But nothing could be more futile, he told himself as he bent to a duty for whose difficulty he wasn't quite prepared. Although he was stronger than most men of his size whose life is a more or less sedentary one, he had to make several attempts before he got Elkins lifted into his arms. He made staggering progress through the patio and knew, when he came to his destination, that his face was apoplectic. He had to catch his breath in gasps and was afraid, as he tapped on the lower panel with his toe, that blood was going to gush from his nostrils as it had from Bohannon's, drenching himself and the intolerably heavy bulk which was racking his muscles.

He didn't try to speak when Mrs. Elkins opened the door, but pushed through sideways and lumbered to the nearest bed, where he laid his burden with what dignity he could manage. Even so, his act wasn't far short of dumping.

He slid onto the bench and for several moments gave more heed to himself, to the trip-hammer blows of his heart and the worms of fire that swam before his eyes, than to Mrs. Elkins. She was sitting on the edge of the bed, brushing her fingertips over her husband's face, loosening his tie, lifting one of his hands and then the other, rubbing them and letting them fall. She didn't cry or make any sound at all, otherwise she might have been a frightened

149

and ineffective mother hovering over an injured child before the doctor arrives.

How long she would have kept this up, Rennert had no idea. It wasn't until he shifted his position, with a faint creaking of the wooden seat, that she turned and looked at him with bewildered eyes.

"Do you want me to stay awhile?" he asked.

"Oh, God, yes!" She got up and came to him. Her touch, as she flicked raindrops from his shoulder and straightened the collar of his coat, was entirely mechanical and conveyed no message. "Your feet are soaked," she said with a suggestion of eagerness. "I'll get you a pair of Jesse's slippers. And some dry socks."

"I'd rather you didn't, Mrs. Elkins."

"Yes, yes, you must let me. I made Jesse change his socks when we came back here tonight. I was afraid he'd take cold." She caught her breath sharply and gave a high-pitched laugh. "I've got to do something. For just a minute. Until I start thinking again. I'm not trying to—"

"I understand." Rennert smiled naturally and stretched his toes toward the stove. "I *would* be grateful if you'd get me those things. My feet are wetter than I realized."

"You're just like Jesse. He fussed around about being cold and wouldn't have thought of putting on his other shoes unless I'd reminded him."

Rennert watched her hurry to the open suitcase on the second bed and pore over its contents. Hers was a familiar reaction: a pitiful attempt to stave off contact with reality by frittering away time on trivialities. With it was mingled, he guessed, an impulse to perform a vicarious service. For the moment, desperately, she was using him as a man of straw who had some of the needs which one of flesh and blood had once had. Better let her get what compensation she could in this manner. It would be short-lived enough. . . .

While her attention was diverted, he went quietly across the room and pulled a Texcoco blanket over the man who would feel cold and damp no more. Odd, he thought contritely, how far wrong he had been in his calculation of the affection Jesse Elkins had inspired. That was no pose of his wife's.

She handed him black leather slippers and thin silk socks and interpreted correctly his motion of withdrawal to the bath. "Stay here. I don't mind." She returned to the rocker and leaned back as if in exhaustion. "We aren't in civilization now. And what difference does it make, anyhow? In Tampico I'd have seen your bare feet on the beach. So why be finicky because we're in a house?"

Rennert said quietly as he bent over: "Tampico?"

"Yes. That's why Jesse wanted to see you tonight. He was going to invite you to be our guest down there. He was as excited as a kid over the prospect. Planning things you'd like to do. You have a bandage on your foot."

"Merely a jab from a cactus."

Rennert took just time enough for his changing that he didn't appear to press the conversation. When he had on footwear which was at least a size and a half too large for him, he brought out his cigarettes. "Try my brand, won't you? I managed to buy some."

"Thanks. I don't know where my case is."

Rennert was at her side with a match. "I can't tell you how flattered I'd have been by that invitation. All the more so because it would have come as such a surprise. I didn't know I had any of the qualifications of a week-end guest. Are you sure Mr. Elkins didn't have someone else in mind?" he asked as he went back to his seat.

She stared up at the ceiling and laughed with the same piercing note of hysteria.

"Someone else! After he sat on that bed and warmed his hands at that stove and talked about you! He was waiting for you to come. And you didn't, so he went to find you. And he was singing when he left. The first time I ever heard him sing out loud. Why didn't you come as you said you would? Then he'd have stayed here and nothing would have happened to him."

Rennert's voice was low. "I had no idea that he was expecting me, Mrs. Elkins. He told me where your room was and said to come to him if I needed any help. I didn't understand what he meant. And his *hasta luego* is a very indefinite phrase. I'm not trying to excuse myself, only to explain the circumstances. I've been busy, but I daresay I should have looked him up eventually. If I had hesitated, it would have been because—" He shrugged and lifted a foot with its loose slipper. "You see how much difference there was between us physically. That same disparity carried over into the affairs of this world. Your husband was an important man, and I might, I say, have thought twice before presuming on what I took to be a mere offhand gesture."

He drew the empty envelope and the metal pencil from his pocket and passed them to her.

"I found these on the floor beneath his chair. It would appear that he was designing a letterhead. I'm at a loss as to why my name should be on it."

Mrs. Elkins looked blankly at the paper for a moment, as if unable to focus her eyes properly.

"'Hugh Rennert,'" she read then, almost inaudibly. "He printed 'Private Inquiry Agent,' then 'Private Investigator,' and scratched both out. He must have decided to leave your name just as it was, without any title. He had 'Jesse Elkins, Consultant,' in small type. With a blank space for the address. And he'd been making dollar signs, thinking how much you'd need."

Her face contracted with pain, she crumpled the envelope and let it drop to the tiles. "God, why did that have to be the last thing he did—make a dollar sign!"

Rennert said nothing, knowing that she was going to continue, that in her condition a spate of words would bring relief. When she asked, "You're thinking of the Jesse Elkins they used to call the Monk of Tampico, aren't you?" he merely nodded.

"And you thought of him as important! More so than you!" Her voice rose, then fell to a listless monotone. "There was once a Jesse Elkins who was of importance, I've been told. But that was twenty-five years ago. I never knew him except by the scars he brought from Tampico—scars and the stories that they proved. Tell me, you never heard of Jesse Elkins after he left Mexico, did you?"

"No, only in reminiscences."

"No one did outside a little town in Kansas. And they only looked on him as a rich man who was generous with his money, who'd give to charity and listen to hard-luck tales. He was strong and healthy. He was a crack shot and a good fighter. He was brave. But what did that matter? He was useless except for manual labor and signing checks. Life was passing him by, and he didn't want to be passed by. Not after he found out what it meant to be inactive. He tried everything. He went back into the oil game in Kansas and Oklahoma but gave it up in disgust. There wasn't any kick in it, he said. Too tame after Tampico. And more money in itself wasn't any object. He thought for a while that politics would give him the excitement he wanted. But the leaders in his party soon made it plain that he was doing more harm than good by his charging about. They told him he'd better sit back and be satisfied to furnish funds. He didn't care about reading. He joined the country club and bought some golf clubs, but he gave them to the caddie the first time he tried to play. Do you understand now that the man you're thinking of died in Tampico?"

"Yes. I'm beginning to understand several things, Mrs. Elkins. He was under the impression that I'm a detective—is that right?"

"Yes." She glanced at him quickly, and he saw the slackening of the muscles about her mouth. "Aren't you?"

"Not professionally, but let that go for the moment. He had a proposition to put to me?"

She nodded, and her eyes didn't leave his face. "He wanted to back you for any amount you needed. He was going to give you an office, laboratories, everything. He was going to make you financially independent, so you could take only the cases that interested you. We were going to move to whatever city you chose and have you live with us. I don't know whether I can make you understand how Jesse felt. He wasn't patronizing; he really respected you and was anxious to show it in the only way he knew. At the same time he was thinking about himself. He saw himself helping you, advising you, getting you out of danger. Oh, you don't need to tell me! I know how impossible it was. He got his ideas of detectives out of comic strips. He'd only have made a nuisance of himself. But he'd have been happy. I was going to explain everything to you when we went to Tampico. I was going to ask you to do it for my sake. I think if you'd been with Jesse awhile you'd have seen what a simple and lovable soul he was. And he'd have made a hero out of you. You could have twisted him around your little finger. We might have become allies—you and I—both of us bored with him but helping him. And I'd have done anything in my power, Mr. Rennert, to make up to you for what you were sacrificing for Jesse."

Rennert got suddenly to his feet and walked over to the bed, where he stood with his back to her and his hands jammed deep in his pockets. His eyes followed the contours of the blanket without seeing the grotesqueness of the humps. Another image was shaping itself before him, clear-cut by the morning sunlight of Monterrey. . . .

He turned, frowning, as a fist began beating on the door.

"I'd better answer it for you," he said to Mrs. Elkins.

She nodded absently. When he moved away, her gaze remained fixed on the spot where his face had been, as if unaware of his departure or patiently awaiting his return.

Rennert wrenched at the knob, to put a stop to the persistent pounding.

Dr. Damson was almost precipitated into the room. He recovered himself, shook water from a yellow slicker over Rennert's clothing and pushed a yellow rain helmet back from his forehead.

"Oh, there you are, Hugh! I thought I'd find you here. Listen. I've been glancing through those books in the library, and I've come across some interesting passages about Mexican snake lore. They bear out your theories. Why have you been so long coming back?" One foot blocked the closing door while he craned past Rennert's shoulder. "Ah!" He nudged Rennert in the ribs. "I see. A pretty woman."

18
NIGHT-BLOOMING

"DAMSON," RENNERT SAID sternly when the door was shut, "there's a limit to everything. Even my patience. *Please* get it through your head that I've given you no lien on my time." He moderated his tone. (The maddening thing about this man was the fact that he always held a desideratum, cigarettes at first and now information, which could be bought only by conciliation.) "I don't know how long I'm going to be occupied. But I'm sure I'll not be able to resume our session tonight. By the way, how was Mr. Elkins when he helped you carry your luggage? Did he complain of not feeling well?"

"Oh no, he was in good spirits. Kept whistling and humming. Why, did he go off somewhere before you went looking for him?"

"Yes," Rennert answered slowly, "he went off somewhere."

Damson seemed highly pleased. He unbuttoned Rennert's coat and yanked at the points of his vest in the manner of a clerk who has an eye to the fit. He made little henlike noises with his tongue. "And you've been in there alone with his wife! I see. You always have a surprise in store for me, don't you, Hugh? I've been thinking you were a bit—shall we say colorless?—for the role of detective. Your only hobby I've been able to uncover is growing grapefruit, and I suspect your heart's not in that. Anyway, readers don't want a detective associated with anything as commonplace as grapefruit. I've been at my wit's end as to how I was going to work you over before I put you in my book. But you don't have as much lead in you as I thought you did. I'll draw a picture of you with that touch of gray hair at your temples. The ladies will think that's romantic—"

Rennert buttoned his coat and rested his hands on his hips. "Damn it, Damson!" To heighten his exasperation his tongue got twisted. "Mr. Elkins is dead. That's the reason I'm asking. That's the reason I'm here. Now think! Did you hear any sound from that east room after you and Elkins separated?"

"No, only his whistling. It disturbed me, it was so silly, and I hinted as much to him when he came back in. But he went on with it in the bathroom."

"He came back into my room? Why?"

"To see if you'd returned. He stayed in the bath awhile, then went through the door, and I didn't hear him any more. But tell me, Hugh,"—Damson was pawing at his clothing—"how did he die?"

"Heart failure," Rennert said and, unable to hold his temper any longer, went inside and closed the door. He waited a moment, afraid that the insufferable ass would start pounding again. It might have been a mistake to tell him of Elkins. . . .

Mrs. Elkins was sitting on the edge of the bed now, one of her husband's hands in her lap. Her face was white and stiff, so that her eyes looked larger and darker and their pupils dilated as she stared at Rennert. He didn't think, however, that she had heard anything except Damson's first words.

As he told as much as he thought necessary of their conversation, she rose and came toward him. "What was he saying about snakes?" She made the question sound like an accusation.

Rennert was silent for a moment, marshaling phrases which would be unequivocal yet not needlessly alarming.

"You mentioned, Mrs. Elkins, that the Smith girl was sweeping the front room when you arrived. You may have noticed since the close attention she, her father and Kerwick have given to that floor. Two explanations would account for it. Either there was something valuable there that they wanted to find or—something dangerous that they were afraid of finding. Now I'm being perfectly honest with you. My first thought was of some poisonous reptile or insect that they had seen. It may sound melodramatic to you, but I know from experience there are such things not far from this locality. Have you spent much time in this house?"

She glanced down for an instant, then raised her eyes and looked directly into his, with a hint of challenge.

"I've been here twice before. Once with a party. Once with only Mr. Bjerregaard—"

"The circumstances don't matter. The question I wanted to ask you before supper was this: Do you recall any talk of insects or reptiles—anything poisonous—infesting the house or the garage or the grounds?"

She shook her head slowly. "No. We didn't go out of doors much. I believe Snorre said the cook had trouble keeping ants out of the supplies stored here. And—oh yes!—there are spiders. You'll notice their webs on the windows and in the corners. A woman in the crowd asked Snorre about them once. We'd been having that black-widow scare up home. But he told her they were harmless. He said there wasn't any danger of crawling things this high up in the mountains. I remember that very well."

"I was almost sure such would be the case. And when I saw the pains Kerwick took to keep any shoes from being worn out of the room, I went over to the other theory. I decided there was something on the floor which might have adhered to our damp soles."

"But you weren't quite satisfied, were you?" She was watching his face closely; on the alert, he knew, for some betraying sign of perturbation. "If you had been, you wouldn't have talked to that Damson man about snakes."

Rennert tried to look and sound sheepish. He wasn't at all. Granting the fact that his effusion to Damson was a piece of folly for which he deserved to be kicked, he had not spoken a word which did not have, here in Mexico, a very special, well-authenticated and sinister significance.

He said: "Oh, think nothing of that. Damson's writing a book about Mexico, like every third tourist who comes here. He got excited about tonight's events and kept pestering me to spin him some yarns that might account for them. I pulled his leg a bit in order to get some cigarettes from him. I became quite glib on the subject of serpents in Mexican life. I went clear back to Quetzal-coatl, the Feathered Serpent, and the history behind the Apizaco cane that Smith carries. I'm ashamed to say that I kept on until I had him digging out his snake serum." Rennert hesitated, then went on: "He did that when I told him how intimately snakes are connected with rain in Mexico. No one seems to know exactly why, except that rain seems to bring them from their holes and hiding places."

"Is that true?"

"I don't know. I doubt it very much. I think it's merely a part of the lore that has grown up about reptiles in a country where they have always been associated with religion. There's no reason"—his voice was even—"why we need give it any further thought."

"But there is!" Her fingers were on his sleeve, twisting the cloth. "Something in this house killed Jesse. We don't know what."

"I'm convinced his was a perfectly natural death, Mrs. Elkins. It was probably heart failure, as I said before. This altitude puts a terrible strain on hearts that aren't accustomed to it. And excite-ment only makes it worse—"

She stopped him, shaking his arm.

"It wasn't his heart! It couldn't have been a natural death! All the time we've been talking, that same thought has been running through my head. Mr. Rennert, listen to me. I know what I'm say-ing. I'm not a hysterical woman, so don't treat me like one. Jesse was in absolutely perfect physical condition. He prided himself on keeping fit. He had so little to think of that health got to be an obsession with him. The least little ache would send him to the doctor. He had an examination just before we started on this trip. Only eight days ago. At the best clinic in Kansas City. He showed me the report. It was thorough. His heart, his lungs, his kidneys, his teeth, his eyesight—everything was sound. They said"—her voice almost broke—"there was no reason why he shouldn't live to be a hundred. Now will you believe me?"

Rennert's eyes had narrowed. "Did he complain of feeling the altitude tonight?"

"No, no! I did when we first began to climb up from the desert, but not Jesse. He spoke of it several times. Said that altitude never bothered him."

"What about the effects of his life in Tampico?" Rennert was grasping at straws. "He must have had malaria in his system. Tampico was a regular fever swamp in those days."

"But it didn't touch Jesse. He boasted about that. He used to say he bested the malaria with less quinine than any other man in Tampico. I tell you, Mr. Rennert, he didn't die of any natural cause. There's something dreadful and deadly loose in this house! Something we can't see! I've always hated these mud walls and these sweating tiles. And tonight the very air is foul. Like the air in a cellar. It makes me dizzy. Mr. Rennert, let's get out of this house! Take Jesse with us. You've got to help me—"

Rennert gripped both her shoulders and held her firmly, facing him. Consciously he tightened his fingers so that she must feel the pain.

"Mrs. Elkins!"

"Yes." He felt her body sag, then stiffen.

"I'm here to do anything in my power. For you and for Jesse. You see, I'm using his first name. He's that near to me now. And I'm depending on you to keep your head. Don't fail me. Will you not?"

She nodded. "I won't let go again, I promise you. I'll do whatever you say."

"Fine!" Rennert released her. "It's impossible for us to leave here tonight, or I'd most certainly take you away. The roads will be almost impassable by now. And I doubt whether Kerwick would let us go. I don't think he means any harm, but he's armed and we're not. And we'd have to get his permission first."

"You mean we're prisoners?"

"It amounts to that. But he won't interfere with us back here. I haven't told you, but when I found Jesse I searched the room for some live thing which might have caused his death. I discovered nothing. Now I want your permission to make doubly sure he wasn't bitten. I want to examine him—his clothing and his body. The light's poor, and I'm no doctor, but if there is any trace of a wound I ought to be able to locate it. Will you go into Miss Pirtle's room or rest on the other bed until I'm through?"

She used both hands to push back the hair from her forehead. "I'd rather stay and help. I can hold the candle for you. Please let me."

Rennert's eyes were searching. "It won't be very pleasant to watch. I may seem callous. I'll be awkward, I know."

"I don't think you will. I don't think," she said with emphasis, "you could be anything but kind and efficient and strong. I think you were sent here for that reason."

"Don't forget," he spoke gruffly as he glanced at the bed, "Jesse might not be lying there if I hadn't come to this house. That's the thought I can't get rid of. Shall we start?"

"Yes, Mr. Rennert."

It wasn't, Rennert found, as odious a task as he had anticipated. Stripping off the clothing wasn't much different from undressing a friend (that's how he had come to regard Elkins) who has had too much liquor. Only at his first sight of the mounded hair-grown trunk was he touched by any repugnance. It was so much like beef.

If there was a tremor in the hand that held the candle he didn't know it. Neither of them spoke, but he was aware of the momentary break in her regular breathing each time his fingers tested the consistency of the flesh about the scars. Tampico's bullets had left most of these while on the back was the long path of a knife which must have sought and almost found the heart. Scars to prove tales of adventure and one, the brand of a long-ago fire, which made Rennert wonder if the celibacy speculated about by Tampico hadn't been due to the only fear the Monk had known, that of ridicule. And if the tremendous vitality which manifested itself in Napoleonic coups wasn't in part the release of energies which were denied the ordinary outlet. And if the result hadn't been a premature sapping . . .

None of his concern at all.

On the outside of the left ankle was a fresh raw rash. He bent over this, then looked quickly up at Mrs. Elkins. "What caused that?"

"The cactus out in the patio. He ran into a trailer of it when he was coming back here in his socks. He got the spines out but kept scratching it. I couldn't make him quit."

Rennert sat down on the bed and lifted that foot onto his lap. He held the light close to the ankle and was glad to have a moment's respite from observation of his face. He didn't want the woman to see how deeply he was worried. He had scanned, to the best of his ability, the entire body—literally from head to foot. Nowhere else had he found any breakage of the skin. And these cactus pricks were insignificant injuries. Entirely insignificant. They wouldn't have been fatal to a baby.

God knew cacti had no secrets from him, who had seldom been out of sight of them for the last quarter of a century. Frantically he ransacked his memory for a hint from some old wives' tale or from the unwritten toxicology of the desert. It was a species of the night-blooming cereus against which Elkins had brushed. *Junco espinoso*, the Mexicans call it; snake cactus, the Americans, from the resemblance of its tentacles to the twisted bodies of serpents. (Turn where you will in Mexico, the ophidian stares back at you.) But there was no note of the sinister in the associations which it evoked: the beauty of the creamy petals on the single night each year when they open and loose their tuberose fragrance; the warmth and quiet of early-summer skies and limitless space into which a man can drift while his body lies flat on the earth; the deep healing peace of Mexico. . . .

Rennert laid the bare foot upon the bed, drew up the blanket and at last met the inquiry in Mrs. Elkins' eyes.

"You've seen as well as I. His skin is whole save for the scars and the irritation from the cactus. My own skin has been nettled in the same way many a time. I never suffered any ill effects. That particular cactus is no more harmful than the interlacing spine variety I stepped on tonight. Did those old wounds ever bother him?"

"No." He knew from the obstinacy of her voice that, so far as satisfying her was concerned, his work had been in vain.

"Then we must fall back on natural causes."

"I told you what the doctors said."

"I know, but a diagnosis can never be absolutely perfect. Or some trouble may have developed since."

"In eight days? What?"

Rennert shrugged in answer. Depression and weariness were settling heavily on him, while his head swam from prolonged breathing of that imprisoned air. Gases from the stove were rank and mingled with vapors from the moisture exuded by the porous tiles. Yet to open a window would bring only increased coldness and little relief, for it wasn't adobe walls which had this suffocating effect, but the downward pressure of the *chipi-chipi*. . . .

Mrs. Elkins' voice was a little whip flicking at him persistently: "A bite or a sting would be small. You might have overlooked it."

"The puncture, yes. But I wouldn't have missed the swelling and the inflammation that surrounded it. I've done the best I can, Mrs. Elkins. When daylight comes I'll look again."

"Daylight!" She swayed and put a hand on his arm for support. "We'll have to wait until then—without knowing?"

"Not necessarily. I may be able to get some information from Woodmansee about what was on the floor in the front room. When I left him he was going to try to make friends with Miss Smith and find out. If he had no luck I'll approach Bohannon. I'm convinced he knows or suspects. If he won't tell me, I'll call Kerwick's hand. Now we've got to decide what you're going to do."

"You'll come back?"

"If you wish." He saw her quick glance to the floor. "You might feel safer if I searched the room."

"Yes, if you will. It's foolish—"

"It's not at all foolish, Mrs. Elkins. I'll get busy at once."

"And I'll fix Jesse so he'll be comfortable for the night. I'll try to think nothing has happened. That he's just sleeping."

As Rennert stooped and knelt and stood on tiptoe, his fingers stung by drippings of hot wax, her voice came to him with some of the dull monotony of the rain on hollow tiles:

"If you could only have met Jesse when he went out that door, Mr. Rennert. When he started singing. He'd just told me how happy he was. He'd come to Mexico hoping to find a little—just a little—of the old joy of living. And by accident his path crossed yours. You carried him with you into adventure, into youth again. That's what he was imagining. Mexico hadn't forgotten him, he said. He told me what the Mexicans would call his meeting with you. It was a word I'd never heard before."

Rennert was on one knee, running the candle along the base of the wall. He turned his head and asked, "*Vacilada?*"

He was in time to see Mrs. Elkins touch her lips, very lightly, to the white tonsure.

"Yes," she answered without looking at him. "That was it. What does it mean?"

Rennert went on with his work, a faintly sardonic smile drawing down the sides of his mouth.

"Sometime," he said, "I want to tell you a story. A story that began twenty-five years ago and ended tonight." The drumming of a fist on wood—Damson's fist, of course—interrupted him. He got to his feet and jabbed a thumb in the direction of the door. "But there's your answer. *Vacilada*. The step from the sublime to the ridiculous."

19
THIS MORTAL COIL

RENNERT SLIPPED through the door and closed it so quickly that Damson's glimpse of the interior must have been an unsatisfactory one.

"What is it?" he asked, his voice more resigned this time, since he had come to feel that perhaps after all the fellow had his uses as a counterirritant.

Damson sidled up eagerly and plastered a hand on the small of Rennert's back. "How're you doing, Sherlock?" he spoke in a stage whisper.

"You really can't expect me to do very much if you keep interrupting me," Rennert told him gravely. "I have to concentrate my thoughts, remember."

"Now, now! I always suspected that was a stall on the part of the detective when he wanted to sit down awhile. Listen, Hugh. I don't like to criticize, but I think this dalliance of yours has gone on long enough. I have something to say which will probably startle you. But if you'd been up to snuff you'd have thought of it yourself. I don't think this Elkins died of heart failure."

"Why not?"

"Look at the attendant circumstances. We've agreed there's an unknown quantity or thing, whatever you want to call it, at large in this house. Very well, a man who has every appearance of being in the best of health walks into an empty room and dies. And you calmly tell me it's heart failure. Come, Hugh! You're losing your grip."

"I won't dispute that. But—"

"Very well." Damson shifted his hand to Rennert's shoulder. "Now here's an incentive for you to get busy. I've been looking over my outline and I find I can give this affair more space than I thought at first. My chapter on Mexican politics can be cut out altogether. It's very confusing, anyway, because all the political leaders I interviewed said the same things. I'm sure a true mystery story will interest my readers more. It'll be somewhat of a novelty, too, in that the killer isn't a human being but—what shall we say?—a secret agent. An inconscient agent. It has no motives that we need be concerned with. It can't be asked for an alibi or fingerprinted. It's simply moving about, guided by instinct, and that makes the detective's job a harder one. I sounded out your friend Mr. Woodmansee to see how that kind of a plot would appeal to him as an average reader. Whether he'd consider it a legitimate solution or feel cheated because there wasn't a murderer who could be handcuffed in the last chapter—only stepped on and squashed. He informed me that he didn't read mystery fiction, although he sometimes felt tempted to commit a good gory murder. And I'm not sure," Damson said thoughtfully, "that he was joking."

"Where is Woodmansee?" Rennert cut in, before the other's chant could exercise further spellbinding effect on him.

"In your room. Making himself very obnoxious. He brought wood and refreshments and seems to think that gives him a right to oust me. But I've been thinking, Hugh, that it would be much better if you and I stayed together tonight and sent him into that east room. I've come to know your ways and won't ruffle your feathers as much as he will. And if you're going to fill two chapters, it's high time you and I were getting our heads together. Come on, let's go send Woodmansee packing."

"I can't leave now, Damson. And to save a squabble I'll move in the east room myself. Tell Woodmansee I want to see him, though, in a few minutes. And ask him to take Miss Pirtle's medicine kit to her, as well as some blankets out of that chest. It slipped my mind. Now I don't think we'd better stand out here in the wet any longer." Freeing himself, Rennert hurried inside.

Mrs. Elkins was sitting on the edge of the bed, as before. She was smoking, however, and her face was more composed, as if weariness were making itself felt. The eyes which she raised to his were remote, with a fixed and faintly ecstatic gleam.

He lighted a cigarette and glanced about. "Where was I?"

"You were going to tell a story."

"I was thinking of my inspection of the room. But I *had* embarked on a story when Damson knocked, hadn't I? I'm afraid the mood's gone now, but I'll try to recapture it." Rennert began to work along the base of the wall again.

"This tale," he said, "concerns a man who was young and just out of college twenty-five years ago. A queer sort of fellow, always groping. For what, he didn't know. A complement, I suppose, for something he happened to have in his make-up. Or a fixative that would bring all his inconsistencies together and make 'em stick so he could present a front to the world. It had to be powerful and at the same time gentle in its action. Because this youngster had a lot of little sensitive places which had been rubbed rather raw by college and what he'd seen of the marts of trade. If it hadn't been for them he'd have got a job and buckled down to it, as he wanted to do. For he wasn't lazy, as so many people thought. He wasn't innocent, at least mawkishly innocent, and he wasn't altogether a dreamer. At base he was just as lusty and meat-eating an animal as the next."

Rennert got up and grinned at her. "I won't try to explain the young cuss any further because he never understood himself any too well. But am I making myself clear?"

"You're making yourself very clear, Mr. Rennert."

He laughed. "You caught me off guard there. Let's see. A thorough search entails this." He walked to the east bed and lowered himself to a recumbent posture on the floor beside it. "Not an orthodox confessional. But you asked me what *vacilada* meant, and I'm doing my best to illustrate. That young man I'm telling you about would never have been guilty of a stunt like this. He'd have been embarrassed by the mere thought of lying flat on the floor and poking his head under a bed. Much less giving away his innermost secrets as he did so. I haven't brought him to Monterrey yet, have I?" Rennert's head and shoulders and the candle disappeared.

"No." Mrs. Elkins rose and came to stand by his feet. "Why don't you speak of him in the first person?" she suggested softly.

"All right." Rennert's voice was muffled. "I don't have the slightest idea why I drifted to Mexico. I like to think there was a magnetism about it that drew me. But probably it was the advertisement of a tourist agency. I spent some few days along the border and finally got as far as Monterrey. The novelty of being in a strange country wore off then, and a revulsion set in. I hated—with a very personal hatred—the brutality and the violence and the obscenity. There was something reptilian about the quiet and the sunlight and the bright flowers. Everywhere I turned I met the scent of blood and death. I was disgusted and, though I wouldn't have admitted it, scared. That's the effect Mexico has on a lot of people, and I made my entry in Revolutionary days. I felt as if I were escaping from some incubus. That morning when I packed my grips and left my hotel room." He wriggled out and sat tailor fashion, looking up at her. "The morning I stepped into the same elevator with Jesse Elkins."

She stared at him incredulously. "You knew Jesse all those years ago? Why, he didn't say anything about it tonight."

"Of course not. The meeting was so brief, so unimportant as far as he was concerned, that he'd probably forgotten about me a couple of hours after we'd separated. He was in his heyday then. Famous, feared, his favor courted. I don't think he so much as glanced at me as we rode down in the elevator. But I didn't take my eyes off him. He had one arm in a sling, I remember. He wore boots and corduroys and a Stetson hat. And a six-shooter. He was slim and hard, somewhat on young Woodmansee's build. I recognized his face from newspaper pictures. I don't know whether I got the thought from something I'd read about him or whether it was my own, but I compared him to one of the crusading monks who came over with Cortez." Rennert's smile became a wry one as he got to his feet without pretense of grace. "Have you guessed

that I was somewhat of a hero-worshiper? Very naïve in that respect."

"I can understand," Mrs. Elkins said quietly, moving to the
chair. "I've seen pictures of Jesse—as he was then. And something
of his youth was left when I married him."

Rennert stood for a moment by the bed on which Elkins lay.
"He was leaving the hotel, too, so we checked out at the desk together. I kept watching him, and it came over me suddenly that he
was only a very few years older than I. But in every other respect I
was a mere infant compared to him. He was so sure of himself.
Not cocksure, but in a quiet, grave way. I think it was that discovery about his age which gave me courage to ask him if I could ride
in the same carriage with him to the station. That was before the
days of taxis in Monterrey. He merely nodded. I remember he was
looking at the sunlight clearing away the mists on old Saddleback.
I supposed his mind was on oil wells and a business deal. I wouldn't
have believed he was gazing at that mountain exactly as I'd been
doing every morning from my window. All the beauty I'd found so
far in Mexico was in Saddleback, but I'd probably have blushed if
anyone had caught me admiring a mountain. That simply isn't done
by young fellows my age in the United States."

Rennert was on the floor again, holding a candle under the
springs which sagged with their load of flesh and bone.

"It wasn't until we lost sight of Saddleback for a time that Jesse
turned to me. 'Leaving us?' he asked. I said I was, and before I
knew it I was telling him why, how I hated Mexico and was disappointed in it. He smiled a little and listened. I thought I was only
furnishing him amusement. But just before we got to the station
he put a hand on my knee. 'I know how you feel,' he said. 'I was
that way when I first came. They've got a saying down here, though,
about Mexican dust. Once it settles on you you'll never find peace
anywhere else. Why don't you stick it out a little longer? Got enough
pesos to take you down to Guanajuato?' He had to tell me where
Guanajuato was. 'I have an interest in an *hacienda* down there,'
he went on. 'Not much there but mountains and dust. I'm on my
way to Tampico, but I'll give you a letter to the major-domo if you'd

like to visit the place. Stay as long as you want. Life's simple there, but you might find what you want.'"

Rennert rose, dusted himself off and lighted a cigarette.

"You went?" Mrs. Elkins asked.

He nodded. "Yes, I went. I stayed a long time. I found what I was looking for. And the dust of Mexico settled on me so heavily that I was ballasted for once and for all. I went back to the States finally and got a job that kept me with one foot in Mexico. That foot's still planted here, and as long as it is I'm happy. If I hadn't met Jesse Elkins that morning I'd have taken the northbound train instead of the south. I'm satisfied I'd still be groping. Rather feebly now but always frustrated. Bitter probably. I wrote him when I left the *hacienda*, but he never answered, of course. I never saw him again until tonight. When, by accident or some conspiracy of the clouds and rain, our paths crossed again. If things had worked out right, those paths would have joined, and their tracks back over twenty-five years would have made a design. Not one with any significance, maybe, but at least one with a little symmetry. But it was like a play where the actors all miss their cues in the last scene. A girl in Mexico City got drunk and broke her roommate's glasses. Therefore I walked along one side of the patio and Jesse on the other. The cue may have been the song he was singing. A silly song, without any meaning at all. If you hear laughter offstage at the way it all happened"—Rennert shrugged—"that's *vacilada*."

20
SCATTERED ASHES

As Rennert came in, Woodmansee sprang like a jack-in-the-box from the depths of a leather chair and raised his hand.

"Welcome home!"

It wasn't until he smiled and spoke that Rennert knew for sure that gesture was neither a warning against entry nor an admonition to silence but something quite different: an automatic imitation of a salute which certain European Men on Horseback have borrowed from the mores of ancient Rome. It seemed out of place, but that was as far as his thoughts went, for his attention turned to the setting in the midst of which Woodmansee stood.

The fireplace was crammed with blazing logs, while on either side of the hearth were stacks of fuel for replenishment. The wicker table had been drawn within reach of two chairs, so that the ruddy light made merry over a board which would have enlivened the eyes of a man less in want of physical stimulation than Rennert. There was an imposing array of familiar bottles, glasses and—most surprising of all—an open carton of cigarettes.

Rennert looked up. "I've suspected several times tonight I was suffering from hallucinations."

"You needed a drink." Woodmansee passed a hand over his smooth hair. "Don't you think I did pretty well foraging?"

"You're the commissary henceforth. Damson told me you'd brought refreshments, but I didn't expect a groaning table like this. Where is *el buen doctor?*"

170

"He got sleepy and trundled himself off to the next room. He left you his cigarettes and his blessing."

"I'm surprised he went so soon. He seemed to have his mind set on staying."

"Maybe he wanted to go dream about his book. God, that guy's a weird 'un! But sit down, Mr. Rennert, and let me do the honors. See here, do I need to keep on calling you Mister? Can't we make it Colonel or something like that?"

"Did you ever see anyone less military-looking than I? Why on earth bother with any title?"

"Well, I didn't want you to think I was taking too much for granted, like Damson. What'll it be, Rennert? Scotch, rye or cognac? Ginger ale for a mixer. No ice, but I don't think we'll miss that."

"Cognac, please. Straight." This had been Rennert's goal all evening, to stretch his limbs catlike before an open fire and abandon himself to its warmth. It was an occasion which never came to a dweller in the border sun.

He watched Woodmansee uncork a bottle of Hennessy and was surprised at the unsteadiness and lack of dexterity in the young man's hands. Unobtrusively his gaze rose to the bronzed intent face. There, too, a change was apparent. It was as if some acid had been at work, deepening lines and etching new ones. The lips were compressed and flanked at either end by wrinkled half-moons. The nose was tense, with hollows above the flaring nostrils. The sibilance of Woodmansee's breathing was more pronounced than ever, and the glitter in his eyes was almost febrile in its brightness.

He jetted cognac into two glasses and put one at Rennert's elbow. "How's the foot, Rennert?"

"Sore, but that's to be expected. The reason for all the pother about it was that Damson saw a chance to use his precious kit."

"Did the spine go in very deep?"

"Not very."

"Did any dirt or dust or anything of the sort get in the wound?"

"I don't think so. It was well bathed with alcohol, and I put disinfectant on it. It'll be healed over by morning." Rennert had shifted his position and thrown one leg over the chair arm so that he could study Woodmansee without seeming to do so. The mood induced by the fire had gone now.

He decided the fellow hadn't been drinking. More likely he was endeavoring to repress some excitement which whipped at his nerves. Even that explanation wasn't quite satisfactory. Why, Rennert wondered, was he refusing to accept the more obvious one that Woodmansee was afraid? Probably because to a first impression created by military bearing he had gone on subconsciously adding daredevil qualities. And all the time the man might be the veriest coward.

No, Rennert wasn't ready to concede that he had been that far wrong. Fear was an imponderable thing, and every individual nursed phobias, for whose unmanning effect he wasn't to be blamed. One of the oldest and most universal of these was the antipathy to those creatures, frequently harmless, whose blood is cold. Rennert felt it to a considerable extent. He preferred to ascribe it, not to a survival of the instincts which scaled monsters aroused in the days of primeval slime, but to childhood lessons in a religion which had chosen a reptile as its symbol of evil.

And (he fingered the cognac glass) there had been as yet no hint as to the information which Woodmansee had garnered.

Woodmansee tilted his glass in Rennert's direction.

"*Salud!*"

"*Salud!*"

They drank, and Woodmansee dropped into the other chair, lighted a cigarette and shot smoke through his nose.

"Tell me about this Elkins. I didn't know how much of Damson's story to believe. He was so scared."

"Damson scared?"

"Darned right. That death coming on top of your line of bull scared the socks off him. He probably tried not to show it when he was with you, but thought I didn't matter. What happened?"

Briefly Rennert told of his discovery of Elkins, his search of room and body and Mrs. Elkins' evidence as to her husband's health. He admitted frankly that he was at a total loss to account for the suddenness and apparent painlessness of death. He gave his interchange with Kerwick for what it was worth.

Woodmansee poured himself another drink, downed it in one gulp and sat forward, staring into the fire.

"It *must've* been heart failure," he spoke a little crossly. "What Kerwick said doesn't mean anything."

"I'd feel the same way if Mrs. Elkins hadn't been so positive that nothing ailed him. If it hadn't been for that physical examination. I confess I'm stumped. But let's hear what you learned. I judge you found somebody in a friendly mood."

Woodmansee's laugh was short and nervous. "Yes, I got acquainted with Miss Smith. A nice little girl. We talked about this and that, and she let me bring all the wood I wanted from the kitchen porch. I raided a shelf of liquor and made away with an extra coffee pot and a can of coffee. They're up on the mantel, ready for breakfast." He sent his cigarette spinning into the flames and lighted another.

Rennert waited for several seconds, then asked: "But what information did you get about the Smiths?"

Woodmansee hunched his shoulders and rubbed the seat of his trousers from side to side as if he weren't sitting comfortably.

"You were right," his words came jerkily. "Smith *is* a manufacturer of religious articles down in San Luis. Kerwick has charge of the plant. He's a sort of foster son to the old man. He's been on a trip to New York. The Smiths drove up to Brownsville to meet him. They got caught here by the rain like the rest of us. This isn't their house. But they were the first ones here and decided they might as well let us think it was. They'll contact the owner and fix it up with him. I'm sure they're perfectly reliable people."

Again that sharply defined, peculiar hiatus in an inconclusive story. Woodmansee slid still further forward, so that all Rennert could see of his face was the hinge of his powerful jaw, one slightly pointed ear and a corded temple where the hair was beginning to recede.

Rennert refrained from any comment. He didn't speak until the other's silence made it plain that he either had reached the end of his account or for some reason wasn't going to continue without prompting.

"But what about the floor? Our shoes? Miss Pirtle said you had some theory about Kerwick wanting to compare them with footprints."

"Oh, that! I just told her the first thing that came into my head. I thought it'd keep her from worrying. By the way, I took her the medicine kit and some blankets. Thanks for visiting with the old soul. You made quite a hit with her."

"Is that so? But why did we have to remove our shoes?"

Woodmansee laughed in the same abrupt manner and shifted his weight from one hip to the other in a way which approximated squirming.

"I certainly felt silly," he said carelessly, "when I found out what the trouble was. There is something on the floor in that front room. But I bet you'd never guess what it is."

"I've guessed until my brain's fagged. What's the answer?"

"Ashes."

"Ashes!"

"Yep." Woodmansee nodded vigorously. "Ashes. The remains of Kerwick's father. It seems he was an old pal of Smith's. He died in New York recently. Kerwick had his body cremated and was bringing the ashes back to San Luis for burial." He turned his head, exchanged a glance with Rennert, then looked away again. "This is just between ourselves, Rennert. I promised Miss Smith I wouldn't tell anyone. And I'd rather her father and Kerwick didn't know I'd been talking to her. So forget about it as soon as I'm through, will you?"

"Why, certainly. But see here, Woodmansee, do as you like about going ahead. You understand why I was curious. But I don't mean to pry into something that doesn't concern me."

"That's all right. I think an explanation's due you. Let's have another drink." He splashed cognac onto the table as he filled the glasses. He took his and leaned far back in the chair with it, sniffing at the bouquet.

"This is what happened. They stopped at this house and asked the caretaker if they could spend the night. He gave them permission, and they brought their things in. There was quite a bit of confusion, starting fires, getting washed up and so forth. Kerwick had the box with the ashes in his pocket. But he shed his coat and left it on a couch in the front room while he was carrying wood. The old man was in the bathroom, and Miss Smith was in and out of the kitchen. None of them paid much attention to the Mexican. When Kerwick went to put his coat on again he noticed it wasn't lying just as he'd left it. He looked at the box and saw the lid had been pried open. The ashes were gone. It was perfectly plain that the man had thought the box held something valuable. While nobody was in the room he'd broken into it and either spilled or hidden the ashes. Kerwick accused him, but he denied it."

Woodmansee drained his glass and stared into it fixedly for a moment before he returned it to the table.

"Maybe you'd better take this part of the girl's story with a grain of salt. I don't know. She claims Kerwick's hotheaded but has a heart of gold. He looks to me like a numskull with a damned ugly temper. But no matter. He tried to browbeat the Mexican into telling him what had become of the ashes. Probably a dumb thing to do, because it only made the fellow think there was some value in the stuff he'd got hold of. Anyway he wouldn't talk. So Kerwick threatened him with the water cure. Know what that is?"

"Yes," Rennert said tonelessly. His eyes were cold and thoughtful between slightly narrowed lids, and the cigarette burned unheeded in his fingers.

"I used to be with the Marines," Woodmansee went on grimly, "in Haiti and other places. I've seen how it's done. It almost always works. Well, Kerwick grabbed the caretaker by the collar and hauled him outside, where one of the waterspouts that come down from the gutter would do as well as a funnel. The Smiths thought— and still think—he only meant to scare the man. Personally, I'd hate to have the bastard sitting on top of me and propping my mouth open that near a stream of water. And he was gone some time, Miss Smith admitted. When he came back he was alone. He told 'em the Mexican had broken loose from him and run off into the rain. He'd been looking for him but hadn't been able to find him. So there they were—up the creek without a paddle."

Woodmansee got up and kicked a chunk of burning wood back into the fire. He remained standing, with his hands buried deep in his pockets.

"You see the fix they were in. If the Mex. brought the Highway Patrol he could have 'em arrested, probably. Or at least there'd be a lot of tramping around on the floor and they never would be able to collect the ashes. So they sent the chauffeur on down to Victoria to get in touch with some of the higher authorities that Smith had influence with. They were going to wait and try to locate the ashes. Just then a car stopped outside, and a couple of men—Bohannon and Lurcott—wanted to stay all night. Kerwick was afraid to send 'em away for fear they'd get suspicious and tell the first patrolman they met to take a look at the house. So he pretended Smith owned the place. Then the Elkinses, Miss Pirtle and I, and finally you came. And the mess got worse and worse. Bohannon and Lurcott spotted the box and thought, just like the caretaker did, that it must contain something valuable. Lurcott's dead, and they've got a murder charge staring them in the face—as well as unlawful entry and God knows what else, now that Elkins has chosen this night and house to give up the ghost in."

Woodmansee's chin was touching his chest, and his face had a rather saturnine cast as his eyes became absorbed in the quandary of the tiny ants which the heat sent scurrying out of the dry logs only to be crushed, just at the edge of the tiled mosaic, by his polished square-capped toe.

"It's none of our affair," he said, "so we might as well forget about it till morning."

There was a long interval of silence during which Rennert found himself watching with a perverse sort of fascination that little game of life and death which was being enacted on the tiles. His reasoning, such as it was, led to the conclusion that he deserved a breathing spell before he began to replace the house of cards which Woodmansee had sent sailing into chaos. The truth probably was that a sense of being victimized by an anticlimax allied with the grape to saturate him momentarily in a mood of reckless, self-protective fatalism. So that he watched, from an Olympian distance, the haste of insignificant legged things to provide an instant's diversion for a higher being whose legs were covered by tan tweed.

"Rennert," Woodmansee released pent-up breath, "I'm going to take a bath."

Rennert looked up, nonplussed by the force with which the announcement had been made. "Well?" was all he could find to say.

The other didn't meet his gaze but waited, with foot poised, until an ant reached the margin of what for it was safety. The toe came down and ground against the surface of the tile as Woodmansee said:

"This is the first chance I've had since I left Mexico City. And traveling in this country makes me feel unclean. I suppose you want one, too, after driving through that hot desert. I'll tell you what let's do—use the patio for a shower. It's dark, and no one will see us. The water in these pipes is rusty—I washed and shaved in it before supper." He laughed and fished a coin out of his pocket. "I'll match you to see who goes first. I'm carrying quite a bit of money and would rather not leave it in here without someone to watch it."

As the slate-blue eyes rose to his face, Rennert cleared from his forehead the frown which had gathered there.

"No contest, Woodmansee." He shook his head. "I could do with a good warm tub, I admit. But frankly I don't have the nerve to attempt a cold shower tonight. I'm not as young as I used to be or as hardy. I'll sit here by the fire like an old man and take about one more drink. Then I've got to be going. I promised Mrs. Elkins I'd come back to her room."

Woodmansee flipped the coin into the air, caught it on his palm and closed his fingers about it. "Heads or tails?" he spoke in a forcedly bantering tone. "Old man, hell! You haven't got many years on me. Don't be a piker."

"No, nothing doing."

"Well, use the shower in the bathroom, then. You'll feel a lot better."

Rennert looked at him steadily for a moment, then smiled and said dryly: "Let's cut out the tactfulness, Woodmansee. Even one's best friends speak plainly in Mexico. You're unpleasantly aware of the fact that I need a bath. Is that what you're trying to tell me?"

Confusion worked on the other's face, removing the last trace of its former masklike hardness. "Yes," he blurted. "It's a hell of a thing to say—"

"No, it's not. I appreciate it. I'm not hunting an alibi, but I wonder if we can't throw the blame on the caretaker. I expect he's in this room frequently and never troubles to air it out. I suspected as much when I first came in."

"I'm sorry, Rennert, but—but I don't think that's it."

"All right. I apologize for being so careless. Go ahead and hit the water. I'll fortify myself with Dutch courage and follow you."

Woodmansee started to speak, reconsidered and walked away, stripping off his coat. Just as he passed out of Rennert's sight the latter saw that he was wearing an empty shoulder holster.

Rennert remained in his chair and went in for rigorous self-criticism. His body he was ready to exonerate from Woodmansee's imputation. While it was far from immaculate, he felt he knew its functioning too well to suspect it now of a lapse from grace. His clothing was another matter. He couldn't remember when this suit had been condemned as unworthy of a visit to the cleaners. And, what with mopping up damp floors tonight, he might very well have let it give him too many of the attributes of a tramp. . . .

Sheer nonsense! If he was offensive to any of the senses it was to that of sight alone. Some other impulse than that toward propriety was actuating Woodmansee in his untimely insistence on these rites of purification. This was part and parcel of the accent on the unwholesome which had pervaded every one of the night's incidents and which might have been bred, like a fungus, by natural elements gone contrariwise on this mountain at the crossroad of Mexico.

Thoroughly puzzled, increasingly disquieted, Rennert listened to the sounds of a man's undressing and of a man's clothing being tossed upon the floor.

"Well, I'm off to have intercourse with Mother Nature," he heard Woodmansee call. "Don't get cold feet while I'm gone."

Rennert peered around the side of the chair in time to see him stride naked to the door.

21
WATER CURE

A QUARTER OF AN HOUR later Rennert was sitting in front of the fire again. His appearance wasn't the same, however, for he wore a white terry-cloth robe, slippers and nothing else. Parting with his clothing had produced in him, too, a distinct psychological effect which he was doing his best to counteract by an additional cognac and cigarette.

He felt that he had given up a post of advantage, precarious though it was, on the solid ground of normalcy and was being lured onto unstable terrain where he would cut a helpless and ridiculous figure. He made resolves to put on again the dignity and raiment of a civilized man, knowing full well that as soon as Woodmansee returned he would complaisantly strip off his last stitch and step naked into the night like a primitive nature-worshiper. And in the meantime he sat and stared at the tiles which Woodmansee's shoe had littered with mangled insect bodies.

These were Talavera tiles from Puebla, white with a blue border. The lettering on them was black and ornamental, so that Rennert had no difficulty in reading the ancient Aztec poem with which a man whose sense of the fitness of things was entirely Mexican had blessed his hearth: *"To-nantzine 'cuac ni-miquiz . . ."*

Yes, Rennert thought, he would like to meet this Snorre Bjerregaard whose personality had left its stamp throughout his house. He liked to play with the fancy that the oft-noticed affinity between Scandinavians and Mexicans was a survival of the relationship inaugurated in the hazy past by a shipwrecked Viking who had found, on these shores, the feathered mantle of godship.

He looked around as Woodmansee bounded in, a gleaming statue come to life.

Puffing and gasping and making animal noises, the fellow snatched up a towel and approached the fire.

"Great stuff, Rennert!" he managed to articulate. "That'll put spunk in you."

"I daresay," Rennert commented as he got up and threw away his cigarette. "But that's not the reason for my bath, is it?"

"No." Woodmansee was scouring his face. "It'll wash off the Mexican dirt, too. Leave you pure as driven snow. But watch out for that damned cactus."

Rennert sank onto the arm of the chair and said, "Cactus?"

"Yes. There's a lot of it climbing up those posts. I got the hell scratched out of me." Woodmansee fell to with vigor on his body, rubbing and slapping at the muscles as he flexed them.

Rennert regarded him for a moment in silence, then said: "I'd like to see those scratches, if you don't mind."

The blue eyes swung to his swiftly. "Why, sure. But they don't amount to anything. I was just kidding."

"I want to look at them, nevertheless."

"Up there on my right shoulder." Woodmansee knotted the towel around his middle and turned his side to Rennert.

The latter inspected the tough wet skin and carefully extracted a few flexible cactus spines. He laid them on his palm and bent toward the fire with them. They were weak little processes, creamy white and brown, dark-tipped, and belonged indubitably to the *Junco espinoso.*

He straightened and ranged them on the mantel.

"This shows you," he observed to Woodmansee, who was standing with arms akimbo, following his movements, "how skittish I've become tonight. Those spines are from a perfectly ordinary and harmless cactus. They'll leave your hide with an itchy and burning sensation, but if you don't irritate it there'll be hardly a trace in the morning. I'm positive of that. But"—he shrugged—"a man died in the next room. He was in sound health and had a whole skin, as far as I can learn, except for punctures from that same species of cactus. Put me down as an alarmist, a damned fool—anything you like—but I'm going to keep you close company for a while. I want bulletins every few minutes to the effect that all's well with you. Let me know if you feel the slightest unusual symptom." He had to laugh. "Have I got you in a morbid frame of mind?"

"No." There was a bit of constraint in Woodmansee's manner. "That's white of you, Rennert, to care what happens to me. I'm really not worth it. But—"

"Don't scratch that!" Rennert said sharply, as the other thoughtlessly moved his left hand in the direction of his right shoulder. Woodmansee let the hand fall sheepishly.

Rennert was on the point of mentioning a guinea pig, but refrained from such an uncomplimentary allusion.

"I feel like a doctor," he grinned. "But not an M.D. Nor yet a Ph.D., like Damson. A Mexican witch doctor, rather—a *curandero* who plays safe by conjuring against all of the unknown evils that may hover about his patient." He started to move off, untying the cord of his robe.

"Maybe that's what I'm doing," Woodmansee spoke quietly.

Rennert turned, and they exchanged a long glance. "Yes," he said, "I think it is. That's why I'm following your prescription."

Rennert was proud of his exit. He left robe and slippers with his clothing on the couch and walked without unseemly haste across the tiles. He didn't shiver. He didn't bundle his arms together as he wanted to do. If goose flesh stood out all over his timorous and shrinking body, only he was aware of it.

When the door was closed and he stood in the passage, however, he tossed his dignity to the winds and was again a small boy poking a toe tentatively into an icy stream and summoning up courage to take the first plunge of the season. Except that his thoughts were on colds and pneumonia and like penalties as much as on bodily discomfort.

The lamp was completely extinguished now, and there was no faintest ray of light anywhere. The only sounds were echoes from a world given over to deluge, a universal rustle and restlessness which had in it the essence of melancholy.

He felt his way along the wall, gained the edge of the eaves and, without daring to risk another pause, dashed blindly out. The shock left him breathless, a broken wretch cowering for mercy. That passed, and in its place came a wild exaltation as he pitted his strength against the water that slid over him, sculpturing and defining his body, streaming to gain entry at every opening.

It was a spasmodic twitch and fluttering in his left side that warned him where the real danger in this performance lay. Sobered, he groped his way to shelter and backed against a wall to give his heart some deserved pampering. Adobe was a cold and unclean hand laid on flesh that had been chastised into purity, but for the instant he was oblivious of defilement.

Neither did he make the effort to orient himself until he was startled to an upright posture by sounds from close at hand. A window had been opened and shutters slammed back, and a feeble light was flowing past crisscross bars.

He realized then that he was on the west side of the patio, between the door of the room occupied by Bohannon and the kitchen wall, which ran at right angles to it.

A thick voice which he identified as Kerwick's was so loud in his ears that he judged the fellow was standing by the window.

"What in the hell's the matter with you?" Kerwick asked.

Rennert was afraid for a second or so that the question had been put to him, but then came the response from within, a voice which was recognizable as Bohannon's but which had in it a new note, shrill with terror:

"I guess it's my heart. I can't get my breath. Open another window."

Rennert flattened himself against the wall (his flesh crept at contact with the adobe) and heard Kerwick throw wide the shutters on the other side of the door. Of all the unheard-of situations he had ever got into, he told himself as he clamped his jaws shut, this was the worst. All that was needed now to make this slapstick comedy was the advent of Miss Pirtle, who would blunder along and collide with his naked uncouth self.

He thought Bohannon was lying on the bed between the window and the bathroom door, for the man's raucous breathing, mingled with little whimpering sounds, came to him plainly.

"There!" Kerwick must be standing over him. "Stop the belly-aching. You'll be all right if you lie still. I've got to talk to you. I couldn't while Mr. Smith was here. Are you going to listen?"

"Yeah." Bedsprings creaked as if Bohannon were rolling over.

"Want to make some more money?"

There was a moment of silence.

"Maybe." The voice was now more like the fat man's as Rennert had first heard it. "What's on your mind?"

"I want you to get rid of another body in the morning."

"Another!" Bohannon gasped. And gasped again. "Whose?"

"Out in the garage"—Kerwick's words were evenly spaced—"there's a dead Mexican. I want you to cart him away with that pal of yours. Put both of 'em where they'll never be found. Not anywhere close to this house. Don't say anything to Mr. Smith about it. There's forty-two bucks in it for you. That's all I've got. Take it or leave it."

"That's not very much."

"Good God, you'll clear fifty thousand out of the other deal. What in the hell do you want?"

"Well—O.K. What's the dope on this Mex.?"

Kerwick's reply was so long in coming that Rennert had time to envisage several disagreeable endings to this eavesdropping episode. Kerwick had probably entered through the bathroom that led to the kitchen. He might have used the patio, however, before Rennert got there and return by the same route. Someone else might put in an appearance and discover him. Or—Rennert decided this was the most likely eventuality—he himself might give vent to a loud and lusty sneeze, betraying his presence. A sneeze was called for by all the laws of melodrama and, since this showed no signs of developing into comedy . . .

It was suggestion, perhaps, but Rennert was positive he felt a sneeze coming on.

Kerwick said: "He's the caretaker we told you about. I didn't mean to hurt him. I held his head by a spout and told him I was going to give him the water cure. He got scared and threshed around and did get a mouthful of water. He broke loose then and ran off, and I couldn't find him. I don't know what happened to him. He must've fallen down. Maybe unconscious. Anyway, a car ran over him."

"Whose car?"

"I don't know. But I'd be on the spot if the Mexican police found out about him."

Bohannon's laugh was ugly. "Just like old man Smith. Maybe this'll teach both of you to be kinda careful how you push people around."

"Stow it!" Kerwick cut in on him. "It's a bargain, then? I'll give you the money when you're ready to drive off in the morning."

"Yeah, it's a bargain. But say—does anybody know about this dead Mex. besides you and me?"

Kerwick said hesitantly, "Only Mr. Rennert."

"Rennert! Not so good. What're you goin' to do about him?"

Again a long dead pause while the subject whose fate was being considered hugged his ribs with one hand and with the other kept a finger pressed firmly between his upper lip and nostrils.

"You don't need to worry." Kerwick was moving off, but not (*Gracias a Dios!*) in the direction of the outer door. "I'll take care of Rennert."

"How?"

"In a way you'd never dream of."

A door closed, and Rennert, heedless of his sore foot, sprinted over the stones.

22
EXIT MR. WOODMANSEE

RENNERT'S ENTRY into his room had none of the pretensions to dignity and boldness of carriage of his exit. Beyond false modesty, he let trembling body and clicking teeth show that he was chilled to the marrow.

Woodmansee, fully dressed, was seated on the hassock, the crown of his head to the fire as he ran long fingers through his drying hair.

"For a man who had to be pushed off the bank, you stayed in the water a long time," he observed after a brief upward glance. "You must've found a mermaid to play with."

"Only water snakes," Rennert informed him through the folds of his towel. "And slimy things."

"I didn't include those in my order."

"I know you didn't."

"Chase 'em away with that drink I poured for you." Woodmansee nodded toward a glass on the edge of the table.

Rennert interrupted his rubbing long enough to swallow the cognac.

"Hit the spot?" Woodmansee asked him.

"Absolutely."

"Then you can hear the bad news. There was an accident while you were gone."

"An accident?"

"To your clothes. You must've dropped a spark from your cigarette while you were undressing. I smelled something burning, and when I looked I found your pants on fire. I had to throw several glasses of water on 'em. Made a hell of a mess of your whole outfit, I'm afraid."

That was putting it mildly, Rennert discovered when he reached the other side of the room. His trousers, shirt, underwear and socks, all of which he had left in some order on the couch, were a sodden heap on the floor.

"You'll have to change," Woodmansee called.

"Yes,"—Rennert was eying the garments thoughtfully—"it *does* look as if I'd have to change."

His face became more and more thoughtful as he took fresh linen and another pair of trousers from his bag and slipped into them. The old trousers he picked up from the tiles, shook and carried to the fire.

"This caught me rather unprepared," he explained. "The other suit I have is my best one, all cleaned and pressed for an engagement in Victoria. And you know what sticklers these Mexican families are for dress. If I can make these pants at all presentable I'll wear them the rest of the night. I feel the veneer of civilization getting thinner and thinner."

He draped the faithful blue serge over the front of a chair facing the fire and ascertained that it had suffered no material damage beyond a slight hole in the seat.

"Wonder if I'd shock anybody's sense of decorum in these?"

Woodmansee's eyes fell from the trousers to the tiles as he continued tufting and pushing fingers through his hair. In an uncombed state that hair betrayed a scantiness which hadn't been apparent when it lay like a smooth straw helmet on its owner's head.

"*I* wouldn't wear 'em," he said flatly. "You can have those you've got on pressed tomorrow."

"Evidently your experience with Mexican cleaners has been different from mine." Rennert sat down and began drying his hair. "I'll be careful not to turn my back to my audience. And darkness and coattails can cover a multitude of shortcomings."

There was no answer. It was restful there by the fire; Rennert's body was warm and glowing, and the steady massaging of his scalp made him sleepy. Soon he had to cover a yawn.

"Planning to stay up all night?" Woodmansee asked quietly.

"Yes. Mrs. Elkins will probably want someone with her husband. I think I'll make some coffee before I go."

"Why don't you let me make it while you get some sleep?"

Rennert considered. He had no intention of giving in to his drowsiness, but he did want very much to be alone with his thoughts for a few minutes. He wanted first of all to decide just how certain he was that he had *not* been smoking when he undressed. . . .

"I believe I will," he acquiesced, rising. "Wake me up in half an hour."

"Sure thing." Woodmansee went to the chest in the corner, hauled out two thick blankets and carried them to the couch upon which Rennert had stretched out. "I promised Miss Pirtle I wouldn't let you take cold. A good kind man, she called you. How does it feel to be one?"

Rennert grunted and pulled the blankets up to his chin. "Sounds like an obituary."

Woodmansee stood stiffly, looking down at Rennert. "It does, doesn't it?" he said lamely and walked away.

Rennert's eyes followed the tweed-clad back. There was a flare on the left side of the coat, under the arm pit, which told him Woodmansee was wearing the holster again. And in it, doubtless, the automatic which had been on top of the clothing in one of his Gladstones.

The principal reason for Rennert's uncertainty about the presence or absence of a cigarette in his lips was the swiftness with which he had moved once Woodmansee was out of the room. The young man's luggage, he had learned before he undressed, was well stocked with apparel of excellent taste and quality, most of it bearing labels from New York stores. But not a single object, except the gun, had furnished a clue as to Woodmansee's mission in Mexico or any connotation as to his true personality. . . .

In front of the fire Woodmansee turned and shoved his hands into his hip pockets. His face seemed, in the glimpse which Rennert had of it before he closed his eyes, to have assumed again its saturnine cast, with a peculiar quirk drawing down one side of the mouth.

For at least ten minutes Woodmansee stood without moving and without taking his gaze from Rennert's face. When he was sure that Rennert was asleep he sat down, drew a memorandum book and fountain pen from his pocket and spent the next quarter of an hour or more in the throes of composition, tearing out and wadding three sheets and tossing them into the fire before he was satisfied that what he had written didn't sound too sappy and soft. This was an altogether new experience for Woodmansee, and he wasn't sure he liked it.

He got up, folded the paper and stuck it under the glass from which Rennert had drunk the cognac.

He stepped to the chair where Rennert had left his trousers, hooked a finger under the belt and, after a moment's hesitation, emptied the pockets. The coins which he found he put on the table beside his note. He made a roll of the trousers and shoved them far back in the fireplace so that the smell of the burning cloth would go up the chimney. Damp as they were, they smoldered and smoked for a time before they caught fire.

Woodmansee tiptoed across the room and gathered together Rennert's underwear, socks, shirt and necktie. He added these to the flames and on his next trip brought the coat and vest which had been hung over the back of a chair. He went through their pockets and deposited a watch, a billfold and a few old letters with the silver. The leather case which contained the keys to Rennert's car he slipped into his own pocket, leaving Miss Pirtle's key case in its place on the table. He fed coat and vest to the fire and thought that that took care of Rennert.

He brushed off his hands, held them up in front of him and saw that he was nervous as a cat. He choked. The draft in the chimney was poor, and smoke was drifting out into the room.

He'd better be going, he told himself. He tied together the clothes which he had taken off before he bathed and threw them into the passage. He went to the bath and combed his hair, returned and put on top-coat and hat. He blew out both candles, hoisted up his Gladstones and took a last look at Rennert, at the little tent which his right foot made of the blankets. There was nothing to be done about that foot.

Woodmansee braced his shoulders and went out the door.

PART THREE

"FOR DAYS at a stretch the sun is obscured," an old writer has it, "and the Mexican, muffled in his sarape, smokes his cigarrillo and mutters, '*Ave María Purísima, que salga el sol!*'—Holy Mary, let the sun come out!"

—*Heigh-ho, Mexico!*
by Gulliver Damson, Ph.D.

23
SANCTUARY

RENNERT'S RIGHT EAR hurt, so he turned over on his face and rooted at the pillow with his nose, to loosen the feathery softness which was always there. But the tip of his nose encountered a round hard button that was unfamiliar and had no meaning for him. Sleepily he opened his unobstructed eye and saw, not the paper of his own bedroom, but a gray-white wall across which trailed wavering bands of reddish light like the reflection of a sunset on water.

He rolled over, kicked his feet free of blankets and sat up. Too suddenly, however, for things seemed to collide at the back of his head and send vibrations of the shock to converge in his eyes. He closed his eyes and sat very still, fighting down a slight queasiness of his stomach. Sleeping without a window open . . .

"'I'll never do it again. *Never*.' Always get that out of your system the first thing." A voice, mocking and yet solicitous, was coming toward him. "Then drink this and put the old skull back on the pillow till the room makes up its mind what it's going to do."

It was Mrs. Elkins. Rennert blinked and wondered what sort of unnatural light this was which gave her white face and dark jacketed body such tenuous indistinctness.

"Don't try to talk," she said softly. "Just drink this." "This" was a glass of effervescing liquid whose sizzling was a pleasant sound.

Rennert shook his head and spoke a little testily: "I'm all right. I don't have a hangover. There's no reason why I should."

"Of course not. Just keep saying that and swallow this." The cold glass was put in his hand. Light fingers were brushing the hair

193

back from his forehead. "That last one slipped up on you, didn't it? It always does. But don't take it so seriously. I'm going to tell you a secret. I like you a lot better now that I know you're only human."

Rennert looked up and knew how close her lips had been to following the caress of her hand. He knew too that she had been drinking, not to the point of intoxication but enough to lend her a nervous excitation which would be easily collapsible. He saw hysteria in the offing and groaned inwardly at the prospect of coping with it on his own responsibility.

The defensiveness in his eyes and manner must have been apparent, for she turned away, laughing slightly. "I'll go away now and leave you alone. The coffee will be ready as soon as you are."

Rennert downed the contents of the glass and remained where he was for a moment, studying the room. The fireplace held a great bank of brightly glowing embers, but instead of the expected darkness outside its range there was a dreary half-light which washed over objects and obscured their outlines. He glanced at the windows, saw that while they were closed the slats of their shutters had been pushed to the horizontal, letting in that strange grayness which was neither day nor night. And over everything lay a heavy stillness. Uncanny, that stillness. The rain, of course, had stopped.

Rennert felt for his watch and for the first time gave attention to the outer man. He was in shirt sleeves, with no tie, and wore a pair of trousers which had been neatly pressed when he lay down.

"What time is it?" he asked as he got up and immediately shifted his weight to his left foot.

Mrs. Elkins held the coffee pot in one hand and raised the other to consult her wrist watch. "Seven-twenty."

"Morning," he told himself redundantly.

"The cold gray dawn of the morning after."

He stepped to the end of the couch and looked about him. His coat and vest weren't on the back of the chair where he had left them. He couldn't see any of the clothing that had been drenched. His bag was on the floor, but Woodmansee's luggage was gone. Woodmansee's topcoat and hat were gone.

"Where's Woodmansee?"

"The tall and handsome city slicker?" Mrs. Elkins' back was to him as she made sure the pot was securely roosted upon the embers. "I haven't seen him since we left the front room last night. Why, was he in on your party?"

"Yes." Rennert approached the table to set down the glass and saw an unfamiliar key case beside his watch, money, billfold and letters. He noticed the folded paper tucked under the other glass, pulled it out and read it. He slid the hand with the note into his pocket, stared into the fireplace for an instant, then freed some of his own dammed-up tension in a laugh.

Mrs. Elkins faced him, eyebrows raised and a quizzical smile on her lips. "I knew that stuff would help. Snorre buys it by the case and keeps it in every bathroom. This house may be lacking in some respects, but it's well stocked for serious drinking. Are you aware yet that we're locked in here?"

"Locked in!" Never in any circumstances at his best early in the morning, Rennert went to the door and tried the handle.

"I got dressed and came in a little after midnight. I wondered what had happened to you. When I saw the bottles and you passed out, I decided I might as well stay where it was warm. My heater had burned out. I helped myself to the cognac, and about that time I heard someone outside and the key turned in the lock. You were sleeping so peacefully I didn't like to waken you. And there really wasn't anything to be done about it. So I made some coffee and sat here all night."

"Was there any disturbance in the house?"

"No. Just before I came out of my room I heard a car. I wasn't sure whether it left the garage or was passing by. After that and after the door was locked it was just like the night before Christmas. 'Not a creature was stirring, not even a mouse.' You didn't even snore. I kept listening. I'm so used to Jesse's snoring. But you didn't. Not once." Mrs. Elkins was moving toward him by degrees, her eyes fixed steadfastly on his face. There was brittle laughter in her voice which should have warned Rennert of the trouble that was brewing for him.

But for the moment he was intent on another concern, forget-ful of the fact that he hadn't washed as yet.

"It's a rather embarrassing question to ask," he said as he glanced about furniture and floor, "but do you know what became of the pair of trousers I left on that chair?"

"Trousers! You've lost your trousers!" Her face was convulsed. "When I met you I wondered if you weren't too formal and digni-fied even to put on a bathing suit. And now here you are looking helpless and bothered because you can't find your pants."

Rennert felt a tightness and surge of warmth about his neck which he would have ascribed to his collar, had that been buttoned. "I am making a rather ridiculous figure out of myself, I suppose. But, seriously, I want to know about those trousers. Did you see them when you came in last night?"

"No, I didn't see them. Oh, Hugh, don't be worrying about your clothes now. Think about me. And Jesse. And tell me what I'm going to do." She lurched toward him and pressed her face against his shirt front. "And, Hugh, don't be so darned standoffish. I like you. I always have. I wasn't making fun of you. Put your arms around me. Just for a minute. Tell me I don't need to worry, that everything will be all right. I feel so lost. I thought and thought about Jesse last night. Something must have been wrong with his heart that I didn't know about. He was excited, that would be bad for him. I know there wasn't anything mysterious about his death. But just the same it was awful sitting here by myself. I was so"—sobs choked her—"so damned scared."

Rennert held her, felt her trembling gradually subside and her warm tears soaking through to his skin. Still the straw man, he reminded himself. Stuffed. If he was ludicrous when he hunted for a pair of pants or was pictured in a bathing suit (why in the hell did she keep harping on that?), what would he be if he showed how alive he was to the fragrance of the loose hair which tickled his nose and to the odor of clove pinks which he drew in with every breath?

He got a little ironic amusement out of putting a Mexican, even a middle-aged, unhandsome Mexican, in his place. The latter would have taken grandiloquently all that the moment offered, making of it a soaring gesture against the propinquity of death and drab circumstance, a flower plucked from bleak soil and worn debonairly behind the ear. Rennert made consolatory noises with his tongue, watched the coffee pot approaching the boil and sought what payment for big-brotherliness he could out of the thought that the Mexican who was such a gallant lover in a dramatic dawn would be one hell of a dud when it came to facing the practicalities of the rest of the morning. Exceedingly sour grapes, of course. It was a dull and thankless job, this facing of practicalities.

He said: "You don't need to worry. Everything's going to be all right. The night's over now. I'm taking you and Jesse back to Brownsville with me. To my house. It's one I just built. A little place exactly like a hundred others in town, I suppose. But I think it's different. The Magic Valley, they call that country. You can rest there. I'll show you my fruit trees. I'll put on my overalls and do my farmer act for you. It's only a few miles away. Now,"—he had his handkerchief out and was drying her eyes—"are you going to trust me? And forget how I failed you last night? I wasn't drunk. But I was stupid enough to take too many sleeping tablets."

"I'm glad that was it. I didn't want to think you'd go off on a drinking bout and leave me all alone. Hugh—"

"Yes."

"You don't mind me calling you by your first name, do you?"

"Of course not."

"Don't ever let yourself get thick and meaty, like Jesse. Stale and dull. It was so hard to keep on loving him when everything he did was so cut and dried. The way he talked and ate and dressed. His solitaire. I didn't really know, until I was sitting here hour after hour and thinking, that I did love him. I suppose you don't see how I could—and still come here with Snorre? You blame me for fooling Jesse. You disapprove of me, don't you?"

"Not at all." Rennert got ready for the imminent eruption of the coffee pot. "I don't see anything inconsistent in taking a little vacation, let's say, from the job you love."

"And Jesse was my job. What a perfect way to put it!" She stood away from him, caught his arms at the elbows and looked up eagerly into his eyes. "You mean that?"

"Certainly."

"I'm so glad you understand. I wasn't sure how you felt about me. It'll be so much easier now to tell you— What is it, Hugh?"

It wasn't boiling coffee which had distracted Rennert's attention but another, somewhat similar sound: the muffled drone of a car approaching from the south, along the road that Damson had traversed.

She heard it too and glanced quickly at the east window. "Can't we call to them? Make them stop?"

He was moving toward that side of the room. "My guess is it won't be necessary. This should be the car the Smiths and Kerwick have been waiting for. Maybe not. Let's see."

He opened window and shutters and stared through the bars in complete frustration. Mist shut them in. It hugged the rocky soil and the adobe walls, a gauzy gray blanket which had dropped like a hood upon the house. There was no movement in its depths, no rift or thinning, and his experience held but one parallel for the trapped feeling which it gave him. This was the claustrophobia which had taken him so utterly by surprise in the subterranean passages that honeycomb the pyramid of Cholula. Not that there was any danger of his giving way to such panic again, but it was disquieting to scent here the same mortuary atmosphere which had been walled in with him at Cholula and which, as much as the sense of enclosure, had sent him scurrying into the sunlight.

At his side Mrs. Elkins shivered. "It's got thicker. I opened these shutters early this morning. I thought the sun might come out after the rain stopped. But— it's just as if something had happened to the sun. And we're in a ghostly world of our own. Oh, Hugh, what would I have done if you hadn't been here!"

Rennert put an arm about her and listened to the low whine of a powerful motor which came intermittently through the murk. So difficult was it to localize sound that it took the shrill blast of the horn to tell him the car was close at hand. Again and again the warning note blared out.

"Aren't you going to shout?" Mrs. Elkins whispered.

He shook his head. "It's the Smith car, I'm sure. Listen."

At the front of the house a door slammed. The horn ceased its noise, and the automobile came to an abrupt stop. Voices drifted faintly to them and faded away. They heard nothing more.

Rennert closed the window and turned to her. "We'll let well enough alone for the present and see what develops."

"But couldn't we make an attempt to signal the next car? If we both shouted— They can't hold us here forever!"

"They can hold us," he said grimly, "just about as long as they want to. Our voices wouldn't carry any distance at all. And there'll be little if any travel on this road as long as the mist lasts. Reports of the weather and the detour will have got down to Victoria. I doubt whether the highway people will permit any cars to start out from there this morning. So let's make ourselves comfortable. And look on this room as a sanctuary, where harm can't come to us. Because that's what I think it is."

24
SMOKE TEARS

RENNERT WAS SCRUPULOUS about his shaving that morning, undeterred by cold and roily water which might have been shot through with blood instead of particles of rust. He worried for some time at his hair. Its slight waviness was gone since its wetting of the night before, and it was lank and lifeless and alarmingly thin on top. With slight pouches under his eyes he looked, he thought, very much like a tout.

He finished, but still he stood, fingers tapping on the rim of the lavatory. On the shelf above was an almost empty bottle of lilac toilet water which Woodmansee had left behind him. With a brusque movement Rennert poured the remainder into his palm and slapped it on his face. He sniffed and, instantly regretting his action, did his best to rub the stuff off with a towel. For the last fifteen years or more Rennert had used the same mild and odorless astringent, put up at the drugstore. Consequently it was in a state of acute self-consciousness that he sat down to inspect his foot.

Some soreness remained, but the swelling had almost entirely disappeared, and the puncture was a mere dark pinpoint. He didn't bother to replace the bandage, and if there was a frown on his forehead it was because a word which he had used a few minutes before kept plaguing him.

A sanctuary, he'd told Mrs. Elkins their room was. The term had come unsought, but the more he pondered it the more he became convinced that this was the salient fact which emerged from Woodmansee's message. Within those walls was safety.

He brought the letter from his pocket and reread it, slowly and perplexedly. When he began, the script was sharp, economic, clear:

> Dear Rennert:
>
> You'll probably have a funny feeling in your head when you read this. But don't worry, it's only the effect of a couple of Pirtle's sleeping tablets and will soon wear off. You took them in the cognac. I had to borrow your car to get to Brownsville, and that seemed the only way to avoid explanations.
>
> I'll leave the car in a garage and pay for all the repairs it needs. You'll find a card in your mailbox telling you which one. Pirtle will be glad to have you drive hers back, I know. The keys are on the table. You can't make much speed in it in its present condition, that's why I'm using yours.
>
> Now get ready to laugh. I never in my life hated anything as much as having to double-cross you like this. I've done everything I know to protect you from— [a word had been blotted out here and "every possible danger" inserted] so don't think too hard of me. Stay in your room in the morning until Kerwick tells you it's safe to go out.
>
> We won't see each other again, I suppose, and maybe it's just as well. You might make an honest man out of me. Best of luck, Rennert, and don't ever trust another stranger. He might be like me.
>
> Very respectfully yours,
George Woodmansee
>
> P.S. I'm a damn fool to be writing this. Want to tear it up and say nothing to anybody about me? Thanks.

By the time Rennert finished his perusal, the dampness which was in the little tiled room with him had so impregnated the paper that the ink was running and the words were losing their legibility. As if water were hastening to comply with Woodmansee's wish. . . .

Let it. Deliberately, with the full realization that he would have been at a loss to justify his act, he tore the letter into bits, dropped them into the bowl and sent them down the drain. Curious that he should find in himself no anger or resentment toward Woodmansee. One simply didn't harbor that sort of feeling about a bright hard blade which has flashed across one's vision and vanished.

Rennert passed a hand over his face, smelled it and grimaced. Still like a breath from a Mexican barbershop.

He stepped to the door of Damson's room, listened and, when he heard no sound, turned the handle and looked inside.

Damson, covered to the shoulders by a blanket, lay on the east bed, his face to the wall. His snores were ample reassurance that no harm had come to him in that room where Elkins had died.

Where Elkins had died. . . .

Rennert tiptoed in and across the tiles. His eyes were fastened on the white bald crown that pressed into the pillow. Startling how at a distance the back of Damson's head resembled that of Jesse Elkins. When you got closer you saw the dissimilarities. This pate was egg-shaped, whereas the other probably came in the mesocephalic range. Here the fringe of hair over the nape of the neck wasn't arclike enough to give the effect of a tonsure. But, viewed in this weird predawn light or by the rays of a candle, it would be easy enough to mistake one man for the other.

The discovery, fruitless though it seemed, was what Rennert had needed to galvanize him into his usual wide-awake inquisitive self. About the room he went with springy steps, circling the chair which had held Elkins' corpse; assuming squatting, kneeling, upright positions; sighting imaginary points in the air. He found the door to the patio locked. He stood for some time before the closed window on the left, staring at the aperture in the shutter where a slat was missing and where water had streamed in the night before.

He didn't make his exit until a creaking of bedsprings told him that Damson was stirring. The last thing he wanted then was to be pestered by Damson's questions. He wasn't sure, as he returned to the other room, that he welcomed Mrs. Elkins' presence. This wasn't due to misogyny or lack of sociability on his part, he would have been at pains to explain, but to the fact that he had a bee buzzing in his bonnet. And he would have liked to listen to it in peace. However . . .

"Sorry I kept you waiting," he said to Mrs. Elkins, who was standing by the mantel, scuffing at the tiles with the toe of her shoe. "I decided to shave."

"You shouldn't have done that. I didn't mind."

"Oh, I feel much better this way."

Rennert put on a necktie and got from his bag the coat and vest which matched these trousers. While he was at it he made sure his missing clothes hadn't been hidden among his other belongings or under the couch or in any of the corners. That aspect of Woodmansee's maneuvering puzzled him more and more. By no stretch of the imagination could he conceive of anyone going to such pains to steal garments which would be rejected by any secondhand dealer.

As he joined Mrs. Elkins he was playing with the theory of disguise. Rather farfetched, but all the fellow's actions were those of the fugitive: his hasty departure from Mexico City with an individual of a type least likely to attract suspicion, an American schoolteacher; his apprehensive manner; his own admission that he was expecting trouble. Rennert's eyes narrowed a bit as he recalled the distinctive salute with which Woodmansee had greeted him the night before. What color of shirts did they wear in Mexico, the members of that party?

He poured two cups of coffee and handed one to Mrs. Elkins.

"My second," she told him. "I hope you don't mind if I went ahead."

"Sure not. I always let my coffee cool before I drink it. I don't think it can be really enjoyed as long as it scalds the taste-buds."

"Mm!" she exclaimed before he could back away. "You made an elaborate toilet. I love that smell. Eau de Cologne, isn't it?"

"Yes," he said uncomfortably. "I don't use it very often. It's so strong."

She looked at him for a moment, searchingly, then glanced down. "I've been trying to remember what these words mean," she spoke as if resuming a previous conversation. "They're Aztec. Snorre translated them for me once. He was quite proud of his idea of putting them in the mosaic here."

"Thanks for giving me a chance to show off." Rennert was at his ease now. "I noticed those last night. That's a poem said to have been composed by Nezahualcoyotl, King of Texcoco. I'm not posing as an Aztec scholar, but John Hubert Cornyn, of Quetzalcoatl Palace in Mexico City, got me interested in pre-Spanish literature once. I think I can give his translation of those lines."

As he spoke he brushed away the debris of ants which was such an unpleasant souvenir of Woodmansee's companionship:

> "'Oh, my mother, when I die
>   Bury me beneath your hearth.
> When you go to make the bread
>   There is where you'll cry for me.

> "'And if anyone should ask you:
>   Noble lady, wherefore weep you?
> You will answer: *Green the wood is,*
>   *Much it smokes and makes me cry.*'"

Reminded by this that the room was growing chilly, Rennert stooped to lay some logs on the embers.

"Smoke Gets in Your Eyes," Mrs. Elkins murmured. She had sunk into a chair and was neglecting her coffee in a contemplative study of his face.

"Yes." He straightened and went to get his coffee. "The same thought found expression five hundred years ago."

"That's why it stayed in my mind, I suppose. Snorre had a record of the song. And last night it was so appropriate. There was so much smoke in here that it made my eyes water. That started me crying. I had a nice quiet little weep. It was what I'd been wanting to do but somehow couldn't. It helped."

Rennert paused in the act of sitting down and stared at her. "You say there was smoke in this room. Could you identify it as any particular kind?"

"Well," she hesitated, "it smelled like burning rags. I didn't investigate. Why, you don't suppose your trousers caught on fire accidentally, do you?"

"No, no." Rennert slid so far back upon the leather that his face was partially concealed from her. "No, they couldn't have."

There was no need, he felt, to share his virtual certainty that her lachrymal glands had been stimulated by nothing more poetic than his soiled clothing. Clothing which had held so active and contagious a menace that Woodmansee had resorted to subterfuge to get it off his body and to effect a cleansing of the flesh which it had touched.

Rennert sipped coffee, scarcely tasting it, and a "cauld grue" went over him at the thought of how intimate he must have been with something unclean and malignant to require this double purge of fire and water. And what of the others in that house who hadn't had Woodmansee's safeguarding? Mrs. Elkins there. Her husband, who lay an apparently unscathed corpse across the patio. . . .

It wasn't the most propitious moment to face a crisis in one's life. When Mrs. Elkins asked quietly, "Hugh, why are you farming?" Rennert started and said, "Oh, I beg your pardon. What was that?"

25
BARS IN THE MIST

WHY ARE YOU FARMING? The question was to Rennert like a gentle jerk upon the reins, to remind him that he wasn't alone and at pasture. Mrs. Elkins couldn't know that he had shied and was staring at phantoms in the air.

"To earn a living," he made the only answer possible.

She was silent for a time, studying the hands which for all their brownness and muscularity were so obviously not farmer's hands.

"You don't really like it, do you?" she asked thoughtfully.

"Well,"—Rennert sat up and forward and knew as he did so that her gaze shifted to his profile—"I wouldn't go so far as to say that. I will admit I have doubts at times that I was cut out to be a farmer." He hesitated, then plunged ahead, thinking that this subject would do as well as any other for their conversation.

"Here's my situation in a nutshell. I went into the customs service and stayed there because it offered me a chance to eat bread and butter regularly and at the same time to—well, to mix with it the grit or the spice of the sweetness of Mexico. However you want to look at Mexico. My father died recently and left me a small sum of money. More capital than I'd ever had. I cast about for a way to invest it and decided on a citrus fruit farm. I thought it'd give me enough income to live on, a home and a little leisure. I've done very well so far, waiting on my trees to bear. I don't know how well I'll like a taste of real work. I'm afraid sometimes my approach is dilettantish, that I want to be a gentleman without being a laborer. Maybe I've browsed too deeply in Horace. But"—he laughed and shrugged—"don't pay too much attention to what I'm saying. I'm only letting off a little steam. Really, I'm very fortunate and am duly thankful."

Mrs. Elkins was, he thought, curiously persistent. "I wonder how you'd have taken Jesse's offer to set you up in the detective business?"

He frowned. "I don't want to sound ungrateful, but I'd have had to refuse it. I think when I understood the situation I'd have made Jesse see how impossible it was and have diverted his enthusiasm in another direction. Because I'm even less qualified to be a professional detective than I am to be a farmer."

"Why?"

"For one thing, I don't have the scientific training."

"You could get it."

"But I don't want it. You may be surprised to hear this—I have a hard time convincing people of it—but I'm not particularly interested in crime detection, either from the scientific or the moral viewpoint."

"Then why—"

"I know what you're going to ask. Why have I got involved in so many murder cases? Oddly enough, I didn't know why myself until last night. I always thought it was because I was interested in people. I am. In the true personality that's hidden behind the everyday exterior. The only way to get a glimpse of that is to live with an individual intimately—or to be thrown into his company when some unusual circumstance has cut him from his moorings. The moorings being the social pattern where he's a chameleon. Take our present experience, for example. I've seen some human beings in their real colorings."

"Myself?"

"Yes. And it's worked both ways. Had we met in a normal manner, you'd have formed an altogether different impression of me. I'd never have talked about myself as freely over a tea table as I did while I was lying flat on my back on that floor. I got an insight into myself there, too. I'll have to mull over it some more when I get time, but I think—I think I know the reason I've continued to poke and pry into cases that others have found gruesome or terri-fying. I'm glad. Because some of my friends have accused me of giving way to a morbid hankering after thrills. That's not it at all. At least *I'm* satisfied it's not." Rennert got up. "But let's have more coffee. And please don't let me chatter away any longer about my-self. You can't possibly be interested in all this."

She said as he filled her cup: "You don't know how interested I am. I'm going to make you tell me these things sooner or later, so you might as well do it now. Besides,"—she gave him a quick upward glance—"you can't escape. You've got to keep me company till Kerwick doth us part. Don't you think I'm a sympathetic listener?"

"Of course. I'm glad you're here. I was just afraid I was boring you."

"You know now you're not. So go ahead and tell me why you've done this poking and prying, as you call it. You're interested in people and in Mexico. What else?"

Rennert resumed his seat, lighted a cigarette and watched smoke drift slowly toward the chimney.

"It never struck me before last night that what I'm primarily interested in is death itself," he said. Then hastened on: "Now that's not as morbid as it may sound. And right there's the whole point. Death in Mexico isn't the ugly thing it is in the rest of the world. Instead of dreading it and standing back from it in awe, the Mexi-can hugs it, sleeps with it, dances with it. Death's a gayer partner for him than life itself. He plays jokes on it just as it plays jokes on him. It tries to slip up on him unexpectedly, and he fools it by being ready with a curtain line. His line may be sentimental or ribald or swashbuckling, but for that moment he's the star of the show. And he loves it. And he almost welcomes death because it gives him a chance to strut in the limelight." He looked at her. "The Mexican would call Jesse's exit from the stage a grand one. He had his line letter perfect. I wonder if that isn't a more sane and healthy atti-tude to take toward the inevitable than the one we're accustomed to in the United States?"

She nodded slowly, and her gaze wandered away, to follow the coil of smoke from his cigarette. Her face was calmer, not empty of expression, as it seemed on first glance, but rapt in meditation on some subject which must be a pleasant one, judging by her faint fixed smile.

"I've thought over what you said, Hugh. About Jesse's death. Last night it seemed irreverent to look at it the way you did. But I see now that you were right. You helped me more than you know by taking away the ugliness. You learned that from Mexico?"

"Yes. I think I've been at it more or less consciously for a long time. Getting close to death rather than avoiding it. Trying to make a boon companion out of it as the Mexican does. I believe that's why I've meddled in so many murder cases. Not so much because I wanted to solve a problem or study people, but because in each instance death has been dramatized. I'd like to keep on until I get rid of more of the fears I absorbed from our own civilization. Until I can be nonchalant rather than tense when death grins at me. Then, when I've got myself worked over to my own satisfaction, I'd like—"

Rennert finished his coffee, put the cup on the floor and threw away the stub of his cigarette. He slid for ward and clasped his hands between his knees.

"But this is so utterly stupid of me!" he exclaimed in sudden irritation. "To sit here building castles in the air when I ought to be thinking about what we're going to do. I was sure Kerwick would unlock the door before this. If I could get outside awhile—"

"What would you do?" she interrupted quietly.

"Well, I don't know. I'd at least be active."

"Aren't you being American now rather than Mexican? I thought you wanted to learn not to get tense. I believe I'm being calmer than you are."

"Yes," he conceded, "I think you are. But that was all a day-dream of mine about taking the Mexican attitude toward things. I'm just a Texas farmer who's got to return to his grapefruit. It's futile to imagine myself ever being anything else."

"Maybe it isn't, Hugh. Go on and tell me what you'd like most to do if you could arrange the rest of your life to suit yourself."

Rennert popped his knuckles absently and stared into the fire, a sober-faced, sun-tanned man whose only claim to good looks resided in his clear, tolerant, thinker's eyes.

"I'd like—" He got that far and stopped, at a low hesitant tapping on the north shutters.

He was on his feet instantly, murmuring an apology to Mrs. Elkins and moving toward the window.

He threw up the pane and pushed back the shutters and looked at Wilma Smith's face as through a still screen of smoke. Behind her the patio was so choked in mist that the walls on the opposite side were indistinguishable.

"Good morning!" He spoke as naturally as he could, noting the pallor of her face, the evidence of sleeplessness in her eyes, such significant items as the hat and suit which she wore and the leather handbag which she carried.

"Good morning." Her voice was little more than a whisper. She came close to the bars which separated them and glanced nervously over her right shoulder, in the direction of the passage. "I've got to talk to you, Mr. Rennert."

"Fine." He smiled pleasantly. "The prisoner was beginning to be afraid he was being held *incomunicado*."

"Oh, don't say that, Mr. Rennert." Her eyes came back to his face. "I'm so sorry Keith locked you in. He'll be along in a few minutes to let you out. Don't hold it against us. Me especially. Because I want you to do something for me. Something important. It's about George Woodmansee. Did you see him when he left last night?"

"No," Rennert said carefully. "I was asleep. I was surprised to find him gone when I awoke. Did he—er, escape?"

"I helped him." A slight flush crept into her face. "I unlocked the side door and the garage for him. Father and Keith didn't know anything about it until he was driving away. They still don't know about my part." A hint of malicious humor crept into her voice. "Keith'll be awfully mad when he finds out. He thinks he's the only one who can manage things. But George and I are going to show him. I want you to give George a message from me. Will you?"

"Why, certainly. He's coming back, then?"

"Oh yes, he'll be back in a few hours. He'll expect to find me here. But Father and I are going away."

"To Victoria?"

"No, to the border. You know very well, Mr. Rennert, he was justified in killing that man last night. But he's getting old, and his health isn't good. We can't run the risk of the Mexican police putting him in prison. So he and I are going to Brownsville until we learn how things turn out. That's what you're to tell George Woodmansee. We'll be at the States Hotel. He's to bring—what he has—to us there. That's all. I can't stay any longer."

"Listen, Miss Smith!" Rennert felt the impulse to shake the bars. "You folks can't leave like this. You'll only make things ten times worse. Go tell your father and Kerwick that I must talk to them at once."

"Well,"—she stood undecided—"Keith said he'd talk to you after we'd gone. I don't think that right now—" She turned quickly as a door off the passage closed.

Rennert thrust his head out of prison and saw the girl's father emerge into the patio, a shrunken mummy swathed in a gray top-coat which, judging by the size and turned-back sleeves, must have belonged to Kerwick. He wore a black fedora which had doubtless been a jaunty thing when new, and in other circumstances would have presented a ludicrous spectacle as he stood peering through the mist at the two of them.

"Oh, there you are, Wilma!" His voice was weak with relief. "I didn't know what had become of you. We must be starting, dear. Good morning, Mr— Mr—"

"Rennert. I was saying to your daughter, Mr. Smith, that you're doing a very rash thing in going off like this. Will you open the door and listen to me and give me a few minutes to investigate? I think I can convince you that you're making a mistake."

"Why, yes," the old man faltered, wincing as if his head were aching, "I believe we should. Why don't we open the door, Wilma?"

She kept her eyes averted. "Keith has the key."

"Oh yes. Well. We must listen to what you have to say, Mr— I'm afraid I've forgotten your name. I seem to be a bit confused this morning. Let's see. You're the man who had oil wells. You were telling me about Tampico—"

"No, no, Father. This is Mr. Rennert. He's a detective. We can't talk to him." She spoke as if to a child and put an arm about him. "Come on. We're ready to go."

"But just a minute, Wilma. So this is Mr. Rennert. I remember him now. I wonder if we oughtn't to ask his advice. Yes, I think we should." Smith brushed pettishly at the mist as if to get a clearer view of Rennert's face. "There was a hotel in Baltimore. The Rennert House. I used to dine there years and years ago. A famous place. The best cooking in Baltimore. Terrapin. I must have seen you there. You will be a son—"

"There's no connection so far as I know, Mr. Smith," Rennert cut in on the doddering speech. "But won't you please get Mr. Kerwick's key? I'm not a detective. I'm merely a man who wants to help you."

But there was no need to go on, for the slamming of a door and the tramp of heavy feet down the passage announced Kerwick's approach.

"What are you doing out here, Mr. Smith?" the thick voice demanded. Then Rennert found himself under the truculent gaze of bloodshot blue eyes which had sunk during the night into a bull-dog face. "Oh!" Kerwick said. "I see. Take your father to the car, Wilma. It's waiting."

The big hands moved like flappers as he herded the Smiths into the passage. "I'll be with you in a minute," he told them, came back and stood before Rennert with his hands jammed into his trousers pockets.

"Don't stick your neck out, Rennert. I'm handling this, and there's not a damn thing you can do about it. Don't worry about having somebody to turn over to the police. I'm staying right here. I told you I wouldn't take a run-out powder, and I won't. I'll settle that with you later. In the meantime attend to your own business."

A cold gleam shot into Rennert's eyes. "I've a good mind to do exactly that, Kerwick," he called to a rumpled and soiled seersucker back that was disappearing around the corner.

26
KISS

"To hell with them!" Rennert muttered disgustedly as he sat down, lighted a cigarette and flung the match at the fireplace. "You'd think I was trying to land 'em all in jail."

Mrs. Elkins was on a low footstool which she had drawn up in front of his chair so that she would be unseen from the window. She stayed there and rested her back against his knee.

"So Woodmansee got the girl to let him out! She looks like an innocent little thing. She probably fell for him hard."

"Yes,"—Rennert was consuming his cigarette with quick puffs—"I suppose any woman would." And, he was thinking, confide her secrets, if she confided them at all, without reserve and without prevarication.

She gave him a quick glance. "What makes you suppose any woman would?"

He laughed and shrugged and wished he could sit for a few minutes without conversing. "Well, the fellow's young and good-looking: Isn't that enough?"

She smiled slightly and turned her head. Both of them were silent while a car drove away from the front of the house.

When the stillness was again undisturbed she spoke firmly: "Now forget about them, Hugh. We don't care what happens to them. Let's talk about yourself. You'd just said, 'I'd like—' when you were interrupted. Go on from there. You're arranging your life now. What would you like to do most of all?"

Rennert studied the side of her face. "I'd give a nickel for your thoughts. I'm not by any chance being razzed, am I?"

She looked straight up at him. "I'm perfectly serious, Hugh. Go on. 'I'd like—'"

"I'd like to write a book. There!" He took a deep breath. "I've got it out. That was almost as painful as dislodging a fishbone from my throat."

"A book." She nodded. "I guessed it was something like that."

"You did? How?"

"How? From being with you. Watching your face. Listening to you talk."

"I didn't know I was that bad. But it's the truth. I'd like to do the very thing I've railed at other people for doing. Damson and his crew. I'd like to write a book about Mexico. Now if you let my secret out to any of my Brownsville friends I'll never dare show my face there again."

"I shouldn't be surprised if they'd guessed it, too. But tell me about your book."

"I wish I could. But it's only a hazy idea. It'd be about myself. Not as an individual, but as a type of American who can't find peace in a machine age, who isn't satisfied with the usual sedatives. It would concern my search for that peace in Mexico, my success or failure in approaching death in the spirit of *vacilada*. *Vacilada*, I believe, is the very essence of Mexico. Yet it has barely been touched on in any book published in the United States. One journalist defined it in categorical terms. A novelist animated her characters with it. That's about all. If I had a magic lamp to rub, I'd ask for nothing better than an opportunity to absorb *vacilada* at my leisure, then try to interpret it for kindred souls."

Mrs. Elkins leaned against him, one arm crooked and laid over his knees.

"That's exactly what you're going to do, then, Hugh. You have a whole lifetime free of worries about grapefruit and your living." She laughed happily. "Don't look so blank. I'm trying to tell you that Jesse's legacy makes you independent. You can sell your farm, live where you want to, do what you want to. You can start your book right away."

Rennert said quietly, "Legacy?"

"Yes. Don't you see what I've been working toward? Finding out what your ambition was. Whether it was that detective agency Jesse had in mind or something else. Because that was his last wish, to help you. And I'm going to see that it's carried out. It's just as if you'd been mentioned in his will. You're taking enough out of his estate to live on very comfortably and to travel. That'll all be arranged. And you'll have Jesse at your side all your life, big and simple and well meaning. That was his wish, too. To share your experiences. He won't understand about writing a book, but if it's what you want to do, he'll give you a desk and a typewriter and whatever you need, then stand patting you on the shoulder and asking if he can't be of some assistance. Because I'm leaving the two of you together, Hugh Rennert. Forever." She nestled her head against his knee and asked, "Happy, dear?"

Rennert didn't say anything for a long time, didn't move, but sat staring unblinkingly at the mirage which had swum over the flat horizon of his life. This was tantalizingly close, he had but to put out his hand to touch it—but nevertheless it was mirage.

His hand passed over Mrs. Elkins' soft black hair in a way which to an onlooker would have suggested a benediction rather than a caress, and he spoke evenly: "Yes, I'm happy to know there is that much kindness in the world and that I and my dreams are of importance to someone besides myself. I'll just say 'Thank you' and hope you understand how sincerely I mean it. Jesse has played too large a part in my life ever to be forgotten, I assure you. I don't need to put my hand into his pocketbook for a souvenir. I'm going to speak frankly now, at the risk of offending you. Jesse left, I expect, a considerable fortune. If I were in your place I'd look at it as a responsibility, not as a largess to be scattered to the winds. I had no idea what you were planning or I wouldn't have put up my hard-luck story. Please consider it untold. I'm not dissatisfied with my life. Quite the contrary. You're going to be surrounded now by

people trying to get their hands on the spoils. And if you start hand-
ing out money to every stranger like myself, you're letting yourself
in for a lot of disillusionment. You'll be shirking your duty, too.
Because you got a lot of power, and it's up to you to use it sensibly.
Think about the most good that money will do and forget about
me. Of course,"—his tone changed—"if you want to buy your grapefruit from me hereafter, I won't object. How's that for a compro-
mise? Give me a standing order and I'll ship it to you every week."

Her head didn't budge, but held him there effectively.

"I knew that'd be your attitude at first, Hugh," she said patiently. "You've made your speech, you were quite sincere, and I
respect you for it. But it's all settled, and your conscience doesn't
need to bother you. Your story didn't affect the matter one way or
the other. If Jesse had made a will last night he would have left
you some money. You'd have been surprised, but you'd have taken
it, wouldn't you—if nothing had entered in but legal forms?"

"Yes, I daresay I would."

"Look at it that way, then. I'm not concerned at all. It's you
and Jesse. And you can't argue with him or make any protest. And
you mustn't worry about the uses your money might have been put
to. Jesse has taken care of all the charities and so forth in Acropolis. He built a church that's far too big for the town and a perpetual
burden on the congregation to keep up. He built civic centers and
monuments that are eyesores on the prairie. He lined the highway
on both sides of town with shade trees. Most of them died and had
to be replanted. Then they changed the highway and left the trees
to be cut down for wood. He sent a local boy to the state university, and the kid was thrown out for cheating on exams. That's the
way everything turned out for Jesse. Poor old fellow. He was big-
hearted enough, but he was thinking of himself, too. He was desperately afraid of oblivion. He wanted to leave something behind
him that would keep him from being forgotten." She paused. "I
was too selfish to let him adopt a child. I persuaded him he didn't
want one himself when I knew very well he did. I'm still selfish, I
suppose, Hugh. I'm asking you to be the one who gives Jesse a little
bit of immortality. Dedicate your book to him, if you want to. Or—

what would please him even more—reminisce about him and tell tall stories of his Tampico days every time you get a chance. Keep his name alive. I won't."

"I was wondering about you."

"I'm going to be Mrs. Bjerregaard." Her hand closed over his. "So you can let down your guard, Hugh."

Rennert was staring with suddenly keen eyes at the face of her watch, where the tiny luminous hands marked so many minutes sped, and in his distraction was quite honestly innocent of her meaning.

"My guard?" he echoed.

"Yes. Your precious bachelorhood is not in any danger. I'm not included in the legacy. Get me into the United States again, and your duty's done. I like you a lot, and—I mean this, Hugh—I hope we can always be very good friends. But as your wife I couldn't make you happy for long." She stopped abruptly and scrutinized him closely. "What's come over you? Have I— Oh, Hugh, you don't—"

Neither of them knew that the bathroom door had opened softly, that a chubby, intensely interested face had peeked in and that Dr. Damson had got his stomach through the crack and was being drawn irresistibly closer on his plaited Oaxaca sandals.

"No, no." Rennert was quite rattled. "Don't misunderstand me. I wasn't conceited enough to think you had designs on me. I—oh, hell!—my mind was on something else. I had a thought."

"A thought!" She laughed, rather hysterically. "You look as if it had startled you."

"It did. See here." He leaned toward her. "Let's postpone our discussion of the money till we get to Brownsville. Shall we? I can't decide right now. We'll both think it over. You've never even seen me in full daylight, you know. When you get a good look you'll be surprised what a poor specimen of humanity I am. You'll wonder why you ever thought a plain fellow like me was worth helping."

She regarded him fixedly. "Hugh, you actually believe that, don't you?" She put up both hands impulsively, linked her fingers over the nape of his neck and drew his lips to hers.

The obscurity of the room almost defeated Damson's avid gaze. He thought at first that Rennert was going to be awkward or reluctant, but decided the next instant that Rennert was neither; he had merely been sitting in a position that required a bit of adjustment. Damson let out the breath which he had been holding and carefully took in another. While doing so he missed something. Mrs. Elkins withdrew her arms as suddenly as she had put them up, sat back on the footstool and looked at Rennert with an expression which was meaningless for Damson. "So that," she said, "is a semi-Platonic kiss."

Rennert's face was all red and confused, and he kept kneading with the fingers of one hand the spot at the back of his neck where her fingers had been. "No." He spoke in a voice unlike his own. "Really. I don't know why it had to come right then—"

"What?" Mrs. Elkins' face was working. "Not another thought!"

Rennert nodded and brought out a package of cigarettes.

She covered her face with her hands and let them sink down upon his thigh. Her shoulders shook with silent, convulsive laughter. "Hugh, Hugh, Hugh! This is the funniest thing that ever happened. You have such odd moments for your thoughts. You ought— you ought to get married. Then the next day you—you could write your whole book."

"Book?" Dr. Damson said aloud without intending to. "What book?"

27
FEAR IN A HANDFUL OF DUST

¡Aquí fué troya! Thus would a Spanish narrator have epitomized the collapse, at Damson's ill-timed entry, of all the props upon the scene of Rennert's discomfiture.

Mrs. Elkins sat up, stared at the newcomer for a second, then added to the confusion by going off into a wild gale of laughter.

While he gathered together what was left of his wits, Rennert rose, went to the table and poured himself a stiff drink. After it was down he was still unable to think of an adequate remark, so he put a cigarette in his mouth and began to hunt through his pockets for a match.

Even Damson seemed to have been momentarily silenced. He stepped to the fore now, however, and favored both of them with a little smirk.

"I suppose," he said nicely, "that this has been going on all night. Don't be embarrassed. I am very broadminded. Now I can see that neither of you is very sober. So, lady, don't you think it's time you went to your room and got a little sleep? I will take care of Hugh. He mustn't drink any more. I'll put him under a cold shower and give him a rubdown. I'll get him into condition—"

A renewed outburst of uncontrollable laughter from Mrs. Elkins drowned him out. She curled up in the chair which Rennert had vacated and wiped futilely at her eyes with a handkerchief as she choked: "I can't leave! None of us can. We're all locked in here together. Oh, Lord, this is too much, Hugh! I've compromised you. Your reputation's ruined."

"Oh no," Damson assured her. "On the contrary I should say his reputation is made. Rightly handled, this incident will give him some of the glamour that he needs. Both of you locked in. Very good." He had been eying Mrs. Elkins rather uncertainly, but came closer to her now as if gaining confidence. "I don't believe we've met. Formally, that is. I am Dr. Gulliver Damson. You spoke of Hugh's book. I'm afraid he let you get the wrong impression when he was telling you about it. I'm the one who's writing the book. Hugh is merely one of the dramatis personae. I suppose it's natural that he should feel a proprietary interest in it, but he shouldn't have gone so far—"

"Here, Damson," Rennert found his tongue at last, "have some coffee or a drink. You're making an ass out of yourself. Neither Mrs. Elkins nor I is drunk. I can explain everything."

Damson winked at him. "Of course, of course. It was the altitude, wasn't it? Very tricky, this altitude. I will have some coffee. But nothing to drink. Mr. Woodmansee prevailed on me to take a glass of cognac last night. He said it would prevent the ague. An exploded theory, of course. All it did was make me sleepy. That's why I didn't sit up for you." His eyes had been taking inventory of the objects on top of the table. They rose now, suspiciously, to Rennert's face. "Odd," he said, "that my cigarettes should have found their way in here after I went to bed."

"I understood you left them here."

"I suppose Woodmansee told you that?"

"Yes."

"Well, I didn't. I took them to my room with the rest of my luggage. Where is Woodmansee, may I ask?"

"He's gone."

"Gone! Like a thief in the night. Have you missed any of your belongings?"

"Nothing of any value."

"You'd better make sure. I hate to say this, Hugh. But you were very very gullible as far as that fellow was concerned. When you've traveled more you'll learn not to trust a stranger simply because he's smooth-looking and wears good clothes. I should have insisted on staying with you last night. But my hands were rather tied, since you showed such marked partiality for Woodmansee. It will serve you right if you find he stole all your money."

"Woodmansee stole nothing from me," Rennert said curtly. "And he had every chance. And I can't see that you have anything to complain of. There are your cigarettes. I'll pay you for the ones that have been smoked."

"But cigarettes aren't all he took. I haven't checked up on all my stuff, but I saw as soon as I got up that one more thing was missing."

"What?"

"My snake serum."

Rennert, who had begun to regret that he had let himself get involved in a wrangle about Woodmansee, made an abrupt about-face. "Your snake serum?" he repeated. "Are you sure?"

Damson gulped the last of his coffee and set down the cup. "Hugh, that's a habit of yours that's very annoying. A person makes a statement, and you immediately ask, 'Are you sure?' Yes, I'm sure my serum is missing. I had it, you remember, when you went out with that schoolteacher woman. I carried all my luggage into the other room then, since you had made it so very plain you wanted Woodmansee with you. I laid the serum on the table. It's gone now. Although why Woodmansee should take it, I couldn't say. It's expensive, of course. The hypodermic needle and the fluid together cost fifteen dollars. But there was my kodak, which is worth much more."

Rennert glanced at Mrs. Elkins, who had quieted and was watching Damson as if utterly bewildered by him.

"Will you pardon us a moment?" he asked. "Damson, I'd like to see you in your room."

She nodded, and Damson started at once for the door, saying, "Yes, yes, Hugh, come on."

In the bedroom he carefully closed the door of the bath, approached Rennert from behind and gave him a smart slap on the coattails. "Now then," he said eagerly, "tell me about it."

Rennert caught his breath, bit his lip and promised himself a very special treat before many more hours were passed. It would require the toe of a good hefty shoe. . . .

He got the table between himself and Damson and asked, "Was that box with the serum and the needle here when you went to bed?"

"I didn't notice. I was so sleepy. Hugh, your tie's crooked. Let me—"

"Never mind my tie, but listen to me." The noise of a car, departing from the garage, he thought, distracted Rennert momentarily. "The serum was lying on this table when you left Elkins here, wasn't it?"

"Yes."

"In plain view?"

"Yes. But, Hugh—"

"In a few minutes Elkins went through the bath and spoke to you. How long would you say he was out of this room?"

"I really don't know. He stayed only a moment with me. I was busy with my notebook and didn't want to get into a conversation with him. He stopped in the bathroom on his way back. I rather think he spent some time there."

"And that's the last you saw or heard of him?"

"Yes. Hugh, you're onto something—I can tell by your face. This Elkins didn't die of heart failure, did he? You remember that's what I said all along. Let's sit down over here on the bed, and you can tell me all about it."

"Hugh!" Mrs. Elkins called through the connecting room. "There's someone at the door."

"Coming," Rennert shouted back. He turned to Damson and forced himself to assume a confidential tone: "You want to help me, don't you?"

"Yes, yes." Damson was edging around the table. "I've been wanting to help you all along. But you've formed such hasty and, I must say, promiscuous friendships. First Woodmansee and now this Mrs. Elkins. I wouldn't see any more of her, Hugh. You're just putty in her hands. She has probably wormed all your secrets out of you—"

"What you're to do, Damson, is stay right here and guard this room until I come back. Don't touch anything, and don't let anyone else touch anything. If I were you I'd lie on the bed—"

"There's something here! The thing that killed Elkins!"

"There's nothing here now. But there may be traces. I don't want them disturbed until I have time to look at them. I knew I could depend on you." Rennert was at the door.

Damson shuffled after him. "Wait a minute, Hugh! Was I right? It was something vile?"

"Vile," Rennert said and, in his haste to get the door closed before Damson could reach him, struck his right foot against the jamb. He pushed the bolt into place and started across the tiles.

Suddenly he stopped and stared straight ahead of him with slowly hardening face. He sank back against the wall, his eyes went shut, and he pressed a doubled fist upon the pit of his stomach. Thank God he was alone!

How long he remained there he never knew, but after smoking part of a cigarette he thought that he was steeled. As he passed into the next room he was resurrecting, to an appositeness they had never had before, those lines from "The Waste Land":

"I will show you something different from either
Your shadow at morning striding behind you
Or your shadow at evening rising to meet you;
I will show you fear in a handful of dust."

Mrs. Elkins was standing in front of the fireplace, smoking as if she were giving vent to renewed nervousness.

"It was Kerwick," she told him. "He left your shoes there by the door. He said to come in the front room when you got ready and he'd talk to you. He was almost speechless when he saw me in here."

Rennert didn't say anything but picked up his shoes, in which he discerned no alteration save a drying and caking of the mud, carried them to the couch and put them on. He sat there, not caring to have her see his face too plainly as yet, and studied the shoes with vague eyes.

"Do you have the keys to your car?" he asked at length.

"Yes, I got them from Jesse's pocket last night."

"I want you to give them to me. And I want to use your car to catch up with some of the party that left this morning. You're perfectly safe here. I've locked Damson in, so he won't bother you. In any event I shan't be gone long. Will you let me do this?"

"Of course, Hugh. But can't I go with you?"

"I'd rather you didn't."

"That means you're going to do something dangerous." She was walking toward him, frowning and trying to read his face.

"Nothing more than reckless driving."

"That's not the truth!" Her hands framed his jaws, and she forced him to look up. "Hugh!" her cry was sharp with alarm. "There's something in your eyes. If it weren't you I'd say—"

His voice was quiet: "You'd say it was fear?"

"Yes."

"Then"—he gazed at her steadily—"you must stay with me while it disappears. Mexico has put her apprentice to the test too soon. And in a way he didn't expect. She has shown him 'fear in a handful of dust.'"

28
ROCKET IN THE SKY

SAP RAN STRONG in Rennert. But if he felt fresh and mettlesome, surprisingly youthful, as he squared his shoulders and stepped out the door, his face was composed and unindulgent. His eyes were steady and clear, with a metallic brightness, and there was no vagueness in them as they fixed themselves on Kerwick.

Kerwick was leaning in a slouchy attitude against the wall of the passage. He looked considerably chastened, and his bewhiskered face was more glum than pugnacious.

"Well?" Rennert spoke brusquely. "Are we still playing jail?"

Wearily Kerwick straightened and went to the door at Rennert's back, where he had left the key and the ring to which it was attached. He turned the key in the lock and dropped the entire bunch into the left pocket of his coat. In the right, Rennert noted, he still carried his pistol.

"Yes," he said as he started to lead the way to the door of the living room. "I'm keeping everybody here awhile longer. You know why, of course. To let Mr. Smith and his daughter get to the border. As soon as they're safe, you can have everything your own way. Come on in here. I'll talk to you now."

"I'm not so interested in talking as I was, Kerwick. I have a thing or two to show you. Come along."

"Where're you going?"

"To the northeast room across the patio. Did you lock it last night when you locked mine?"

"Yes."

"Look inside?"

"No."

"You should have. Let's go." As Kerwick, after a moment's hesitancy, accompanied him through the mist, Rennert went on; "I'm surprised you didn't skip away to the border with the Smiths."

"I told you last night I'd stay and hold everybody here until the police came about that body we found behind the garage. I kept my promise as near as I could. It wasn't my fault that Woodmansee fellow got away. And the Smiths were in the car with me when we drove up, so I know they didn't have anything to do with running over the Mexican. And Bohannon— See here, Rennert, I'm going to take all the responsibility for that caretaker's death. I didn't actually kill him, but it was my fault." Kerwick came to a stop in front of the Elkinses' door, took out the keys and stood twirling the ring about his index finger. "I'll go down to Victoria with you," he said, "and give myself up."

"You've changed your mind since last night, haven't you?"

Kerwick's hand fell to his side, and he stared at Rennert. "How did you know?"

"I overheard your conversation with Bohannon in his room."

"Oh. I'm sorry you did. I'm ashamed of myself now. But I thought it'd be so easy to get him to take that corpse away with the other and hide it. You wouldn't have any proof then, and it'd be your word against mine. But I told Bohannon this morning the deal was off."

"That last car which drove off was Bohannon's?"

"Yes." Kerwick's jaw shot out. "He's got Lurcott's body with him. He's going to bury it where it can't be found, and he's not going to prosecute Mr. Smith. And if you've got any decency in you, Rennert, you'll forget about it. You saw how Mr. Smith came to strike him. He didn't intend to kill him. But a Mexican court's liable to stick a heavy jail sentence on Mr. Smith. And at his age—"

"Yes," Rennert said, "I'm well aware of what might happen. I have been all along. You should have stated your case to me last night. At the time, say, you assured Bohannon you'd take care of me in a way he never dreamed of. Would you mind telling me what you meant by that? Just to set my mind at rest."

Kerwick looked away into the mist. "I was going to appeal to your mercy. That's what I'm doing now. It doesn't make a damn bit of difference what happens to me. I've never done the world any good, anyhow. But Mr. Smith has. And he doesn't have many more years to live. You don't look like a hard man, Rennert—"

"Since you've come to that conclusion, you might have assumed I'm a fairly intelligent one, too. Suppose you open that door now."

"All right." After an interval of experimentation Kerwick fitted the proper key into the lock and threw wide the door. He stepped inside, leaving the bunch dangling against the wood, as Rennert had expected, and peered about the dim room.

Rennert followed and opened the shutters. He went to the bed opposite the door and drew back the blanket which covered Elkins.

"God!" Kerwick swore hoarsely. "Is he dead?" Rennert nodded, sat down on the pillow and gently lifted the heavy bald head.

"Who's there?" The unsteady query, followed by a hacking cough, was Miss Pirtle's and came from the bath.

Rennert glanced up. "Will you ask Miss Pirtle to stay in her room?" he said to Kerwick. "And tell her there's nothing to be alarmed about."

"Why don't you?" Kerwick seemed unable to take his eyes from the bed.

"I haven't been acting as host in this house."

"Well—" The young man walked unwillingly toward Miss Pirtle's quarters.

Rennert bent close over the back of the thick stiff neck and passed his hand from the fringe of hair down to the top of the pajama coat. He struck a match and held it in his left hand while the fingers of his right pressed and squeezed for a moment. He stood up then and swiftly pulled the blanket back into place. But not so swiftly that he failed to see the transformation which death had wrought on the countenance of Jesse Elkins. The well-fed grossness was gone, and in its stead was the hungry questing look of a young man in a Monterrey elevator.

Imagination, perhaps, or the effect of the fog-obscured room. Or Rennert's will to see what he wanted to see. There would be time for that later. . . .

"I'll bring you some breakfast," Kerwick was saying to Miss Pirtle as Rennert moved past the half-open bathroom door to the wide-open door of the patio. He went through the latter, quietly drew it shut, locked it and pocketed the keys. He risked a slip by racing across the stones, but was urged on by the knowledge that once Kerwick became aware of his incarceration his gun or powerful shoulders would make short work of that barrier.

He entered the living room, secured the entrance from the passage and gave himself a few moments for exploration. By unlocking and propping open the front door he gained both illumination of a sort and a means of hasty exit.

In the chimneys fires had burned low, and on the floor near by were strewn blankets and dust coverings which might have been used—which had been used, of course—to darken the room. An object on the west mantel caught Rennert's eye, and he approached to examine it. It was a gallon water jug of glass into which protruded a metal rod with two small wings of silver tinfoil attached. An impromptu substitute for—in his distraction he couldn't think of the scientific name for the thingumajig, which he had read of but never seen. No matter, it had verified his hypothesis.

He glanced at the phonograph and whistled "The Hall of the Mountain King" as he made for the door and freedom.

At the rear of the house Kerwick was shouting and hammering without much spirit.

The garage doors were folded back, and as Rennert went to the Elkins car he looked at the chains on its tires and on those of Miss Pirtle's roadster. Check!

He slid behind the wheel and dug into the side pocket for Jesse Elkins' automatic. He had a decidedly cocky smile on his face as he started the motor, backed swiftly down the drive and headed northward into the mist. For an oldster he thought he was performing rather well. Rather well, too, for a reserved Anglo-Saxon not given to foolhardy melodramatic stunts such as this. That stirrup cup of cognac had helped.

Better than that, he was filled with the wine of release. Death had touched him, was still touching him, with a sharp dusty finger, in a far more insidious way than any of those he had imagined during the night—and instead of recoiling or cringing he was giving death a banter. He would never have yielded to that first retch of fear, he assured himself, if it hadn't come to him on an empty stomach.

The end of fifteen or twenty minutes' driving didn't find the fine edge of his ardor blunted. The mist showed no signs of lifting. All he could do was to keep his eyes glued on the tracks which two cars, one with chains and the other without, had cut in the mud. Both had swerved frequently, wildly and dangerously. The one without chains, which would be Bohannon's coupé, in particular had had hard going.

Rennert found it, in the *monte* where the cliffs swooped down on either side of the exit from the mesa. It had skidded sharply to the right, plowing deep furrows to the brink of a gully shoulder high to Rennert. It lay on its side at the bottom, partially hidden by the underbrush.

He jumped out of his car and, before he scrambled down the steep bank, took note that another man, wearing shoes bigger than his, had made the same descent and gone up again. He saw Bohannon first through the cracked glass, his olive-clothed fatness wedged behind the wheel. Beneath him, serving as a support, was Lurcott's rigid figure, which had been doubled to an angle that the seat would accommodate.

Rennert opened the door, caught the fat man by the ankles and lugged him out and upon the ground. Dead, of course. He didn't attempt to extricate Lurcott, merely broke the rear glass with a stone, knelt down and through the aperture examined the nape of his neck, as he had that of Elkins.

He devoted a little more time to his examination of Bohannon. The latter had suffered no apparent injury beyond minor bruises which would be accounted for by the fall. But one glance at the pasty face told Rennert what had killed the man: sheer terror. The mouth was half open and had the appearance of that of a person who is sobbing. The eyes were bulging, pink-shot, still staring at the mist out of which danger must have materialized with the swiftness of a striking blade.

Rennert wanted to know what the pockets of the whipcord suit held. He went through them methodically, but to his considerable disappointment failed to find what he was looking for. He was behindhand in this ghoulish business, he told himself as he left Bohannon lying in the mud and climbed to the level of the road.

He paced about there and found it easy to reconstruct what had happened. Another car had been standing, almost blocking passage, some twenty feet ahead of the spot where Bohannon had swerved. The large footprints which had followed the wrecked machine into the gully and ascended led straight to this second car's marks. The man had been running.

Rennert pursued the backward trail of those prints (there could be no doubt as to whom they belonged) across the road and into the bushes on the left. A rude arbor had been constructed there, and on the ground beneath it were the evidences of a long vigil. The way-layer had sat and dug his heels into the soil; he had squatted and tramped about; he had smoked innumerable cigarettes. His must have been a miserable experience, for he had been at his post before the rain stopped and had continued to wait while it slackened to a drizzle and became mist.

Rennert sighed as he got into the Elkins car and set out to overhaul his own machine and its driver. That he would succeed was a foregone conclusion, in view of the relative speeds of which the two automobiles were capable. The tread marks were plain, it was a long road to the border, and there would be few opportunities to shake off pursuit.

At that the end came more quickly than he had expected. As he rounded one of the low bare hills his coupé loomed ahead of him, stationary, its rear jacked up, a spare tire beside it.

Woodmansee stood motionless, the brim of his hat pulled low, his topcoat unbuttoned, and watched Rennert draw up a few feet to the rear, open the door and spring out.

"You asked for this, Rennert," Woodmansee said as, with a lightning movement, he jerked his right hand from under his coat and leveled an automatic. "Reach for the sky!"

29
SECRET AGENT

By OBLIGING COINCIDENCE the automatic in Rennert's right hand was of the same make and caliber and finish as the one which Wood-mansee held.

For several seconds the two men eyed each other over the matching guns. All Woodmansee's trimness was gone. His clothing was sodden and streaked with mud. Mud darkened and coarsened his hard-set face so that his whiskers, where they showed, bristled dead white.

"Looks like a draw, doesn't it?" Rennert said quietly. "Shall we put away these playthings and declare a truce? I think each of us has impressed the other enough."

Woodmansee nodded, thrust his automatic into its holster and buttoned the topcoat, one of whose pockets sagged with an object which appeared to be somewhat larger than a package of cigarettes. His face remained expressionless.

"Let's adjourn to the back seat of the Elkins car," Rennert continued when he had disposed of his gun. "I don't often get a chance to sit amid such luxury. And I imagine you're tired."

Woodmansee said nothing but climbed through the door which Rennert held open, leaned back on the dove-gray upholstery, folded his arms and stared straight ahead of him. He merely shook his head when Rennert sat down and extended cigarettes.

Rennert made himself comfortable with crossed legs. He smoked for a time in silence, played with a tasseled hanger and touched the flowers in a glass vase before he was satisfied they were artificial.

"I brought you a message from Miss Smith," he said. "She and her father will be at the States Hotel in Brownsville, waiting to receive you. I thought, however, you might like me to deliver the radium."

There wasn't a twitch of a muscle in Woodmansee's weather-beaten face or a flicker in the fixed slate-blue eyes and, after a moment, Rennert went on in his conversational tone: "I feel like kicking myself for not having thought of radium at once. My introduction to the whole affair was the sight of a string of beads and a crucifix shining in the dark. Radium paint, of course. It's mixed with crystalline zinc sulphate, I believe. But you don't know about that part of the case."

The account of the discovery of the Mexican's body brought Woodmansee out of his trancelike state. He turned to face Rennert, and his eyes became wary. His silence, however, remained unbroken.

"I'm wondering," Rennert told him, "if those beads weren't a product of the Smith factory. That would account for Kerwick's interest in them. No matter. I didn't tumble to what had been lost when I learned that Smith made such articles. Although I knew Kerwick had just flown down from New York and I'd seen the lead box that had held the radium. Then came your ingenious story of the ashes. That threw me off the scent until this morning when the word 'radium' popped into my mind at sight of a luminous watch. My compliments on your powers of invention."

"Let me get some things off my chest," Woodmansee said suddenly. He leaned forward, propped his elbows on his knees and rested his closed eyes on the heels of his hands. "The Smith girl told me about the radium. I volunteered to waylay Bohannon and take it from him if she'd arrange for me to get out. That's what she did. She even got my gun from the place where Kerwick had hidden it and gave it to me. Now—"

He was silent for a moment, his face drawn as if by pain. "I can't explain very well how I felt. About the danger, I mean. I don't think I'd be afraid of anything on earth that I could see and fight.

I know I wouldn't. But there's something about the unknown or the unclean that simply turns my stomach over. I feel so helpless. And I can't stand"—his fingers raked over the mud on his jaw—"filth. Give me a cigarette, will you? I smoked all mine up last night."

Rennert handed him the package and said, "I'm not forgetting that you risked your show to protect me."

Woodmansee frowned furiously at the match. "It was the least I could do. The hell of it was that I don't know much about radium. I'd read stories about people getting poisoned with it. I knew there wasn't any cure. It shoots off rays that nothing but lead can stop. If it gets into the body it crumbles the bones, and you just— just come to pieces while you're alive. The more I thought about you and me being exposed to it in that front room, having it sticking to our clothes maybe, the more jittery I got. I started to tell you so you could take precautions. But I was afraid if I did you'd suspect what I was going to do, get the damned stuff for myself. So I rigged up that story about the ashes to account for the actions of the Smiths and Kerwick. And I told you you needed a bath. That was true, but not in the way you took it. I wanted to get your clothes off you and your skin washed. I set your pants on fire and poured water over all your things as soon as you were out of the room. I couldn't think of any other excuse to keep you from putting them on again. I burned 'em after you were asleep. I knew if there *was* any radium there Kerwick could find it with that machine the Smith chauffeur had made down in Victoria."

"Electroscope, that's what it's called!" Rennert spoke up. "I couldn't remember when I saw it on the mantel. Let's see now if I've got everything straight. Your story holds all right if we substitute radium for ashes. The caretaker opened the lead box and made way with the contents. The Smiths and Kerwick were hunting for it and waiting on the electroscope when I arrived. If it's worth fifty thousand dollars, as Kerwick said, there must be about a gram. I'm like you, I don't know much about radium. But it strikes me that's a lot to use in making luminous paint."

Woodmansee nodded and looked away. "There's a hospital in San Luis," he said deliberately. "Smith was going to loan it to them to treat cancer with. He was going to take a little bit at a time as he needed it. That's why he got so much."

"Oh, a hospital. That makes a difference, doesn't it?"

Woodmansee refused to meet Rennert's eyes. He blew smoke through his nose and answered with a trace of curtness: "Not that I can see. Smith's got lots of money. He can buy more radium. Because, Rennert, you might as well—"

Rennert was fiddling with the lid of the chromium-plated receptacle into which he had dropped the stub of his cigarette. "Tricky, isn't it?" he interrupted blandly. "Fifty thousand dollars would buy you a car like this. Put you on Easy Street for some time. There's always a market for radium, and no duty on it at the border. Let's see. Is my guess correct that when Miss Smith called Kerwick after supper last night she'd come across some trace of the stuff?"

Woodmansee's face was hard and set again. "Yes. Elkins, you remember, knocked over that cactus stand. Well, she was cleaning up the mess when she found the gold tube the radium had been in. None of 'em knew whether it had been in one of the flower pots or lying on the floor. But anyway, somebody had stepped on it and mashed it flat. Radium looks just like dirty salt in this form—radium salts, it's called—so they couldn't separate it from the dirt without an electroscope. And they had no idea whose shoes it was on or how far it had been tracked into the other room. So Kerwick made all of us take our shoes off before we left."

"So. And now we come to Bohannon and Lurcott," Rennert said as he lighted another cigarette. "Do you know how they found out the Smiths were carrying the radium across country? Because I feel sure they planned to rob them out in these mountains."

"Miss Smith said there was a note in one of the Brownsville papers about it. She and her father spent a few days there before Kerwick was due to arrive, and the old man did quite a bit of talking. Bohannon and Lurcott must have spotted them and kept them in sight when they crossed the border."

"Evidently I don't read my newspapers carefully enough. I missed that item. Tell me what happened this morning. When Bohannon died."

Woodmansee turned his head, and his eyes searched Rennert's face. "I suppose you think I ought to give myself up to the police because of that. A good upright citizen like you would. It's easy enough for you pious fellows who've had everything in your favor to sit back in your pews and shake your heads at those of us who've had to fight for what we got. I was born in a tenement, if you want to know. I've taken care of myself all my life; I got an education and learned how to dress and talk. All by myself. The world never gave me anything but hard knocks." The words had lacked fire, and at the look in Rennert's eyes he lowered his gaze and said gruffly: "O.K. Forget it."

"I have. Tell me about Bohannon's death."

"Well, he told Smith last night that he'd hide Lurcott's body and not prosecute if Smith would give him the radium. He was to dump Lurcott in the mountains away from the house. So I waited there where the road was narrow. I parked your car so anybody passing would have to slow up. The Smiths came by first but didn't stop. The girl must have known I was near, but I'd made her promise not to tell her father. Then Bohannon drove up. I stepped out from the bushes and pulled my gun on him. He went haywire and lost control of the car. When I got to him he was stone dead. And I swear, Rennert, that's the truth. I didn't touch him."

"Yes, I'm satisfied he died of heart failure. Don't feel to blame. Don't waste any sympathy on him. He committed three murders in his effort to get that radium."

"*Three* murders!" Woodmansee stared at Rennert. "I don't get it. Something I found in his pocket did make me wonder about Elkins. Here." He drew out Damson's package of snake serum. "I couldn't figure out what he was doing with that. I knew Damson had had it in his room. He'd told me about it. I remembered that was the room where Elkins had died. I thought I'd take the stuff with me and leave it for you in Brownsville. You might find a connection. At least, if this was the same serum it'd prove Bohannon had been in that room."

"Have you opened it?" Rennert asked as he examined the pasteboard container.

"No, I didn't take time."

"Good. I'm hoping we'll find Bohannon's fingerprints on this." Rennert shook out on the seat between them a phial of cream-colored liquid and a hypodermic and pointed to the broken needle. "The rest of that's in the base of Elkins' brain. A vital spot, easily reached. The puncture was quite small, and there was no blood. I made my examination by candlelight, so I feel I can be excused for not seeing it. It never occurred to me to look there until this morning when"—he busied himself replacing the contents of the package—"something happened to press rather forcibly at the nape of my neck." It had been one of Mrs. Elkins' rings, of course, but no one was ever going to hear of *that* incident.

"Lurcott died the same way," he said, "but from a different kind of needle."

"Lurcott! Then Smith didn't kill him?"

"No," said Rennert. "Smith knocked him unconscious, that's all. While he lay on the chaise longue, Bohannon stood by the open phonograph, saw the needle and doubtless thought how simple it would be to dispose of his partner. Everyone would conclude naturally that he'd died as a result of Smith's blow. Since Kerwick had disarmed him, it must have seemed to Bohannon the only chance he was going to have to get hold of the radium. He had plenty of opportunity to take a needle from its box and push it into Lurcott's brain. The thing was of steel, five-eighths of an inch long or more. I imagine he did it while you and I were sitting on the couch, with our backs to him, and everybody else was at the other end of the room. He closed the lid and waited for an opportune time to discover Lurcott's death. I remember now noticing that the lid of that phonograph was closed, whereas I had left it open when I turned off the record, and that Bohannon kept leaning against it. Probably with the idea of detracting attention from it. He was sucking his right thumb, too, which the blunt end of the needle must have bruised. I'm trusting he was in such haste that he neglected to wipe his fingerprints from the metal box of needles or elsewhere in the interior. I think I can convince the Mexican authorities I'm right, but I'd prefer, for Smith's sake, to have conclusive evidence to show them. Check me up if I leave out anything because this is the first rehearsal of my story."

"All right so far. About Elkins now."

"That was the most ironic part of the whole business. From the moment that ass Damson walked in the door it became a tragedy of errors. In the first place Bohannon made the same mistake we all did of thinking Damson was an M.D. He saw his whole scheme turning into a boomerang once a physician made a detailed examination of Lurcott's corpse. I wonder if Smith didn't refuse to agree to Bohannon's blackmail until he'd had Dr. Damson's report as to the true cause of death?"

"Yes," said Woodmansee, "but I don't think he had much hope that it would be anything but the blows from the cane. I know Miss Smith didn't."

"But as soon as he heard that, Bohannon had to put Damson out of the way. That done, he'd be safe, because Smith wouldn't dare bring another doctor from Victoria. Enter error again and a damnable combination of events. I'm guessing here, but I think I have it essentially correct. When Bohannon went to Damson's room and peered through the broken shutter he saw a bald-headed man. That man left the room, and Bohannon slipped in to murder him when he returned. Perhaps he wasn't able to see that plainly from outside, I'm not sure. He may have merely happened to come in when Elkins, not Damson, was absent. Or he may have stood outside the door and followed his movements by the whistling. Neither do I know how he planned to kill Damson. With his knife, doubtless. But when he got inside he saw lying there on the table, ready to hand, something that would serve him as well as the phonograph needle had earlier. He picked up the package of serum, got out the hypodermic and hid, in the closet doubtless, until Elkins returned and sat down in a chair. Elkins' back would be turned to him and by the light of one candle would resemble Damson's. Bohannon murdered him quickly and neatly—the rain enabling him to slip up from behind unheard—then may have gone out without

discovering his victim was the wrong man. Whether or not he recognized his mistake, he left the body in a natural position in the
chair, the candle burning, so that death would appear to have been
from natural causes. The running water would take care of footprints. A few minutes later Kerwick came, I told him Damson wasn't
a physician, and he and Smith went to Bohannon's room and made
their agreement."

"But the box of serum? Why didn't Bohannon leave it as it had
been on the table?"

"I don't imagine he took time for much deliberation. He may
have simply stuck it in his pocket without thinking. Or he may have
reasoned that it would probably not be missed and if it were lying
in plain sight by the corpse it might give somebody ideas. After
he'd taken it out of the room he couldn't very well leave it about
the house where it would attract attention. He carried it with him,
intending to chuck it out along the road. Luckily, he hadn't done
so yet when he had his encounter with you."

"You think he was the one who ran over that Mexican?"

"I'm sure of it. The tire which passed over the man's face left a
long even bruise, with no broken skin. If it had had chains on it
they'd have cut into the flesh or at least made irregularities in the
contusion. The only cars to travel that bit of road after the caretaker escaped from Kerwick stopped at the house. All had chains
except Bohannon's. The Smith car was without chains and might,
as far as the evidence of the corpse was concerned, have run over
the man while leaving the garage. But when Kerwick opened the
doors for me he was without a doubt looking and listening for
someone near by. That could only be the Mexican, I figured; therefore Kerwick didn't know he was dead. And I didn't think he was
capable of feigning surprise so well when I found the body. It's
fortunate for you that Miss Pirtle's roadster had chains, otherwise
I might have put your and her nervousness down to guilt. Even
after she confided in me I might still have suspected you, since it
was possible that she had been unaware of an accident."

Rennert quite frankly was fishing here for further confidences
from Woodmansee. The latter merely made another query: "You
think the Mexican's death was an accident?"

"Yes. We'll never know just what happened, but I think it's safe to surmise that he ran out to stop the first car that approached—Bohannon's and Lurcott's—and enlist their aid against the strangers who had taken over the house. In the rain and darkness it would have been easy enough to strike the fellow unintentionally. When they found he was dead they tossed him out of sight so he wouldn't be discovered until morning—by which time they hoped to be far away with the radium." Rennert drew breath. "I believe my story's told. Nothing in it very creditable to anyone."

"Except yourself," Woodmansee said gruffly. "You've saved old man Smith from having the rest of his life ruined. But—has it ever occurred to you what your reward may be?"

"This ending to the adventure is enough. You see, I took your note as a challenge, that part about making an honest man out of you. That's the reason I followed you."

"Hell, forget about me! Think about yourself. Your foot, Rennert! That cactus thorn you stepped on was lying there on the floor with the radium." Woodmansee grasped the edge of the seat as if to steady himself. "The least little bit of the stuff would be enough to poison you. And it may be in your system now—eating at your bones."

Rennert chuckled. "I thought of that. But if this old carcass of mine has radium in it, for the first time since it came into the world it won't be worthless. I'll be quite overwhelmed at my own value. And if I go broke—"

"Don't joke about it!" Woodmansee gripped Rennert's knee. "It's slow, sure death. You've got to have yourself examined at once. Listen, Rennert. I was going to leave a letter for you in Brownsville, telling you to come up to New York and I'd meet you there. But now you can go with me. On the afternoon plane. We'll see the best specialists in the country. If there is any radium in you, we'll make 'em find a way of getting it out. I'll spend every damned cent I make from the sale of the rest doing it. And if—if there isn't any cure, I'll take care of you. On Easy Street. What do you say?"

Rennert smiled broadly. "Thanks, Woodmansee. I couldn't have you spending your hard-earned money on me. And we have doctors in Texas, remember." He opened the door and prepared to climb out. "Come on. I'll help you get that tire on. I know its idio-syncrasies. By the way, you can leave the car at the Romero Broth-ers' garage. It's on the street that goes out to the airport."

Woodmansee followed him to the ground and watched him at-tack the tire. After a moment he asked: "Would it help you clear up this business if I went back with you and explained to the po-lice what happened to Bohannon?"

Rennert didn't look up. "Bohannon ran his car into a ditch, that was all. No one else present. Much simpler that way." He grunted as he gave the recalcitrant tube a yank. "Unless you're anxious to stay in Mexico awhile longer."

"No. The sooner I'm over the border the better."

"How about Brownsville? Like it?"

"It looks all right. I've only passed through."

"I was thinking you might like to stick around there a bit. I have a house and can put you up with pleasure. I shouldn't be sur-prised if we located some sort of job that appealed to you. I may possibly be looking for a manager for my farm before long."

Woodmansee's laugh was hard. "Honest work, eh?"

"Um-huh. Oh, if you just had to do something devilish, once in a while you could smuggle a bottle of liquor past the customs officers. What about it? Want to watch grapefruit grow for a spell? You'd look fine in overalls."

"Wouldn't I?" Woodmansee was busy fastening the punctured tire in place. "I'm taking the first plane to New York," he stated flatly. "Got some things to attend to there. Will your invitation hold open for a while?"

"It will." Rennert got up and surveyed his job. "I think that'll carry you to Brownsville." He glanced at his watch. "With luck you can catch the one-fifteen plane. Of course you won't have time to see the Smiths. Any message?"

"There's nothing to say, is there?"

"I thought I'd see Miss Smith in private. I might give her your regrets and all that. Maybe hint slyly at good wishes for her and Kerwick. I think romance is ready to bud there, and we wouldn't want to hinder that, would we?"

"Not I. I really do feel like a heel for putting on the Prince Charming act last night. Nothing happened, though, and she'll forget about me after Kerwick stands on his head for her awhile longer."

For a full minute there was no sound at all in the mist.

Then Woodmansee's left hand went suddenly to his pocket and extracted the lead box, securely tied in twine. "Here!" He thrust it at Rennert. "Take the damned stuff before I change my mind."

Rennert took it and held out his right hand. "Thanks, Woodmansee. How does it feel to be an honest man?"

"Damn you, Rennert! I only hope it's all in that box. None in you."

"Read the last chapter of Damson's book and find out."

Woodmansee grinned. "It'll be a joke on you if that book's ever published. So long, Rennert."

"I believe," Rennert said, "I'd prefer the radium."

Smiling, too sanguinely as it turned out, he watched his car swallowed by the mist.

30
SUNSET

THE CAR SUFFERED no great damage on its trip to the border, since not many months later it deposited Rennert, sound but shaken, near that same spot. Water was churning in the radiator, and to give it time to subside and to rest himself before undertaking the last lap of his southward journey he climbed out and sought the shade of a spur of rock which advanced upon the trail.

An orange-red sun was diving at last for the hills, and as at a signal a blue haze began to creep over the parched and desolate landscape. Incredible that this region had ever known mist and rain, he told himself as he stretched out on a stone couch, lighted a cigarette and watched a *zopilote* balance in the cloudless sky.

As he lay, in one of those moods of deep and sensuous content which came over him so frequently of late, his mind turned idly, very idly back upon his previous visit to Bjerregaard's adobe house and to the characters in the dark little drama which had been enacted there. In the matter of Lurcott's and Elkins' deaths he had found it easy enough to establish Bohannon's guilt to the satisfaction of the Mexican authorities, what with a fingerprint on the plunger of the hypodermic, its broken point in the base of Elkins' brain and the entire phonograph needle in Lurcott's. Bohannon had taken the precaution of wiping his prints from the needle box, but the handkerchief which he had used had been bloodied from his nose, hence left its incriminating marks. It had seemed for a time that there would be a long and wearisome investigation into the caretaker's death, since the evidence here was circumstantial and seemed rather weak, Rennert had to admit, when paraded before nationality-conscious police officers. A doctor's examination, however, did bear out Rennert's contention that the tire which passed over his flesh had worn no chains, and since a chainless coupé of an acknowledged murderer was to hand, the affair had ended with handshaking and effusive compliments all around.

Rennert thought of Woodmansee, that still unexplained young man who had vanished so completely from his ken that morning in the mist. Rennert had been enough interested in him to look over the files of the Mexico City *La Prensa* in the Brownsville library shortly after. He had found only one item which might throw light on Woodmansee's mission in Mexico. This was a veiled allusion to the activities of a group of Americans in the export to Mexico and the transshipment to "a certain European country" of various chemicals which, although known to be of use in warfare, did not come under any of the embargo acts. Several of these agents had died under mysterious circumstances, according to the reporter, and there had been a general scattering of the others. It was all very vague, with hints of a powerful rival organization which had blocked all avenues of escape, of death overtaking the fugitives one by one, and had it not been for his brief acquaintance with Woodmansee, Rennert would have put it down as another hysterical flight of Mexican journalism.

He thought of Miss Pirtle, whom he avoided now that the events of that night had taken on for her legendary proportions, to be lived over in interminable reminiscence. The last time he had fallen victim to her was in the library, where she was seeking the latest and most thrilling in mystery novels. She had become quite addicted, she confessed, to this type of fiction and couldn't understand why she had scorned it before. Had he read so-and-so? Yes, it might very well be that Miss Pirtle was near indeed to actual adventure throughout that drive up from Mexico City, with a young man in a tan suit finding immunity beside her obvious respectability.

Rennert looked at his watch, an expensive gift from Smith, who had said he wanted its luminous dial to serve as a memento of grateful friends in San Luis.

Unfortunately for the success of the old man's gesture, a luminous watch always aroused other thoughts in Rennert. He got up now and walked slowly back to the car, since he would have to be getting along if he arrived at the house of Mr. and Mrs. Snorre Bjerregaard in time for dinner.

He had met Bjerregaard when the latter and his wife passed through Brownsville after a quiet wedding in Corpus Christi. He had found the big jovial Norwegian very *simpático* and had promised to spend this week end with the couple in their Mexican retreat. To Vera Bjerregaard he was going to give an unequivocal answer with regard to the Elkins money, an answer which for reasons best known to himself he had postponed giving to the widow who had disconcerted him by taking charge of his decorous bachelor's establishment in Brownsville during his prolonged stay in San Antonio.

In a clinic there he had submitted to observation, with daily blood counts and tests by newfangled machines which Smith, in an excess of apprehension, had had brought from far and wide. Rennert had got a mild sort of amusement out of all the pother, during which he had nothing to do but grow sleek and lazy. Finally, when his trousers would scarcely meet at the waistline and he had reached page 1107 of *Los Bandidos de Río Frío*, the doctors had hauled him from under the last set of lenses and informed him that they had detected no trace of radium in his system. However— since an infinitesimal but deadly amount had never been recovered, since all machines perfected to date left a certain element of doubt in cases of recent exposure, since a new machine was to be on the market the first of the year, since Mr. Smith had given orders that no expense was to be spared—he had best return for another examination. So Rennert had had to bestir himself, pack his bags and go home.

Only to find his furniture rearranged, a laced and flounced figurine hiding his telephone, and to meet with news which, when full realization of its import came, stripped him of his avoirdupois and salted his temples with gray.

Woodmansee's parting words had been prophetic.

Even now Rennert's fingers weren't any too steady as he opened the door of his car and took a pasteboard package from the ledge behind the seat. He had picked it up at the post office on his way out of town and, knowing what it contained, hadn't bothered to unwrap it. He did so now, thinking it might be just as well not to introduce this topic during the weekend.

It was a book on whose jacket a Mexican landscape had been done, by an artist who had never seen one, in vivid reds and greens and yellows. A *señorita* danced and a peon strummed a guitar. The title was *Heigh-ho, Mexico!* and the author was Gulliver Damson, Ph.D. This, Rennert ascertained as he flicked pages, was the latest "large printing" and marked yet another step up the ladder of best-sellerdom for a volume which "captured the gay and insouciant spirit of the land of *mañana*." On the flyleaf was the inscription: "For my chum Hugh, who never answers my letters, in the hope that we may go adventuring together again one of these days—Gulliver."

Rennert turned on, out of force of habit assuming the hangdog expression he always wore in a crowd, in expectation of hearing that oft-repeated exclamation: "Oh, isn't that Hugh Rennert, the detective who was in that book?" Once or twice, he was quite sure, it had been "funny detective." For his role was at best subordinated to that of Damson, and it didn't take much perspicacity to find clownlike qualities in his words and actions.

For example. He looked with bilious eyes upon a page toward the end, opposite the chapter heading: "A Detective in Bedroom Slippers." This was a sketch of himself, drawn by the author. He was equipped with a magnifying glass and was engaged in removing from the shoulder of his dressing gown a long hair which could belong only to the female of the species. . . .

Rennert closed *Heigh-ho, Mexico!* There was one use to which he would have liked very much to put it. Since that wasn't practicable at the moment he looked about, spied a tall cactus which suggested something obscene, and wondered if he could hit it. He did.

The Cat Screams
ISBN 1-61646-148-9

Vultures in the Sky
ISBN 1-61646-149-7

Murder on the Tropic
ISBN 1-61646-150-0

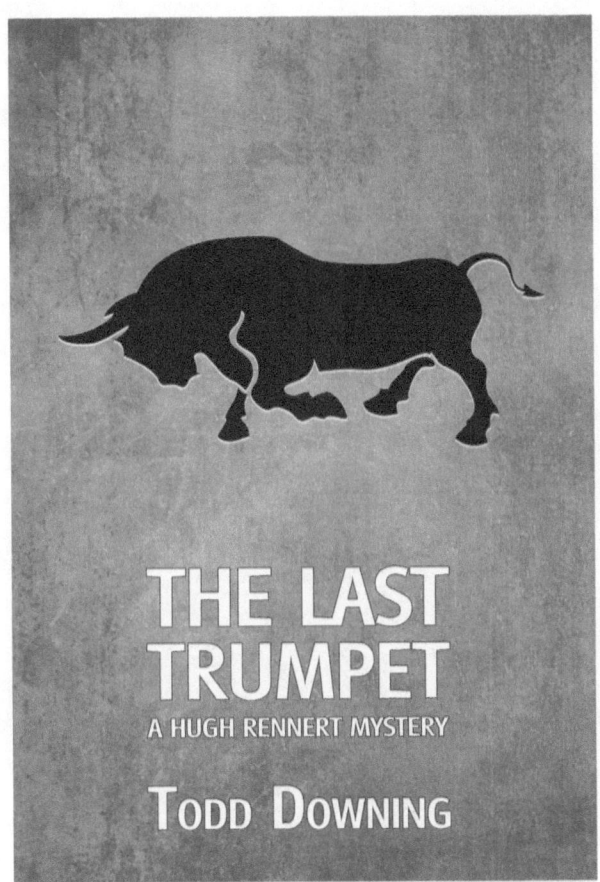

The Last Trumpet
ISBN 1-61646-152-7

The Case of the Unconquered Sisters
ISBN 1-61646-151-9

Clues and Corpses: The Detective Fiction and
Mystery Criticism of Todd Downing
Curtis Evans
ISBN 1-61646-145-4

www.ingramcontent.com/pod-product-compliance
Lightning Source LLC
Chambersburg PA
CBHW020636260626
47157CB00008B/2776